BRITISH BAD BOYS

NANCY WARREN

BRAVA

KENSINGTON PUBLISHING CORP.
http://www.kensingtonbooks.com

BRAVA BOOKS are published by

Kensington Publishing Corp.
850 Third Avenue
New York, NY 10022

All Kensington titles, imprints and distributed lines are available at special quantity discounts for bulk purchases for sales promotion, premiums, fund-raising, educational or institutional use.

Special book excerpts or customized printings can also be created to fit specific needs. For details, write or phone the office of the Kensington Special Sales Manager: Kensington Publishing Corp., 850 Third Avenue, New York, NY 10022. Attn. Special Sales Department. Phone: 1-800-221-2647.

Brava and the B logo Reg. U.S. Pat. & TM Off.

ISBN 0-7582-1043-4

First Kensington Trade Paperback Printing: November 2006
10 9 8 7 6 5 4 3 2 1

Printed in Mexico

Acknowledgments

I want to thank Carol Buckland, Sharon Dennison, and Lynn Miller for their generous help in explaining documentary filmmaking. If I made any mistakes or took artistic license, I hope you'll forgive me.

Thanks to my editor at Kensington, Kate Duffy, for coming up with the idea for *British Bad Boys* and editing the manuscript with her usual brilliance.

Most of all, thanks to all the wonderful people in England who helped with the research of this book whether they knew they were doing so or not. A lot of castles, stately homes and, yes, pubs had to be visited in the writing of this book.

Thanks to my family, both in England and here in North America, especially my stalwart traveling companions, Rick, James, and Emma. You are the best.

Contents

GEORGE AND THE DRAGON LADY

Chapter One

"The public loo in the riding stable's broken again, your lordship. And the head gardener says that if the rabble from the adventure playground stamp on his peonies once more, he won't be responsible for the consequences."

George Hartley sighed and sipped the tea his butler served—along with the bad news—from a Derby cup and saucer decorated with the family coat of arms. Despite his suggestions that he'd be happy with a pottery mug from IKEA, the staff were unbending. He might think that being the nineteenth earl of Ponsford was more of a cross to bear than a cause for celebration, but it seemed he was pretty much alone in the household with that opinion. He sipped the tea and found it strong and fortifying. "Another broken toilet. Excellent," he said with only the slightest hint of sarcasm. "Any good news, Wiggins?"

"An inquiry for a society wedding. If you call that good news," the butler said in a doom-laden tone.

Actually, a wedding was good news. Very good news. Every corporate event and private celebration, every tourist who paid their eight pounds fifty to tour his ancestral home meant more of a chance to hang on to Hart House, the estate that had been in his family for half a millennium. Earls of Ponsford had brought the property through wars, revolutions, and political intrigue. George wasn't about to lose the place to death duties and taxes.

But he almost thought he'd rather face war, revolution, and political intrigue than the long face of the man who'd been the family butler for three generations.

"You know, Wiggins, you should have been the earl. You're much better at it."

"I know you enjoy your little jokes, sir, but what about the loo?"

"Ah, yes. Right. The loo." George turned his back on the large-screen monitor where he'd been designing vacation cottages he didn't have the money to build. "What the bloody hell did Father mean letting me study architecture? I should have been a plumber or an electrician or something useful."

One hundred and eighty-two staff depended on the estate for their livelihoods. Twenty-two acres of gardens, rolling lawns, woodlands, and streams needed tending. Another thousand acres were farmed. The small village existed mainly because of the estate.

George carried the burden of it all, along with a debt to the bank that kept him wakeful on many a night.

There were days when he wished he could give in, chuck it all, sell the old pile with its history, pedigree, priceless heirlooms, and its problems, and move to a loft in Manhattan. No, not Manhattan. Somewhere much newer, where nobody gave a toss about royalty, nobility, or antiquity. Los Angeles perhaps. Or Sydney. The daydream began to take beguiling shape as he imagined beaches populated by sun-kissed girls in bikinis, warm, blue water to swim in, and nobody expecting a bachelor of thirty-two to act as caretaker to an old girl who was nearing five hundred years old, and showing her age.

"Has anybody tried to rejig the loo? Seems to me we had

some luck once with a bent hairclip and some chewing gum."

"One of the volunteer docents discovered water gushing out the bottom of the fixture, sir. She had the sense to turn off the water."

"Right. So it's a job for the plumber, then. Who do we usually use?"

"Phillip Chumley, sir. So long as you catch him before the pub opens."

"And afterward?"

Wiggins merely shook his head slowly. "More tea, sir?"

"Great. The local plumber's a drunk." He heaved a sigh. "In London I know a dozen good plumbers." The things he missed in London didn't bear thinking about. Plumbers were the least of it. His father's death had brought him down here less than a year ago, and grief and duty kept him here. Hart House was only two hours from London by train but it was worlds away to George.

"It would cost a great deal to bring one out here, though, wouldn't it?"

"I suppose. All right. See if you can dig out this Chumley's number. I'll give him a ring."

"And the peonies?"

Peonies and toilets. The life of the titled nobility was an enviable one indeed. "I'll speak to the gardener. Perhaps we can put up a fence between the adventure playground and the garden."

"That would rather spoil the view of the peonies, your lordship."

"Well, maybe he can move his blessed peonies."

"Yes, sir."

George had been as unsuccessful at stomping out the *your lordship*s and *sir*s spilling from his butler's mouth as he had been at getting his tea in a simple mug. Some days he wondered if he could possibly pull this old estate back into the black when he couldn't manage to change the habits of his own staff. "Please tell me you've got some good news."

"I don't know that it's good news, your lordship, but there is a young woman to see you."

"Really? Is she pretty? That would be good news." His fantasy about sun-kissed girls in tiny bikinis hadn't quite left him.

"I couldn't say, sir. She is an American."

"A tourist?" He did get them sometimes, stopping in to say *hey* after touring his house. Far too many young girls from places like Cincinnati and Chicago had seen Colin Firth in some poofy costume on television and decided they'd like to bag a titled Englishman. Usually, the staff took care of them.

"A documentary filmmaker."

George leapt to his feet. "Why didn't you say so sooner? Have you left her waiting all this time?" As he spoke, he found a navy blazer and tugged it on over his sweater. Wiggins tried to help him into it but he shrugged the man off. "It's really important we impress this woman, Wiggins. She works for a production company that's going to make a series of programs about—well, I forget what it's about. But the important thing is, there's a nice fat location fee involved, which God knows we could use to pay drunken plumbers. In addition, I should think the publicity in America would bring in more tourists and more revenue."

There was a tiny flicker of emotion across Wiggins's face, and George knew, as though he'd read the man's mind, that he was thinking back to the good old days, when this had been more of a prestigious estate than a tourist stop. "I will take you to her at once."

"No, no. Don't bother. I'll find her myself."

Chapter Two

Maxine Larraby stared around herself at the opulent décor of the morning drawing room, or whatever this overstuffed museum of a room was called. It was red. That was all she knew. Far too red. God, if they filmed in here her documentary would be mistaken for one of those medical ones where they stuck a camera inside the body. *Inside Hart House* could be confused with *This is Your Pancreas*.

In fact, she wasn't at all sure about this project. Yes, Hart House had some interesting history, had been a hospital in World War II, and there was an American connection, but still, if she couldn't find a focus, and better backdrops than this red-walled frilly china shop of a room, she might as well move on to the next possibility on her list and save herself a lot of trouble.

Especially if she was going to be kept waiting much longer.

Restless, as always, she went to the window and stared out at a landscape that was probably prettier than a Constable painting in good weather, but now merely drooped and dripped in a steady downpour. The rose garden, she'd read, was famous. At the moment every bud and leaf seemed to be bending its soggy head, wishing for an umbrella.

She turned back to the room and spotted a china figure of

a shepherdess. Idly, she picked it up and turned it over, wondering if it was genuine English china or some cheap Taiwanese knockoff.

"It's Meissen," said a deep male voice from behind her. "A gift to the seventeenth earl from a German cousin, I believe."

After almost dropping the no doubt priceless heirloom and smashing it to Meissen dust, she managed to put the thing back on the table and turn, an apology on the tip of her tongue for acting like a flea market browser. What on earth was wrong with her?

But the apology died on her lips.

She blinked. Everything she'd seen so far on this estate was old and crumbling. But not this guy. It was a shock to come face to face with a man—a gorgeous one—who was young and sexy and, well, modern. He had brown wavy hair, and blue eyes that tilted down a little at the corners, giving him the look of a rogue—and how they twinkled. As though life was his own private joke. A smile that managed to be both charming and slightly wolfish. Tall, great body. Wow.

"You're Maxine Larraby? Here about the documentary?" he said, reading from her card. The one she'd given to the butler. Now what? She had to go through some secretary or advisor before she could see the earl? Not that she minded being stuck with the hottie wearing jeans, a gray sweater, and a navy blazer that didn't go together, and still managing to look amazing, but her schedule was tight. She didn't have time to waste.

"Yes. Possible documentary," she told him. She wasn't going to commit until she was certain she could do something fresh.

"Please, have a seat. Would you like some tea? Or coffee?"

"No, thank you," she said, sinking into a brocade chair and glancing at her watch pointedly. Maybe the earl was king of his castle, but she had a schedule. Being kept waiting by his male secretary wasn't helping.

"How was your flight over?" Tall, Dark, and Handsome asked.

"Fine. Thank you."

"Ah, good. I always have a dreadful time with jet lag." He'd seated himself across from her, and appeared very comfy. Like he was planning to stay awhile.

"I slept on the plane, so I'm fresh and raring to go."

"Good. Well, let's get started, then. What would you like to see first?"

"The earl," she said as pleasantly as she could.

"The earl?"

"The Earl of Ponsford," she said with a slight edge. T, D, and H continued to stare at her blankly.

"Look, you're very good-looking and charming, and I'm enjoying talking to you, but I don't have years to make this documentary. My schedule's overbooked as it is. I'd really like to see the earl. Now."

"You are seeing him." He glanced down at himself and then back at her with a disturbing twinkle in the depth of his gaze. "And thank you for calling me charming."

"You are not the earl and this is not funny. Why do Brits insist on thinking Americans are stupid?"

"Not stupid, no. Merely, I would say, a little more free to express your thoughts and opinions. We English tend to be more reserved."

She didn't bother to answer, merely yanked a file out of her briefcase. Opened it in her *I am not to be messed with* manner, and read, "The Earl of Ponsford, a distinguished general, includes in his hobbies cultivating roses and playing with his grandchildren." She raised her brows. "And how are your grandchildren, Lord Ponsford?"

He didn't look embarrassed or let on that he was busted. He said in that same pleasant tone, "I haven't got any. Yet.

I think you must be referring to my father. He died last year. I still miss him very much."

"You know, I'm not a big fan of practical jokes."

He stood, and she had another moment to relish how great he looked in jeans. Then he trod to the back of the room and picked up a photo in a heavy silver frame. He walked back and handed it to her. Inside the frame was a photograph taken by a noted London photographer, and a caption, no doubt for the edification of the tourists who paraded through the place six days a week during the hours of 10 A.M. and 5 P.M. The central figure was the same man in the picture in her file. He stood with a lady who must have been his wife, and his two kids. There was no doubt that the tall one standing behind his father's right shoulder was the guy bending over her now. The caption read: *The 18th Earl of Ponsford, the Countess, Viscount George, and the Lady Margaret.* It had been taken four years earlier.

If she'd been the kind of woman who blushed, she'd have done so. "And Google is usually so reliable."

"Well, your researcher probably typed in eighteenth earl. I'm the nineteenth," he said helpfully.

A long moment ticked by, aided by a gilt clock that appeared to be centuries old and showed a young maiden being dragged off somewhere by a team of horses. Wherever it was going, Max wanted to jump on board.

"You're the nineteenth earl."

"Yes."

"The honest-to-God Earl of Ponsford."

"I'm afraid so." He was still standing over her, very male, very yummy, and taking the fact that she'd challenged his identity pretty well.

"And I've just made the biggest fool of myself."

"Honestly, I've seen bigger fools. Really, among my friends, you're a rank amateur."

She blew out a breath that ruffled her carefully styled

bangs. Well, maybe life wasn't exactly like television, but she was always willing to try for a retake. She held out her hand. "Maxine Larraby, your lordship."

His smile was singularly charming. "Call me George. Everyone does." And he took her hand. Nice, warm hand. Good grip.

If he noticed the extraordinary heat they were generating he gave no sign of it, merely shook her hand as though he were meeting her at the queen's garden party, and asked her how she liked England.

"It's a little damp," she said.

"I know," he said, glancing out the window guiltily as though the rain were his personal fault. "My mother was American, you know." He shook his head. "She never could get used to the weather, or the inconveniences." He glanced out the window into the wet rose garden, and she suddenly realized that he'd lost both parents within the four years since that picture had been snapped. "However, you've got a schedule, and I am at your disposal."

"Yes. Thank you." She pulled out a notebook and pen. Since meeting the sexy young earl she'd been tingling with professional excitement—well, mostly professional. With his father walking the TV viewer through the estate, it would have been good television, depending on how riveting she could make the script. With a young Prince Charming on camera, Hart House could be Heartthrob House. But first, she was going to need his full cooperation.

"We really appreciate your interest in this project," she said, launching into her sales pitch. Producing and reporting were like seduction—you had to go with what worked. Of course, it was difficult to know right away. What would most likely get the earl to cooperate, she wondered, looking at that far too attractive face. Flattery? Should she appeal to his ego, or should she suggest he had an obligation to history and to his illustrious family? She went with a little of all those things. "As you know from our letters, George, this project is tentatively called *Great Estates, Grand Titles*. There will be six one-hour episodes, each exploring one English estate with an American connection. In your case, of course, your late mother.

"We are so excited at the possibility of doing this show with you. It's history, English-American relations, a chance to show the world your beautiful home." She snuck a glance at him and found him listening politely, but not sitting forward in a lather of excitement.

"We'll try and keep disruption to a minimum, and of course there's the location fee."

His gaze sharpened and she felt him straighten almost imperceptibly in his chair. Who'd have thought it, it was the money that motivated him. She named a figure that was in the upper range of her budget. And saw an expression of relief cross his face. Money was tight, then. No huge ancestral fortune to pay for the upkeep of the estate.

"And how long would your crew be here?"

"Probably we'll shoot on location for about a week. It could be delayed if we don't get good weather to shoot outdoors, or sometimes there are unexpected delays. But I'm budgeting a week. Shooting to take place late spring."

"And what do you need from us?"

"All right. Well, I'm not only scouting locations, I'm also getting a feel for the story of this house and your family. I'll want you to talk about your mother, and how she came to leave Philadelphia to marry your father, but also the interesting stories. Ghosts, murders, that sort of thing."

"Air out the family closet."

"I think a good murder story or a house ghost adds a lot of interest to a story."

"Really." He rose. "Shall I put you to the test?"

There was something about him that made her think he

could get a girl in a lot of trouble if she wasn't careful. "What would that require?"

"Wellies," he informed her.

"Wellies?" Was this one of those incomprehensible things the Brits ate, all of which seemed to include some form of sausage?

"Yes. Wellington boots." He nodded, glanced outside and said, "And you'd better bring your Mac."

Since she didn't think he was telling her she'd need her laptop, she merely raised her brows. For her trouble she was rewarded with one of his lordship's mischievous smiles. God, the things he must have got away with in his lifetime thanks to that grin. "Wellington boots. Rain boots. And a Macintosh is a raincoat."

"And you're the Earl of Ponsford." Okay, she'd managed to look foolish in front of her documentary subject, which was bad, but the fact that he, a sexy and naturally charismatic man, would be the focus of the documentary was very, very good. She wondered if he was single. For some reason, she felt too foolish to come right out and ask. She didn't want him thinking she had any personal interest. She'd get a researcher onto it.

"So, you do have a ghost."

"Well, there may be loads of them, but if so they're very polite ghosts. No one ever sees or hears them. No. What I want to show you is the scene of the grisly murder."

A hottie and a murder. This location was looking better and better.

She was too busy for a man, Maxine reminded herself, especially an interview subject. But as he helped her slip into an ancient dark green raincoat, she thought he could literally charm the pants off her.

Chapter Three

George rambled at her side, leading her down a crushed stone path that curved through the damp rose garden. There was a light mist over the river and the white stone of the Palladian bridge stood out like a ghost.

"Is that where the murder took place?" she asked. Could she reproduce the misty atmosphere? Already her mind was working angles, lighting, a little bit of special effects. Maybe an actor or two to play out the bloody scene while the earl described the murder in his wonderful voice.

"That's where the ninth Earl died. He was our naughty earl."

"He drowned in the river?" Not bad, but not terrific television unless his ghost kept tipping over rowers, or spitting water at pedestrians on the bridge or something.

"He was very drunk and took a hankering to ride his horse into the village to the local pub for some mayhem. But he never got there. His body was found the next day under the bridge."

"Was he murdered? Then dumped in the river? Or did he fall in?"

"That, my dear, is as yet, and probably always will be, an unsolved mystery."

My dear was an old-fashioned endearment, but still, for

some odd reason awareness skittered over her skin at the words. With luck, he'd have the same effect on female viewers, she thought, pushing aside her own response. And mystery was almost as good as a murder. Immediately, she began assessing how to dramatize the scene. Maybe a POV shot of the ninth earl, woozy with drink, approaching the bridge. Did he hear a sound? Turn? She scribbled some notes.

"Would you like to see his picture?"

"The ninth earl? You bet."

"I'll take you to the portrait gallery."

They tramped across a lawn and through a grove of fruit trees coming into blossom. He opened a side door and they entered an almost empty room. "We don't use this wing, much. But it's a shortcut to the portrait gallery. It's also a bit chilly, I'm afraid. We save the heat for the main rooms."

It wasn't just chilly. It was freezing, in a damp way that made her reluctant to give up her coat, though she did when he took off his.

"Don't worry about your wellies," he said when she bent to take them off. "The main rooms are open to the public, so the floors are covered."

So she found herself treading beside the earl in slightly too big, borrowed rubber boots that must have looked really good with her black and white Miu Miu suit.

They entered some kind of hallway with gorgeous wooden paneling, high coffered ceilings, and paintings and treasures everywhere. Gorgeous and, thankfully, no red in sight.

The portrait gallery was long. Very long. Long enough to hang huge portraits of an awful lot of earls, their wives, their families, dogs, and horses.

If they set up in here, she'd have to warn the sound tech.

"There are a lot of earls in here," she said, amazed. She knew that her great-grandfather had come from Ireland and her great-grandmother from Sweden, and that they'd met in

Boston and moved to California. She doubted family memories or records went back much further. How incredible to live in the same house and have pictures of all your ancestors for such a chunk of time.

"I'll give you the highlights," he promised her.

"This one's the first earl. Titled by Henry VIII and given the land. There was an abbey here originally, but when the Catholics were tossed out and the Protestants were in, my ancestors found themselves on the right side of the king." The first earl looked very pleased with himself, she thought, as well he might, given that he'd been handed a massive estate. He wore ermine and jewels and was pictured astride a black stallion. Massive sexual symbolism for pre-Freudian times.

Some of the artists were more famous than the men they'd painted. He showed her two Van Dycks, and a Lely, a probable Rembrandt.

"This one's interesting," he said, gesturing to a painting of an earl and his countess. "If you look carefully, you can see that the painting's been sliced in half and a second half painted later and reattached."

She stepped closer. "Wow. And now that I really look, the background is a little different somehow."

"Different artist. You see, the earl remarried and the new countess didn't like her dead predecessor on the walls, so she was cut out and the new one put in her place."

She scribbled more notes.

"And here we come to the naughty ninth earl."

"The one who drowned but was possibly murdered? Why did he have enemies? Did he kill someone?"

"God, yes. Killing people was, as far as we can tell, his only hobby. He shot or stabbed three men, badly wounded two. Drink made him crazy. Luckily he didn't live very long."

"Too bad he doesn't walk around at night rattling chains or something," she said, disappointed in the ninth earl.

"Well, I could show you the spot where he killed his mistress's husband in a duel. Would that help?"

"Are there bloodstains?"

He chuckled. "Better. The mistress, who was a most unwilling one, by the by, kept a diary."

Her eyes widened with excitement. "You haven't got it?"

"In a glass case. Upstairs."

"Is it good stuff?"

"Oh, there's everything in it. Love, loss." He gave her a steady glance. "Sexual longing."

How could the walls of a castle suddenly feel like they were closing in on a person? Even though the castle was chilly, she felt the heat of his gaze on her and the zing of attraction she'd experienced when she first set eyes on him.

"All the ingredients that keep a documentary interesting, then," she said lightly.

"And that keep life interesting," he said softly.

By the time she'd seen the diary, toured everything that was of interest in the house, and met the house staff, she had so many scribbled notes she'd given herself a severe case of writer's cramp. Outside, the dismal day had turned even grayer as the afternoon aged.

"I need to get going," she told the earl. She needed to get to her hotel and type up her notes. And then tomorrow she'd be up early to head to the next location.

"Thank you so much for all your help and for giving up so much time to me today."

"It was my pleasure. I hope we'll spend more time together in the near future." He might have been talking about the shoot, but the undercurrent to his words was clear. Of course, she didn't have sex with the subjects of her documentaries. At least, she never had. It seemed like such a bad idea, not to mention complicating an already complicated business.

But then, she'd never met anyone quite like George before.

"We won't make our final choices for a few weeks, but I have to tell you, I'm very excited about Hart House. Very excited."

She shook his hand, and as she was leaving, heard him say under his breath, "I'm feeling quite excited myself."

She was definitely going to have to do some research on this earl.

"Blimey," George said, after he'd shut the door. He felt a bit stunned. He'd imagined a gorgeous, sun-kissed L.A. girl in a bikini and got a gorgeous L.A. girl in a power suit with an attitude. Much more appealing than a bikini—though he wouldn't mind seeing her in skimpy two-piece. Or, in fact, nothing at all. "That was sudden and possibly extremely inconvenient."

"Just so, sir," said, Wiggins, who happened to be passing.

Chapter Four

Maxine was in a snit. She admitted it, accepted the fact, knew she should wait to confront his bloody lordship in the morning, except that she didn't feel like being wise, and restrained, and sensible.

This was her second day at Hart House. The first she'd spent on preproduction stuff, making final decisions on locations, pulling together a list of scenes. Today, she'd been getting ready, writing the script, preparing for the crew, which would arrive tomorrow. She wanted to walk George through his duties tomorrow. He was going to be on film, telling the story of the house, the story of the ninth earl, the murder, the unwilling mistress, the mysterious drowning. Sure, George's stories would be off the cuff and in his own words, but she needed his full attention while they rehearsed.

Instead, he'd most charmingly put her off again and again. First there was a crisis on the farm, an accident with some equipment. She didn't completely understand what business it was of the earl's, but he had a *noblesse oblige* thing going on that was kind of appealing.

Then they'd started to talk about the history of the house and which parts he should talk about, when his banker called. It seemed the banker was an important person in George's life. Fair enough.

She'd accepted his invitation to stay at Hart House in one of the guest rooms mainly so she'd have easy access to him, but it seemed this was not to be. She'd eaten alone in a cozy room known as the family dining room since the earl had gone to the hospital to visit the injured farm worker.

Tomorrow was looming and she needed the first day of shooting to run smoothly. They only had a week on location, and she wasn't paying a crew to hang around while the earl figured out what to say on camera. Oh, no.

So she went searching for the man. A pretty futile effort in a house that boasted so many wings and rooms that she could get lost for years. At last she stumbled on Wiggins the butler wandering by with a load of his lordship's shirts.

"Where is he?" she asked as pleasantly as she could considering she really wanted to growl and hiss.

"He's round the pub, madam." And the way the butler gave the information with bland-faced terseness told her he didn't appreciate that his lordship had skipped out and gone to the pub either.

Injured workers and bankers she could appreciate, but if his friggin' lordship wanted a pint, he could do it next week, when she and her very expensive film crew were gone.

"Thank you," she said. "Which pub?"

"I would imagine he went to the Royal Oak, madam. The village local."

"Okay. I think I'll go and find him." *And bring him back whether he likes it or not to face his responsibilities.*

The Royal Oak was on the main street of the tiny village outside the castle gates. In Hart House terms, it was one of the closest neighboring buildings. In actual getting-there terms she had to stomp down miles of roadway to reach the end of the earl's land before she could cross the street to the pub. She slipped on her sneakers, grabbed a sweater and her purse, and headed down the drive at a speed-walk. Halfway to her destination it began to rain.

Naturally. When did it do anything else in this country?

The drizzle wasn't heavy enough to soak her, merely wet enough to be annoying, dampening her hair so she knew it would frizz, moistening her face so her makeup smudged. The air smelled of freshly mowed fields, of the damp wool of her sweater, and a little bit like horse.

When she got to the pub, she'd at least marched off the worst of her temper, but George Hartley, nineteenth earl of Ponsford, better not push her buttons or he'd discover she had a temper—and was enough of a republican to let him have it, earl or no earl.

When she dragged open the heavy door of the pub, she was hit by the feeling of warmth and cheer, the sound of laughter, and the smell of beer and centuries of smoke.

There were about three generations of people who had to be related, since so many of them sitting round the big table in the middle sported the same beaky nose; a group of young people laughing and flirting at the bar; a couple more interested in their drinks than in each other; and a few assorted tables of guys who must be mates and a raucous group at the dartboard.

No George.

Her eyes swept the pub once more for his lordship, and only then did she see him rise and take three darts. She blinked. He was part of the boisterous bunch of dart players. Imagine. His company wasn't exactly Buckingham Palace fare. They were working men, and they seemed as comfortable with his lordship as he seemed with them. A new picture of George Hartley sprang up in her mind, and she experienced the zing in the pit of her stomach that helped her in her work.

She could visualize this scene in the documentary: the

earl playing darts with the lads down at the pub showed off a wonderful contrast to the man who could stand on camera in his Saville Row suit and explain, in his I-went-to-Oxford-and-you-didn't accent, the famous paintings in his gallery, including those of his own ancestors painted by the greatest artists of their day.

Okay, so she was still mad at him, but not as angry now she'd had this epiphany. Still, he didn't have to know that. He'd snuck away without a word. She wasn't going to let him get away with treating her like that.

So she walked forward, ready to ask him, rather pointedly, what he thought he was doing. She couldn't be heard approaching through the crowded room, of course, and when she arrived behind him, she didn't have the heart to speak when he was about to throw his final dart. So she waited. She could see the taut line of his body, the stillness of his head as she imagined him squinting at the spiderweb of circles on the board, then his hand came back decisively, and with a graceful arc, he threw his dart. It didn't land terribly near the bull's-eye, but it was a respectable shot.

"Not bad," she said at his shoulder.

He turned, brows raised in surprise. "Maxine. Hello. I didn't expect to see you at the pub tonight. Thought you were working."

Those charming blue eyes were so guileless she'd have believed he'd forgotten all about the fact that he was supposed to be on hand. If she were a naïve woman.

"I came to—"

"But where are my manners?" he interrupted, slipping a hand behind her upper back and urging her forward. "Come and meet my mates." There it was. Mates. As though he were anybody.

"Barney, Dave, Patrick, and that handsome dark fellow over there is the pub owner, Arthur."

"Hello," she said, giving them each a taste of her smile,

then turning to George, by which time the smile was suffering a severe case of rigor mortis.

"Tell your mates you have to leave," she said, managing to squeeze the words out through her closed teeth.

He chuckled, a *Hahaha, you're so amusing for a Colonial* type laugh. "Did I tell you it's my birthday?"

Damn it. No, he hadn't, nor had anybody else, and that little piece of information certainly wasn't in her research folder—or if it was, none of her supposedly keen underlings had bothered to bring it to her attention.

"Your birthday?"

"Yes."

"I wish I'd known. I'd have got you a present." Okay, one of the keen underlings would have picked something out; something tasteful and expensive enough to ensure the good relations remained cordial until the end of the shoot.

"You know what I'd really like?" he asked, as guileless as a sunny day, if they ever saw one in this country.

She had a horrible feeling it was going to be something she'd regret. New sewer pipes, central heating for the entire ancient castle, Internet access in every room. "No, what?"

For an Englishman, his teeth were awfully white, and amazingly straight in a country where orthodontists must be a rare species. "I would love for you to stay and join us for the evening."

She glanced around. "But I'd be the only woman."

"Well, it's my birthday and I want you."

She raised her brows. Somebody guffawed and then tried to cover up the sound by drinking so he sounded as though he were drowning. Without so much as acknowledging the amusement from his buddies, the earl said, "I want to you to stay and play darts."

"Americans aren't big on darts," she said.

"Ah. It's quite simple, really. Shall I show you?"

Oh, what the hell, she decided. It wasn't like she'd get

any useful work done with an earl who was half sloshed anyway. So she relaxed, and said, "Okay."

"Right. We'll have a bit of a practice go, just to get you on your feet."

George walked to the dartboard and retrieved his dart, then presented her with three. "Now," he explained, standing so close to her she could feel the heat off his body, smell the beer on his breath, and see a darker spot on his chin where he'd missed a patch while shaving. She smiled. He was sexy—the kind of sexy that crossed continents, time zones, language barriers, probably centuries.

She felt the sizzle when his shirt—white, with pale blue stripes—touched her. She glanced up sharply, but if he was aware of the current of heat flowing between them, his blue eyes didn't show it. If anything, he seemed obsessed by the dartboard.

He took her hand, put a dart in it. Closed her fingers around the shaft and then closed his hand around hers. Whew. The heat flowing from his fingers into hers was amazing. Scary almost.

"Ready?" he asked softly, into her ear.

"I'm not sure," she answered truthfully.

This didn't happen to her. Not ever. She met all kinds of hot guys, all over the world. They were intellectuals, professors, adventurers, tycoons. The kinds of men a person made documentaries about were not clerks and bureaucrats. But of all the superachievers she'd met, none had affected her so . . . personally.

Until now. And let's face it, she reminded herself, George's main claim to fame was that five hundred years ago, one of his ancestors had backed the right horse in the Catholic versus Protestant wars. It's not like he'd crossed the Atlantic on a surfboard while trying out his new cell phone technology, or climbed Everest, written plays, or discovered the genome. No. He was a throwback to a world that no longer existed—hanging onto a derelict estate by his dirt-free finger-nails. What was so special about George Hartley that she should feel her skin shiver when he brushed close to her, or her nostrils flare when she drew in the scent of him?

Nothing, she reminded herself again. Nothing.

Still, when he pulled her arm back, murmuring instructions into her ear, she did react. A shiver so subtle she hoped he didn't notice it wafted over her. Her nipples tightened.

She wanted to close her eyes and lean back, lean into him, into his warmth and solidity. Naturally, she didn't. Instead, when he asked if she was ready, she said she was. She'd never thrown a dart with someone before. It was surprisingly fun.

Together they tossed a dart that would have taken off the guffawing guy's ear if he hadn't ducked at the last second.

"Oops," she said.

"Never mind," George said softly. "Next time."

Chapter Five

"You've been avoiding me," she said quietly. They were sitting, and somehow she'd ended up beside his lordship, close enough that she could speak softly and not be overheard.

"Nonsense. Busy day, that's all."

"You're not having second thoughts, are you?" And if he was, she was totally up shit creek. She was going to have to talk him back into his initial enthusiasm, whatever she had to do.

"About the documentary?" He blew out a breath. "I don't know. I'm thirty-two years old today and I'm acting like a man twice my age, tied to this falling-down wreck."

"Why do you stay?"

"It's my home. My duty."

"And you love it."

He looked at her ruefully. "It's hard to explain, really. It grows on you. Today was bloody frustrating, though. An injured man, the bank breathing down my neck." He sipped from a pint that was clearly not his first. "There are days I really do want to chuck it all. Maybe I've got more of my mother in me than I realized. She hated it, you know. Spent as much time on your side of the pond as she could. Made my father miserable. You'll hate it, too, being from Los Angeles and all that sunshine."

"I don't hate it. It's a wonderful place. We may have sunshine in L.A. but we don't have all this history." Oh, no. His mother had hated England? One of the topics she'd wanted to go over with him was the romantic story of the eighteenth earl and his American bride. She didn't want their story to be one of bitter misery. Where was the fairy tale? Damn.

"What about you? No wife? Girlfriend?" Of course, she already knew he didn't have a wife, but she didn't want him to know she'd been researching his private life. And she was curious about the girlfriend.

He shook his head. "I had a girlfriend. In London, but she didn't fancy it here. Too far from everything. She ended up wearing wellies more than high heels and a scrubby old jumper instead of designer things." He shrugged. "She chose London over me. Well, who wouldn't?"

Maxine privately thought a lot of women wouldn't.

"And how about you?" He said, suddenly emerging from his gloomy state and giving her a curious glance. "Is there a significant other waiting at home?"

"No."

"I'm surprised."

"I work. A lot. I'm out of town, out of the country." She ran the tip of her finger around her beer mug, frowning. "I'm not home long enough to commit to a houseplant."

"The rolling stone gathers no African Violet."

She smiled dutifully, but glancing at him she could see he understood.

"What about a family? Children?"

"Sure, I want them. But not yet."

Between rounds of darts, when it became clear that she had a natural aptitude as well as a strong competitive instinct, she managed to interview him about his mother. It wasn't as bad as she'd feared.

"Oh, the match was love at first sight, I understand," George said. "Father was over visiting America and saw my mother at her debutante ball. They were married within six months."

"What happened?"

"She loved my father, but hated England. It was all right for the first few years, and then she had my sister and me, so that kept her busy, of course. But as time went on, she began to hate England more than she loved my father. She visited her home in Philadelphia as often as she could and for longer and longer periods. I rarely saw her in the last few years unless I flew to America to visit her. She died over there. Pneumonia. Very sudden."

"I'm so sorry."

"Father was like a broken man after he lost her. Funny, that. It hadn't been a very successful marriage, but in his way, he was devoted to her. He died last year, heart attack."

"A broken heart," she said softly.

He made a short, bitter sound. "Well, I think it broke much earlier."

Privately, she thought his mother had been too young and possibly too impressed with the title. And, if George took after his father, there was the whole sex appeal force to contend with. She'd probably married the man before she realized she didn't really love him at all.

"Same again, George and Maxine? My round," Barney said.

They exchanged a glance and then Max said, "No, thanks. I've got to be up early tomorrow."

"Right, yeah. Me, too," said George, rising. She was surprised his buddies didn't try to talk him into staying on his birthday until she saw the leer on one face, and caught a wink from another.

Men weren't any different here, that was for sure. So she and George had spent some time having a private conversation. It was business. How could they not see that?

Everyone in the pub knew George, of course. And the final well wishes for his birthday ranged from loud and drunken to quiet and respectful. When they emerged into the quiet, damp night, he said, "Thanks for coming. It was great having you there. I know my friends enjoyed meeting you."

She snorted. "Why do I think they are right now laying bets to see whether you get me into bed?"

He glanced at her sharply, that unruly and utterly charming twinkle in his eye. "Why would you think that?"

"Because they're guys. We walked out together."

"Ah, but how would they know who won?"

"Well, you'd tell—"

He shook his head.

She glanced at his profile and noticed his nose wasn't entirely straight. Even the tiny jog was sexy. "Come on. You don't have to lie to me."

"I'm not. I don't talk about my intimate life to my friends." It sounded unbelievably pompous when he said it, but she saw from his face that it was true.

"Why? Is that some aristocratic imperative?"

"No. I may be old-fashioned but I still believe a gentleman doesn't tell."

"My God. You're as archaic as your castle."

"I probably sound like a total prat."

"No. I like that you won't blab. Not," she hastened to add, "that there's going to be anything to blab about."

"Of course not." By this time they'd crossed the street, entered the castle grounds, and were strolling up the path. The tree-lined walk, the castle rising from its surroundings like a fairy tale, the moon streaked with clouds like a coal miner's face.

"Why would anything happen between us?"

"Exactly. This is a purely professional relationship."

"It's not as though we're attracted to one another, is it?" His voice was a caress.

"Absolutely not." She felt as though they were the only two people in the world. It was so quiet here, so romantic. They walked close enough that they were almost, but not quite, touching. "There will be nothing to talk about."

"Not so much as a single kiss under the moonlight," he said, turning her slowly to face him. Oh, he was gorgeous. Sexy and desirable even as he remained as steeped in history and tradition as his property. He was broad of shoulder and slim of hip, exactly as a man should be, and when her arms went around him, she felt the muscles and the firmness, the warmth and gentle teasing that always seemed to be a part of him. "Unless you were to take pity on me."

"Well. Maybe a birthday kiss," she said softly, raising her face. He brought his mouth down to cover hers and she felt the heat of him. He tasted like beer and hot sexy Brit, but he felt even better. Strong, dependable. Someone she could trust.

And suddenly a semi-innocent birthday kiss was heading way out of control and very far from innocent. He held her against him, pulling her off the road and under one of the hefty oaks that had stood here so long Henry VIII had probably carved his initials in the trunks.

When they stopped moving, she realized George was leaning against the heavy trunk of a tree, and she was leaning on him, pressed against him so her breasts flattened against his chest, their bellies brushed as they breathed, and then their hips jammed together as though their bodies had decided to get together long before their minds had caught up. Hers, anyway.

It had been a while for her, she decided. That must have been why she was having such an incredible reaction to a kiss. It was as though he'd ignited something wild in her and she wanted to climb all over him, take him, right here, out in the open. Well, it wasn't as though they wouldn't have privacy. The tree was like a tent covering them and they were probably equally as far from the house as they were from the road.

Probably he'd planned it that way. Not that she cared. At the moment she was blind and deaf to her usual common sense. He kept kissing her, deep, wonderful kisses that made her pulse everywhere with needs she'd either forgotten she owned or had buried in work.

When she pulled away to drag in a breath, he moved down, kissing her neck, that wonderful sensitive spot beneath her ear. Above her was a dark, green canopy of leaves. Her feet were a little cool from standing on damp grass, but it was the only part of her that was cool. She let her eyes close as she took in all the amazing pleasure points dancing for joy throughout her body.

Letting herself go was so rare, and so wonderful, that she ignored all the very good reasons why she—the documentary filmmaker—and he—the subject of the film—should not be getting quite so up close and personal. For once, she let herself follow her instincts rather than her list of shoulds and shouldn'ts.

"You taste wonderful," he mumbled against her skin.

"Probably like the inside of a pub."

"No. Very American. Very . . . clean."

"You're crazy," she said, running her hands over his shoulders and upper back, letting her fingers sink into the gorgeous mop of hair that would cost a couple of hundred pounds in a top London salon to style this casually rumpled, and that she suspected, in his case, came naturally.

She gasped as she felt his questing fingers brush the tops of her breasts, above her bra. Gasped with the shock of finding him there, so subtle she'd barely noticed him sneaking under her clothing, and because it felt so very good. She could feel the tingle and knew she'd come out in goose bumps, and not because she was cold.

When he cupped her breast, a tiny moan of pleasure escaped her. The night muttered to itself, and the leaves above said *shhhh*.

George of the nimble fingers had her jacket open, her shirt open, and her bra pushed up and out of the way. Then he leaned her back a little so he could reach her breasts with his mouth.

Oh, God. The night air was cool and damp, his mouth so hot and wet, the licking and sucking motions setting her on fire. She heard panting and knew it was coming from her. Wanted all of him. To see him, touch him, taste him.

Her hands delved under his sweater, but the little touches of skin weren't enough. She wanted more.

"I want—" she began, and then a breeze blew through their tree, setting the dark leaves above her trembling almost as badly as she was. And suddenly, a shower of water droplets rained down on her naked breasts.

She squeaked with the shock. George laughed and began to lick up the drops, but the literal cold shower also served as a metaphoric one and she pushed him away.

"What are we doing?" she asked in a horrified whisper.

There was a tiny moment of silence. Mortified on her part, and, she thought, slightly amused on his. "I believe you were giving me a good-night kiss," he reminded her, as though they'd done nothing more than peck each other on the cheek.

"It was a birthday kiss," she corrected. "And it's over."

She started trying to shove her buttons back together but made such a mess of it that he helped her.

They were mostly silent the rest of the walk up to the castle. She stole a quick sideways glance at his profile, but he looked the same as he always did. As though nothing had happened.

Right, she reminded herself. Because nothing had happened.

Still, she was going to have to face him in the morning, and try not to remember that his tongue had been wrapped around her nipples, making her moan with delight. Just before they reached the great oak front door, she put a hand on his sleeve.

He glanced down at her, brows slightly raised.

"That should never have happened," she said. "It was totally unprofessional."

He waited, but she didn't have anything to add, so he opened the huge door and waited for her to pass in front of him.

She knew they both had to climb the great staircase to reach their bedrooms and she couldn't stand the idea of going upstairs at the same time. She'd either keep babbling or drag him into her room. Two very bad ideas, so she said, "I think I left my laptop in the dining room. I should go get it."

"Right. I'll say good night, then." He turned to the stairs, then back to her. "I won't say I'm sorry, because I'm not. But consider the matter forgotten."

And with that he started up the stairs with the easy grace of a man not still trembling from frustrated desire.

Irritation spurted through her. Was she the only one?

Chapter Six

Of course she wasn't going to forget what had happened. Her overheated, oversensitive skin reminded her as she walked to the dining room. Her laptop wasn't in there; of course, it was already in her room.

She waited a minute to make sure George was tucked away in his own room, then she made her way up the quiet stairs to hers.

But she was wide awake and edgy. She spent a couple of minutes making some notes about her pub scene idea. She brushed her teeth and hair, washed up, changed into her pajamas, and stuck her feet into the sheepskin slippers she was glad she'd brought along. The castle was often cold. Even the parts they bothered to try and keep warm. The heating bills for this place must have been astronomical.

The book she'd picked up in the estate gift shop with the scintillating title *History of Hart House* was as un-put-downable as she'd imagined. Great for falling asleep, except that tonight it wasn't. She read about the number of local rocks quarried and how long the outer walls had taken to build and didn't even feel sleepy. In fact, it was a waste of time reading since she barely took in a word.

Usually she got more exercise. That was probably why

she wasn't sleepy. Tomorrow she'd go for a run. Of course, it wasn't lack of exercise but being so tantalizingly close to making love and then backing off that had her body feeling so twitchy and irritable.

Yoga. Mind over body. Mental and spiritual calmness. That's what she needed.

She didn't love running, but it was exercise that she could do anywhere, so she'd become a runner by necessity. Yoga was by choice. She had a few DVDs she could play on her laptop, or she could do a simple routine of her own. She chose the latter, kicking off her slippers. All she wanted was a series of calming, sleep-inducing poses. Hauling herself out of bed, she worked through some nice, easy stretching. Her hamstrings were particularly tight, she noticed, so she went into a wall stretch. She debated putting her bare foot on the historic and intricate paneling. Her foot was perfectly clean, but it seemed wrong somehow, so she found a new pair of athletic socks and pulled them on. Of course, that made her foot slippery and she'd no sooner got herself in position and stretched in toward the wall when her heel slipped, catching on a knobby bit of wood. She wobbled on her standing foot and would have fallen if she hadn't grabbed one of the carved acorns. She tried to steady herself, but the acorn moved.

Shit. If she broke a piece off the centuries old paneling . . . But before she'd even finished the thought she realized that a whole section of paneling was opening, like a door.

No, she realized in amazement. Not *like* a door. It *was* a door. A secret panel. Delight filled her. Nobody had mentioned anything about a secret door in her room. Maybe they didn't know it existed. Perhaps the secret had died with one of the earls currently on display in marble effigy in the family chapel.

Since the castle was no stranger to losses of power through

storms and other mischance, her room was equipped with both a decent flashlight and candles and matches. She picked up the flashlight and turned it on. The beam was strong and steady. She shone it into the still-open doorway and got a second rush. It was definitely a passageway, not a cleverly designed closet.

Cool.

Dark, mysterious, and very gothic. She glanced around at the luxurious guest room, then back into the dark, scary tunnel. Naturally, what any sensible woman would do would be to wait until morning and mention her discovery to one of the earl's staff. But a person didn't go around the world making documentaries without being, at heart, an adventurer.

Shoving a single candle and a book of matches advertising the gift shop into the breast pocket of her pj's, just in case the flashlight battery failed, she plunged into the tunnel.

It wasn't really all that exciting. Since it was aboveground, there was no stone walkway that might lead to the dungeons. In fact, her sense was that the plain wood floor didn't dip down, but stayed level. Still, maybe there was some kind of treasure. A forgotten Rembrandt, or diaries from one of the former earls. What that would add to her documentary!

Not to mention possibly helping the current earl out of a financial crunch. She imagined a newly discovered Rembrandt, properly auctioned, could help him out of his monetary troubles a lot faster than increased tourism.

She crept along, smelling dust and stale air, trying to ignore the cobwebs. The passageway was narrow, barely a foot wider than her shoulders, and not more than six inches above her head. Not a good place for a claustrophobic person, she thought, glad she'd left the door open at her end.

The tunnel made a turn and then she was facing a blank

wall. Not a Rembrandt or ancient diary in sight. But, when she played her flashlight over the wall, she saw the thin line of a doorway and a latch.

Without giving herself time to think, she pushed open the latch, and with it the door.

Chapter Seven

"Good God," said George, standing in his shirt, underpants and socks beside his massive bed and looking startled, as well he might. A deep and comfy-looking armchair sat beside a fireplace, and by its side was a table, with a lamp illuminating a book. Obviously, the earl had been trying some prebedtime reading as well. No doubt for the same reason she had.

"George."

"Ah," he said, while she stood there with her mouth open and her eyes blinking. "I see you've found the passage."

Embarrassment flooded her cheeks as she stood there. "I am so sorry," she managed. "I had no idea it went anywhere. I mean, I accidentally found the knob thing and it opened a door and—"

"Naturally, you were curious," he said with his usual well-bred ease, as though people wandered out of the walls and into his bedroom every day.

"Yeah. I was."

"Come in. Would you like a drink?"

She felt so foolish standing there, half in the tunnel and half in his room, that she went all the way in. "No, thank you."

There was a pause. He finished folding his trousers over a wooden stand by his bed. She watched him, fascinated. His boxers were blue and white striped, very genteel looking. He had great legs, muscular but not bulky, furred with brown hair. When he leaned over to put his trousers away the fabric pulled over his butt and her mouth went dry.

"Why is there a secret passage linking these rooms?"

He took a navy dressing gown from a hanger and slipped into it. "The eleventh earl is believed to have built it. For his mistress."

"For his mistress."

"Well, more than one, I fancy. In fact, for a hundred years or so, I think that was a fairly high-traffic thorough-fare."

She stared at him, resisting the urge to smack him. "Three hundred and thirty-three rooms in this place and they put me in the earl's mistress's room?"

"Wiggins' idea of a little joke, I imagine."

"Well, it's not funny."

"No. Quite."

Her eyes narrowed. "Did you know I was in that room?"

"Yes. I didn't choose the room, but I heard that's where they'd put you. Look, I wasn't planning to come sneaking into your room in the middle of the night, you know. And I never thought you'd find the door. It's damned difficult to do unless you know it's there," he said, sounding a little huffy. "I'll have you moved in the morning."

"That's okay," she said, deciding he was right and she'd only look like an idiot if she asked to move. Besides, she realized, flashing him the smile that very often got her what she wanted in life, "There are advantages."

He glanced up, the sexy twinkle in his eye. "There are?"

"Yes. Unlimited access to you."

"I like the sound of that." He walked forward until he was close enough to touch her.

She looked up at him demurely from under her lashes. "For documentary purposes."

He reached out and traced the vee of her pajama top, the smile already tilting his lips so she caught a flash of white teeth. "Is that all?"

Oh, what the hell, she thought. Fate had practically drawn her a map to his bedroom, taken her hand, and led her to his bed. "No," she said, throwing her arms around his neck. "That is not all."

She kissed him, surprising him while the smile was still on his lips. She felt it, the curve of lip, the hardness of teeth, and found herself smiling against him. This, she realized, was about as perfect as mixing business and pleasure got. No one would ever know.

Being an earl definitely had its privileges.

After the way she'd walked away so hot for him, and so unsatisfied, her libido roared from zero to the speed of light in the time it took their kiss to deepen.

Tongues tangled and stroked, hands stroked then grabbed, good manners and caution flew out the window, and all that was left were heat and need.

Her oh-so-proper some kind of distant cousin to the queen turned into a savage. He nipped at her, dragged her nightclothes off her with no subtlety at all, popping two buttons in his haste.

She didn't care. She reveled in it. She wasn't all that shy about exposing her body, but usually the first time involved a certain awareness that a guy who loved big breasts was going to be disappointed, and that her belly would be a lot flatter if she could stick to her running schedule when on location. She'd normally turn away from the lamp, maybe suck in her stomach a bit, but somehow, here with George, none of that entered her mind.

While he was dragging at her top, cursing his own clumsiness—and what had happened to the smoothie out there

under the oak tree who'd buttoned her back up so effi-
ciently?—she was pulling off the sash of the robe he'd only
just put on. When she'd dragged it down and off his arms,
she went to work on his shirt.

When he got frustrated, he tried to help her and more
buttons flew.

Oh, his chest was so nice. Barely hairy at all, but surprisingly buff. Even his muscles were elegant, she thought. They
weren't so big you worried he'd bench-press you halfway
through the act, or so small you knew the guy rarely picked
up anything heavier than a teacup.

"You play sports," she breathed,

"Tennis," he agreed, pulling off one sock. "Polo," as he
pulled off the second and hopped on one foot to keep his
balance.

Polo. Of course.

He pulled her against him so they were skin to skin, and
her nipples had never felt so exquisitely sensitive as they did
rubbing against his chest. The warmth and friction only reminded her that she needed a lot more warmth and a lot
more friction, and soon.

Slipping lower, she hooked her thumbs around the waist-
band of his boxers and slid south, taking the garment with
her.

"Oh my," she breathed, when she found herself face-to-
face with the probable reason the earls of Ponsford had always enjoyed such a reputation with women.

If what she was staring at was a dominant gene—and it
sure as hell seemed like one—then money and position weren't
all the earls had had going for them.

She glanced up and the usually self-effacing George was
grinning down at her, looking anything but. He enjoyed her
surprise. This genteel, urbane, well-mannered aristo was
hung like a moose.

He stepped out of his boxers and when she rose, she

couldn't resist the urge to cup him in her hands. Oh, he felt as good as he looked. Hard and velvety warm.

He liked to use his mouth, she discovered. Everywhere his hands went, he followed with his lips, his tongue. Until she was dizzy with the desire that kept on building, and he finally pushed back a surprisingly modern-looking bed-spread and they tumbled into bed.

She was so hot by this time, so needy, that she couldn't wait anymore. She wanted him, and now. And just as she was about to grab him and guide him to where she needed him most, an unwelcome realization swept over her. She hadn't started down that tunnel with sex on her agenda.

"Um, I have to run back to my room for a second."

"There's a bathroom through there," George said, leaning in and nipping at her shoulder.

"No." She shook her head and whispered. "Condoms."

"Ah, right. I'm sure I've got some."

"You have?" She flopped back in relief.

"I'll ring Wiggins. I'm sure we've got some somewhere."

"You'd make your butler . . . ?" Even as she got halfway through, she realized he was joking. He leaned over and opened the drawer of his night table. And like every man worth his salt, he had protection ready and waiting.

He took care of sheathing himself and she lay back and watched him. Then he was kissing her, rolling onto her, pushing into her.

And she went completely and absolutely wild. It was as though a starving woman had been invited to an elegant banquet—it didn't matter. She would stuff her face with greed and no manners. A desperately thirsty woman would glug water, not caring that it splashed all over her face. That's how she felt. She couldn't get enough of him, urging him deeper, rolling over, taking him, being taken. There was something wild and magic about the way they were to-gether. She felt it, knew he felt it, too.

They didn't have to talk or ask, or murmur questions or suggestions, they simply took, greedily, ravenously until she was sobbing out his name and he was shuddering against her.

When her heart had finally slowed so she thought she might one day be able to function again, she turned her head to gaze at him, chest heaving as badly as hers was. As though on cue, he turned to regard her. She wanted to say, *That was the greatest thing that ever happened to me.* Or, *Wow.* Or, *Thank you.* Instead, she gazed at him, deep red from exertion, a drop of sweat rolling from his forehead into his damp hair, and a giggle snorted out of her.

After a stunned moment, he started laughing, too. And somehow, it felt like they'd said it all.

They talked then, she with her head propped in her hand, doing what she did best, interviewing. Not because of the documentary, or because she was incurably nosy, though both were true, but because she really wanted to know.

She wanted to know everything about this guy. How did it feel to be brought up so upper class that you got sent away to boarding school at eight years old? What were his favorite foods, flavors of ice cream, when did he learn to swim? How did he discover sex? All the things that made him who he was were suddenly fascinating to her.

And so they talked. He turned out to be not a bad interviewer himself, or maybe his curiosity was as ravenous about her.

"Will you stay?" he asked after a while. Her fingers were making patterns idly on his chest, and he was twirling a lock of her hair around his finger.

Stay. The night.

How had they gone from a birthday kiss to spending the night?

She glanced over at him, feeling suddenly uncertain about how far and how fast she wanted this thing to go, but who was she kidding? If she cared passionately whether he preferred Chocolate Chip to Rocky Road, she was obviously not averse to spending the night in the man's bed.

Something of her momentary uncertainty must have shown on her face. He kissed her lightly. "If you stay, I promise to act like less of an animal and make love to you properly."

"Okay," she whispered.

But it didn't work that way. They started out slow and decorous, but in the end the heat and greedy passion caught up with them again. It was like being struck by lightning twice.

But in a very good way.

Chapter Eight

Maxine paused. She couldn't help herself. She was busy and had at least three million things to do today, but the grand portrait of the eleventh earl caught her, as it always did. Of course, it was the family resemblance between George and his ancestor that always pulled her to a halt. As she gazed up at him, in all his splendor, she felt an odd thrill.

"Communing with the spirits of my ancestors?" George said softly from behind her.

She started. "I didn't hear you."

"No. You were deep in thought."

He came up behind her and wrapped his arms around her, kissing her neck. She closed her eyes and leaned into him for a moment, recalling, as she was certain he was also doing, the way they'd made love last night. Slow and tender. As though they mattered to each other. Which was a dangerous game when your lives were so very different, and separated by an ocean.

"I was thinking," she said, "how sure of himself he looks. He stares down at me as though all he has to do is give the order and I'll prostrate myself at his feet."

"Lucky bugger. In his day, you would have."

She secretly thought things weren't so different today, but she didn't share that thought aloud.

"I love his pride and arrogance."

"He's not wrestling with death duties and union wages," George reminded her, sounding a teensy bit aggrieved.

"I'm sure he had his own problems."

"Doesn't look it, though, does he?"

"Well, he must have had some."

"I suppose." She felt George's smile as his cheek wrinkled against her own. "There was all that political intrigue for starters. My ancestors, I'm sorry to tell you, weren't men of highest morality. They tended to change religions whenever it seemed expedient and they were dreadful boot-lickers and arse-kissers. Anything to keep the king's or queen's favor. Then there was the urgent need of a wife to ensure the succession."

"That couldn't have been very hard," she said, looking up at the earl in all his glory. His clothes were sleek with fur and glinted with gold thread and jewels. "Not only is he obviously rich, but he's hot."

"Important for him to choose wisely, though. As well as being wellborn, and hopefully rich in her own right, his wife had to be a good breeder, you see, or who would inherit the estate?"

"What a depressing way to choose a partner," she said, seeing some of the romance of the period dim before her eyes.

"Well, that one didn't waste a lot of time being depressed. Or in his wife's bed."

She turned her head. "You sound like you admire him."

His grin was sudden and wolfish. "I do. He's the one who had that secret passageway built."

"Oh," she said, feeling her own lips twitch. "I knew there was a reason why this picture was my favorite."

"Come on. I think I have to be interviewed and I can't do it without you there."

They'd been shooting for five straight days. The shoot was so smooth it was spooky. George was as natural and charismatic on camera as she'd known he would be. If she said to him, "Why don't you take us through the portrait gallery, and give us the highlights," he could do it without a lot of fumbling or overuse of the word *um*.

So often there'd be an unforeseen delay. Equipment broke, or illness struck, or the roof would start leaking, and the rain would hold things up. But not this week. They'd shot outside in the rose garden and he'd told the story of his parents charmingly, focusing on the falling in love and happy times. She'd cut in some old family movies and stills showing the Anglo-American love match.

Even the dramatic telling of the ninth earl had been comparatively easy since they were able to hire local actors. Soon they'd be done here, possibly a day ahead of schedule.

How ironic that of all locations, this was one where she'd have happily been stranded for a while.

They turned away from the painting and she checked out the current earl with a critical eye.

He stood still for a few seconds while she studied him and then said, "Well, will I do?"

"You're gorgeous. But the tie's too bold. It's going to draw attention away from your face."

"Sounds like a good thing to me."

"Give it up with the false modesty. Something blue and muted would be much better. Want me to go and choose something?"

"No, thank you. I'm capable of selecting a tie on my own." He pulled out a cell phone and dialed. "Ah, Wiggins. Sorry to bother. Can you bring me a tie?

"Yes, I know. I thought so, too," he continued. "But they want something blue and muted. Will do. Thanks."

"I can't believe you sent a servant for a tie," Maxine said. "I would have gone."

"But I need you with me. Besides, there ought to be some advantages to being a relic of a bygone era."

A few seconds ticked by uncomfortably. "You read the intro?"

"Your assistant producer sent me a copy. In error, I'm sure."

"Look, you have to understand that this airs in the States, that's our primary market, so we need to make it . . . I don't know, appealing to people who chose a republic but who still love the pomp and glory of royalty."

"Do you think I'm a relic?"

She stared at him, thinking of how he'd been with her last night, so passionate and—well, there was nothing old-fashioned about the way this man made love.

"No. No. Not at all."

"Well, then . . . did you write the script for today?"

"You mean the questions? No. I gave Suz, my assistant, a general idea and she wrote them. You don't need to worry. We'll edit the tape to make you sound good. I promise."

"It's a question and answer format. Like an interview on the telly."

"That's exactly what it will be. An interview on the television. It's part of the show."

"And you didn't tell Suz what to write?"

"No. I gave her some direction. We want to know about you, the man, as well as you the young earl in an old estate. Why? Is there something that bothered you about the questions? She's got a degree in film and majored in screenwriting. She's great."

He looked at her oddly. "No. The questions are fine. Not to worry. You will be there?"

"Good. I'll be there, of course, so if there's anything that makes you uncomfortable, give me a signal."

"All right, then."

Soft footsteps sounded and she turned to see Wiggins arriving in his slow, genteel way, with four ties over his arm. "All blue, your lordship." Wiggins was too well trained to glare at Maxine, but she thought his respectful tone, containing the tiniest note of censure, was masterful. "All muted."

"Excellent. Thank you." George turned to her. "Well?"

She chose a gray-blue background silk with a restrained paisley pattern. "Here."

He pulled off his current tie and handed it to Wiggins. She took the muted blue tie and looped it around his neck. There was something about putting on a man's tie that always seemed so intimate, so wifely. Weird word to come up with, when she wasn't ready to settle down and he'd all but promised dear old dad not to marry a girl from the States. He lifted his chin and she snugged up the knot.

"All right, then. Are we ready?"

"Yes, be yourself. Your charming, lovable, lordly self. You'll be wonderful." She stood on her tiptoes. "And here's a kiss for good luck."

She'd meant to give him a quick peck on the lips, but he pulled her in close. She held back for a moment, worrying about creasing the silk tie she'd so neatly knotted, then gave in and kissed him back.

"Come on," she said. "We don't want to keep everyone waiting."

They'd decided to do the interview in the great room, where the furniture was the most ornate, and the paintings the most overpowering. She and Simon, her cameraman, liked the juxtaposition of the ancient grandeur with the young, modern earl.

When they crossed the threshold, he said "Good God" under his breath. From his perspective, the setup must have looked pretty overpowering. Not to mention intrusive. Power leads stretched and coiled like thick black snakes across the priceless rug. Two cameras were set up, one to record the interviewer and one for George. Two cameramen, the lighting technician, the sound tech, the interviewer, a gopher, and Suz. The room seemed to be crawling with people who clashed with the furnishings, the décor, the very elegance of the room. The lights were huge and hung like twin suns.

He must have felt that his ancestral home had been invaded by aliens.

"Don't worry," she said, squeezing his arm. "We'll soon be done and you'll get your home back. You must be looking forward to that."

He glanced down at her. "I've never anticipated anything with less pleasure."

His gaze was serious, all the usual light charm and humor gone. She felt her heart skip a couple of beats as they stared at each other. How had it happened? How had they slipped from a light, carefree, secret affair, much aided by the hidden passageway, to this searing intimacy? She hadn't allowed herself to think about how soon they'd be packing up and moving on. She always packed up and moved on. It was part of her job, part of her personality, in truth, so that the job was often a handy excuse.

Now, for the first time ever, she realized she wasn't ready to leave. "Oh, George," she began. She didn't know what she wanted to say, only that it was important, but before she'd gotten more than those two words out, Simon caught sight of them. "Oh, good. You're here."

The spell was broken, and she wasn't sorry. What would she have said? What did she want to say? George was wonderful. Gorgeous, funny, sweet, even rich if you didn't count the burden of debt and the fact that he could never sell Hart House. It was sort of like inheriting a museum, she decided. The responsibilities balanced out, and possibly outweighed, the benefits.

But he'd gotten to her, in a way that no other man ever had. She didn't even know when or how it had happened.

She'd been so busy making the documentary, getting to know him as a subject, and then as a man, that she was half in love with him before she'd realized she was beginning.

She watched George take his seat, and let the sound technician fuss with his lapel mike while she stood frozen in the background.

Suz went to him with the Max Factor foundation powder. Honestly, the way he recoiled you'd think they were going to make him up like *Boy* George.

Love.

That was what made this affair different from every other. She'd gone and fallen in love with George the way an unwary pedestrian falls down a flight of stairs. One minute she was heading straight forward on a chosen path, the next minute she was tumbling head over heels and landing on her ass.

Moving closer, she hovered outside the circle of light. Janine Wilkins, the on-camera interviewer, was going over the questions. Janine had enjoyed a respectable career on Broadway playing the second lead and then the older woman.

Max had seen her in a summer stock production of *Brighton Beach Memoirs* as the mother and thought that she had the right look, elegant but approachable, and exactly the right voice for the talking head of the *Grand Titles, Great Estates* series.

Today, they'd dressed her in a blue suit. She and the earl could sit down to high tea and look perfectly matched. Her blond hair was upswept, her makeup subdued.

Walking up to them, Maxine said, "You look gorgeous, Janine. As usual." They air-kissed. Then Max walked their program host over to George and introduced them.

"Any last-minute advice?" he asked her.

"Yes. Stop being a big baby about that makeup. It stops you shining and makes you look better." He had on his I-will-throw-you-in-the-dungeon-if-I-don't-get-my-own-way expression, so she grabbed the powder from Suz. "I'll do it." She didn't give him a chance to argue, simply went at him with quick strokes. "There. That wasn't so bad."

"I feel like a bloody great poofter," he whispered. "This stuff smells like my old aunt Edith."

"Trust me. It's good. You'll wash it off after and no one will know."

"I can't believe I agreed to this," he complained.

"This time, you don't look at the camera. Look at Janine, or at least in her general direction."

"Right. Okay. Where will you be?"

"I'll be standing at the back, watching." She couldn't kiss him in front of all these people, so she touched his shoulder. "Break a leg."

Janine was settling herself in the chair, getting miked up, when Max leaned over and said, "You're a natural interviewer. Use those questions as a guide, but go ahead and press him a little bit if you sense he's holding back. I think he might be a bit elusive."

"Sure. No problem." Janine flicked her a glance. "Easy on the eyes, too."

Max chuckled. "You noticed."

She checked her monitor. Said to her lighting tech, "There's a shadow on the right side of his face. Can you fill a little bit?"

When she was satisfied, she nodded to Simon, who started rolling. She watched in her monitor. Simon did his wide, establishing shot of Janine and the earl. He then went in tight on Janine for her intro.

"I'm here in the great room of Hart House," Janine said to the camera, "with the nineteenth Earl of Ponsford." She talked about George and his ancestry, including his American mother, of course, and then turned to the earl.

George, Max was pleased to note, looked relaxed and urbane. He'd probably learned interview protocol in nursery school.

The second camera was trained on George.

"You trained as an architect, I understand, and until recently worked for a London firm."

"Yes, that's right. I'm still employed by the firm, but I'm on a leave at the moment. Since losing my father last year, I've had to step in and run the estate."

"That must be a lot of work."

George had obviously read the questions carefully, for his answers were smooth. He gave enough detail about the estate, but not too much. So far the whole interview was going so well there'd be little editing needed.

Max left the monitor and moved around until she was standing behind Janine's chair, but out of camera range. From here she had a clear view of George and the leisure of staring at him without being thought crazy. Or crazy in love.

"You were named by *Hello!* as one of England's twenty-five most eligible bachelors," Janine said. "How did that make you feel?"

Whoa, Maxine thought. *Good one, Suz*. Hah, she was sleeping with one of England's most eligible bachelors. How did she feel about that?

"Bashful. And a little nervous." Here he gave a glance around, as though being pursued by a bevy of female *Hello!* readers, that made Maxine smile. It would go over great in the broadcast.

"What do you look for in a woman? In a future countess?"

"Well, obviously, I'm looking for the woman first. We'll worry about her being a countess later." He paused, crossed one leg over the other. "What am I looking for in a woman? Humor, intelligence, someone I can laugh with and be myself with." He glanced at Janine with his naughty boy, flirty eyes. "I've always fancied the idea of someone who worked in television."

Janine was an old pro, and she handled him perfectly. You could feel the warmth and the slight older woman–younger man thing batted between them like a badminton birdie.

"Of course, any woman who married me would have to give up a lot. I'm running the estate now, and so I can't go off and live in London, say, or Los Angeles. She'd have to be willing to live here a great deal of the time."

L.A.? Odd he should mention L.A. He might have been talking about Max.

Janine waved her hand graciously at the antiques and magnificence of the great room, and smiled. "I think a lot of young women would be willing to live in Hart House."

"It's not all garden parties and spreads in posh magazines," he said. "This is a working estate. The livelihood of one hundred and eighty-two people depend on it, the village depends on it. Frankly, it's a lot of work."

"You wouldn't give it up?" Janine sounded alarmed. She'd gone way off the script, Maxine was fairly certain, but it didn't matter. Janine was a born interviewer. She knew instinctively when to follow a line of questioning and when to revert to her script.

"No, of course not. I was born and raised to be the Earl of Ponsford. It's my duty as well as an honor, but for a woman who wasn't born to it, it might be a bit more than she bargained for."

"Is there a special woman in your life?"

Oh, no, Max thought. If only she'd had time to check the script over, she'd have cut that line. It was personal, impertinent, it was . . .

George's eyes drifted over Janine's shoulder to rest on

her. He'd been following her movements, then; he knew exactly where she was. "Yes," he said. "There is."

Through the bright lights, the cables, the technicians, the whirring cameras, she felt that gaze and they could have been alone. She shivered as she realized he had been talking about her. She didn't realize her hand had moved to her chest until she felt her own heart pounding against her palm.

"So the estate may get a new countess fairly soon?"

"That depends on whether she'll have me," George said. His eyes had never left Maxine.

She wanted to run forward and throw herself into George's arms and yell, *Yes!* Cameras and all. Wouldn't that make a dramatic scene for *Grand Titles, Great Estates?* At the same time, she was conscious of an equally strong desire to turn around and run the other way. Out of the great room, out of Hart House, out of England as fast as commercial air service could take her. She was from L.A. She had a job she loved, a life. George was right, he couldn't be the kind of modern man to follow his woman even if he wanted to. He was stuck here.

That meant that if they were serious about each other, she was the one who would have to move.

She loved George. The feeling was still new and tender in her chest, but it was undeniable. But did she love him enough to give up her job? Her life? Her country?

Chapter Nine

When the last question had been asked, Janine removed her mic and the assistant producer unhooked George. They both rose.

Max joined them, trying to act as if her world hadn't tilted slightly.

"Well," Janine said to Maxine, when she joined them, "I thought that went really well, didn't you?"

"Ah, yes. Absolutely. Yes. Really well, really, really well." *Shut up,* she told herself. *Quit babbling.* The quick smile George sent her was as intimate as his answers to Janine's questions had been.

And she felt as unsettled as she had listening to him.

"Well," she said, "I'd better get down to the pub and see how things are looking. We shoot there tomorrow." And with a wave, she was gone.

The ornate walls, priceless, irreplaceable furniture, paintings, carpets, the thirty-foot painted ceilings seemed to oppress her. Even the marble floor glared up at her as she clacked across it on her way out. Once she'd made her way outside she felt the great weight of the building behind her, grimacing at her back, as though telling her she didn't belong. She strode down the long, oak-lined avenue, her mind in turmoil, her heart the same.

"Max."

She heard George shout out her name but didn't turn. Maybe he'd go away. She wasn't ready to be alone with him. Didn't know what she wanted, what she felt, what she ought to say.

The unmistakable crunch, crunch, crunch of a man running on gravel came to her ears. He was getting closer. Unless she tried to run away—and his legs were so much longer than hers, he'd catch her anyway—she might as well face him.

So she turned.

His muted tie flapped as he ran, his polished shoes were getting dusty, but he still looked aristocratic, elegant, and yet sexy. His long-legged stride was athletic, and he ran like a guy who'd run a lot of miles in his time, whether on the tennis court, the soccer field, or—like now—running after women.

"You scarpered off awfully fast."

"I did."

They walked on in silence. She was aware of him looking at her face, but she kept her gaze resolutely forward. "You're a natural on camera, you know."

"I wasn't thinking about the camera. When she asked me those questions, I was thinking about you."

Max looked out at the acres of land and the lines of ancient trees. There was the tree he'd dragged her underneath when he first kissed her, only a week ago, and it seemed like years. If she'd known that she'd wind up falling in love with him, would she ever have let him kiss her? Would she have kissed him back? Made love with him?

She snuck a glance at him and knew the answer. Of course she would have.

"It's all so complicated."

"God, yes, and bloody inconvenient," he complained, so she had to smile. "I worry that you couldn't bear to live here, that you'd hate it as much as Mother did, but I have to try. I love you, you know." There it was.

So simply said. Such a simple emotion, really.

"I know," she whispered.

"I didn't intend to spout all that rubbish during the interview, but I could see you standing there, and it seemed right, somehow, to announce my intentions to the world. We've been so discreet, I don't think anyone knows about us. But I'm sorry if I upset you."

She turned to him, wanting to throw herself into his arms and say, *Yes, yes,* to everything. But she couldn't.

"I was just thinking about that first night in the pub, your birthday. It was raining and you pulled me under that tree there, do you remember?"

"Of course I do. I remember everything about that night," he said softly.

She nodded. It was the first time they'd made love. She'd never forget it either.

"I was thinking, if we'd only known that our crazy little fling would turn serious, maybe we would have thought about it more carefully."

"Would you have acted any differently?"

She made a weird sound between a sigh and a laugh. "I asked myself that same question and the answer's no. This has been . . . amazing."

"Maxine. I don't want to lose you."

"I don't want to lose you either."

"I want you to marry me."

"Oh, please don't say that," she wailed.

"Why not? I love you. Why shouldn't I want to marry you?"

"Because I live in L.A. And when I'm not there, which is a lot of the time, I'm all over the world. I don't stay still. I'm restless. I love the next adventure, the next story, the next interview, the next show, the next series."

"And I'm stuck here."

"You're not stuck. This is your home, and your life, and your heritage."

"And you hate it. You miss palm trees, and Rodeo Drive, and those frightfully muscular fellows on the beach in Speedos."

She laughed. "No. I don't hate it here. I love it. I love that this land is virtually unchanged over centuries, and I love that you know who your great-great-great-grandmother was and that she loved to needlepoint, and, in fact, her needlepoint and her portrait are in your house. I love this village and the slow pace of life." She drew in a tremulous breath. "And I love you, George. I only realized it today. Bang. It hit me on the way to the interview, so it was a double shock to hear you saying those things only a few minutes later." She rubbed a hand over her hair, pulling slightly on the ends, as she only did when she was nervous or preoccupied. "I . . . What does a countess do exactly?"

"Well, you'd give out the prizes at the local fête, be the hostess for several public events, but mainly we'd live like normal people."

"Except for the title and the huge estate."

"Apart, of course, from those." He took her hand. "I can't leave, you're right. I can't even manage a job in London. Even once I've hired another manager for the property, I'll still have to spend a good deal of time here."

She nodded. "I know."

"But I'm not stuck here all the time. We could go on holidays and visit America. But"—he looked back at the great house looming over them—"this will have to be my home, I'm afraid. And, if you agreed to have me, I couldn't put up with what my father did, or have my children miss their mother half the year."

"I have to keep working, George."

"Of course. And often you'll be away. I understand that.

But if you can't face England, or the estate, then don't have me."

"When a girl thinks of living in an honest-to-God castle, that's usually a good thing. But all those fairy tales never mention the costs of heating, and that you have to live in a house with servants—which is weird when you're not used to it—and you can't someday decide to give it all up and move to Morocco."

"No. Those are decided drawbacks, you're quite right."

"But then I think about walking away from you, and I'm not sure I can do that, either."

He took her face in his hands and she could see that he understood. "Well, that's something. Because I can't bear to think of it." And he kissed her, slow and sweet and tender, so that for a minute L.A. and her home, friends, career, itchy feet, none of it mattered.

Except that it did matter, and when the kiss ended, everything she'd made of herself, all the choices and hard work and guts that made her a successful producer at thirty-one were still there. "I feel like you're giving me the most precious gift, and I'm acting like I don't want it, but I do." She leaned her head against his chest, breathing him in, loving the feel of him, so solid against her.

"I do understand, you know. I want so badly for you to say yes, but I do understand."

"Can I have some time to think about things?"

"As long as you need."

She hesitated. "We'll be finished shooting tomorrow."

He turned to her, alarm clear in his expression. "You're not leaving? Surely. I understood you'd be staying on for a few months."

"I'm not leaving the country, but once the shooting's done here, we move to our other locations. Then I'll have to go back to L.A. to finish the scripts and edit the series."

"So after tomorrow you're done here."

"Yes."

"I didn't know it would be so soon."

She chuckled. "Admit it. When we first arrived you couldn't wait to be rid of us."

"That was before I came to know you," he said with dignity.

Oh, she thought, how could she ever leave him?

And how could she ever stay?

Chapter Ten

The final scene to shoot was the pub. Maxine and the cameraman started outside with the establishing shots. "Pan of outside of the pub, close in on the sign, and then the door," she said.

"Sure. Do you want the street?"

She wrinkled her nose. "Maybe just this section, from the newsagent's to that gift shop."

"You got it."

She left him to it and walked inside, where the rest of the crew were setting up under the curious gazes of the pub patrons. They didn't seem bothered one way or another. She'd dreaded finding the pub packed to overflowing with the curious and those who wanted their faces on TV, and she had a crowd control plan all ready, but it seemed she wouldn't need it.

The pub was about as crowded as it had been the first time she'd stormed in, irritated and looking for George. How different her feelings were now. She saw him not as a slacker trying to evade his responsibilities, but the very opposite. A man who took his responsibilities so seriously that he'd threaten his own happiness.

And hers.

In his place, wouldn't she do the same? You couldn't turn your back on your destiny.

"Maxine? Are you all right?"

The voice belonged to Arthur Denby, the pub's owner and one of George's "mates." He was looking at her in some concern.

"Sorry, yes. I'm fine. I was thinking of something else."

"Must have been something pretty bloody astonishing," he said, the concern softening into teasing.

"Hah, it was." She glanced over at George. "Do you believe in destiny?"

Arthur followed her gaze, then sent her a curious glance. "Do I believe in destiny?" He appeared to ponder the question, while Suz stuck down an electric cord with gaffer's tape to keep it out of the way, and her sound tech checked the ambient noise, and the pub patrons drank, and watched, and chatted among themselves.

"Well, I've always thought a man, or woman," he said, inclining his head to her, "makes his own destiny. But sometimes, sure, things happen and there's no getting around the fact that they throw you off course."

"But you think the man or woman is still in control?"

"Well, when destiny comes along, you can sit back and take what it dishes out, or you can choose what you're going to do about it, can't you?"

She sighed. Still looking at George, as though she could store him up for when she was gone. "And isn't that the kicker? Figuring out what you're going to do?"

"George is a good bloke," Arthur said. She could have protested that her discussion of destiny and George were unrelated, but she respected Arthur's intelligence. "One of the best." He shook his head. "If destiny is pushing you in that direction, you could do a lot worse."

"Have you ever been in love, Arthur?"

"Sure. Lots of times." He had a softened burr, an Irishman who'd lived in England a long time.

She smiled, shaking her head. "One of these times it's going to stick. And you may find it's more complicated than it seems, this love business."

"Maybe you're right," he said with a shrug and the slight insolence of a man who's never had to choose between love and career. *One day, darlin'*, she thought to herself, *I'd like to see you deeply in love and torn apart by it, then see if the superior smirk isn't wiped off that dark, handsome face of yours. One day.*

The roar in the pub dimmed. The sound guy miked George, but they'd decided to go for a boom mic for the rest of the dart players.

Simon was inside now, his camera on his shoulder. "Arthur," she said, "would you mind telling everyone to relax and not look at the camera? We want this as natural as possible. The instructions will be better coming from you."

"All right."

"Attention, everyone," he boomed. The room was silenced in an instant. Wow. Cool trick.

"If you want to be on television, you have to act cool. Relax, don't look at the camera, and have a good time." She nodded, pleased with him. "And, if you're very good, these lovely people have offered to buy a round for everybody at the end of it."

A ragged cheer greeted his final words, and he turned to Max and winked at her. Oh, what the hell. If she couldn't submit that invoice, she'd eat the cost.

Since George had threatened to spank her in a very painful and not sexually fun way if she dared come near him in the pub with the pressed powder, she refrained. He was dressed as he always dressed for darts. Casual shirt, rolled at the cuffs, and today a navy T-shirt underneath. He made aristocracy look sexier than any movie star she'd ever worked with.

She backed out of the camera's sight line. To her it was like being a studio audience or watching live television. She saw the scene before her, but it was apart from her. She was the viewer. A hypercritical one, of course, as she looked with an eye to editing, an overall impression of pace, energy, in-screen design, and overall entertainment.

Simon glanced at her and she gave him a thumbs-up. Then she found George also looking her way and she blew him a quick kiss. The glance she got in return was steamy enough to melt wax.

"Okay, your lordship, go for the darts," the cameraman said.

"We've got sound, speed, we're rolling."

Max stepped back to watch the monitor.

You had to be so careful with a documentary. People wanted to learn something, experience something foreign to them, but they also wanted to while away an hour or two in a pleasurable manner. So she tried to inform and entertain.

This portion of the program was definitely more in the entertainment category. There was the nineteenth earl of Ponsford with a regular-guy shirt on, sleeves rolled up—she'd insisted on that. She liked the visual metaphor of him rolling up his sleeves and joining in the village darts game down at the local pub.

You could tell a lot about a man from the way his friends treated him, she thought.

And George seemed like a man with a lot of friends. He was perfect for her in every way but one huge one. How could she be so sure? She'd known him officially for a few months, spoken on the phone and by e-mail, but only spent a week as lovers. How could she know she loved him? How could she even contemplate marrying the man?

Well, you could learn a lot about a man when you spent a week with him, 24/7, under somewhat trying circumstances. Maybe they'd fallen in love with the fast-forward button on.

When the shoot was over and she'd bought everybody a round, it seemed perfectly natural to stay at the pub and enjoy fish and chips, or Cornish pasties, and a glass of lager or a pint of stout. Since it was the last day of shooting at Hart House, there was a convivial party atmosphere. Tomorrow they'd be moving on to a new location, and chances were they wouldn't be coming back this way again.

As the evening progressed, she found herself glancing more and more often in George's direction, and worrying less and less about who might sniff out that something was going on between them.

When he caught her gaze and held it with his own, she read all the longing she felt reflected in his eyes. Why did this have to be so hard?

The key crew members were staying at the castle—she thought that since she was staying there, George had felt honor-bound to invite Simon and the others. So it was a noisy group who left the pub at eleven and walked back to the castle singing English pub songs that Arthur had insisted on teaching them.

"'Cor, what a mouth, what a North and South,'" Simon bellowed as he tromped up the path.

It was their last night, and she knew George felt it as keenly as she did. She didn't even know when she was coming back or how long she could stay when she did.

Well, for tonight she wasn't going to think about that. George was here, she was here, and for this last night, she didn't plan to get much sleep.

Tomorrow she could worry and fret and plan, and maybe grieve the love that simply wasn't meant to be. But for tonight she was going to enjoy the man she loved. Every inch of him.

When they returned to the castle, however, it turned out that Simon had purchased a fine bottle of scotch from the pub, and insisted on toasting George for his "generosity and for being a stand-up guy." Which was more than could be said for Simon, who was weaving and swaying, the bottle swinging like a conductor's baton, punctuating his slurred speech.

"Well, all right, then. Just a small one," George said. "I'll fetch some glasses."

Janine had the sense to take the bottle from Simon and do the pouring, thus saving the expensive rug and keeping the drink sizes moderate.

Max could have kissed her.

The six filmmakers settled in, and Max, who usually enjoyed these impromptu parties as much as anyone, had never more wished to be spared.

George sat down and appeared a man at his ease, but she could see the tiny movement of his foot tapping. She picked up the rhythm and found her fingernails tapping her knee in synchronization.

God, would Simon never shut up? And did Janine have to encourage him to launch into his stories about his days shooting soap operas? Okay, they were funny stories, and she loved Simon, but not now.

She glanced at her watch. Ten minutes. Then she'd slip away.

When she lowered her wrist, George was looking at her with slightly raised brows. She stretched out the fingers of both hands and he gave a tiny nod. He could wait that long. Well, he'd have to. He'd wait another five minutes or so for form's sake, but she anticipated that within twenty minutes they'd be naked, in his bed, and everything else could be put away until morning.

Her body stirred as she tried to decide what she'd like to do to him first.

She made it to nine minutes. Close enough. She rose, putting aside the heavy crystal glass, and yawned. "Well, I think I'll turn in. We've got a travel day tomorrow. I need my sleep."

Simon, in a most un-Simonlike manner, suddenly rose, too. "Ya know, that's an excellent idea," he said. Then he blinked.

"And Max, before morning, I need to talk to you. Got a problem."

Frustration boiled in her stomach. No, no, no. She did not have time for this. "Can't it wait until morning?"

Simon shook his head violently. "Think we need to make a personnel change. Ted's mother's sick. He wants to go home."

Even though lust was lapping at her nerve endings, she knew this couldn't wait until morning. She'd have to make some calls and try and replace Ted. "I'm so sorry about his mother. Of course. We'll work something out."

"Ted?" George said. "The lighting man?"

"Yes. Crucial member of our team," Simon informed him.

"Will Ted stay on until we find a replacement?"

"You know he will. But she had a heart attack. She's okay, but he wants to get back." Simon knew the guys, but she was the one who got stuck with problems like this. She felt sorry for Ted, sorry that his mother had suffered a heart attack, but also sorry for herself. The timing was bad in every way.

"Okay," she said. "I'll get onto it."

She sat down, and Simon sat with her. They were deeply into a save-their-butts strategy session when George entered the room. "Sorry to interrupt," he said, "but I'm off to bed now. Wanted to say good-bye." Simon rose and the men shook hands.

When Max put out her hand to shake, he leaned in to kiss her cheek. "Pleasure," he said, and gave her the ghost of a wink.

As he was leaving, and she was thinking she'd be better able to solve their problems in the morning, she heard Wiggins say, "Ah, I thought you were in, sir. There's a small matter I think you should be aware of."

With one panicked glance at her, George said, "I suppose it can't wait until morning?"

"I think not, sir. If you'd step into the library."

"Right. Okay." And off he went.

Oh, great. Just great. Their last night and it was like a warped game of Clue. The earl was in the library with the butler. The producer in the sitting room with the cameraman and the scotch.

Finally, she got away from Simon and made her way up the stairs. The library door was closed, she noted, and the lights were on.

When she got to her room, she calculated that it was afternoon right now in L.A. Let them get started on the problem. It was weird to talk to Hank, her boss, and picture him at his desk so far away.

Suddenly, she felt very far from home, from her own life. He sounded delighted to hear from her. "How's it going over there?"

"Well . . ."

"Listen, I've been thinking, what about expanding this series? Why don't we go to Europe and do some castles? Same concept."

Max rubbed her forehead. Lust was interfering with her ability to think. "Um, the title part would be a problem. Not many European nations still have titled families living in castles," she reminded Hank.

"Right. But that's what makes it work for us. Loads of those deposed royals and all live Stateside, right? We could have a whole subseries on kings without thrones. Talk to those guys who are royalty from Russia and places, but work as doormen in Manhattan and car salesmen in Cleveland. Go with them and tour the old estates. What do you think?"

"Honestly? I can't think. It's been a long day and all I can think about is bed." And how.

"Right, sorry. I'm forgetting. So why are you calling so late?"

She explained the problem with Ted. Hank was a take-charge kind of guy, which she liked about him. And he immediately said, "Don't worry about it. I'll get the ticket changed and get the kid home, and I'll find somebody else. In two days you'll have a new sound tech. I promise."

She laughed softly. "You are the best."

"Of course. That's why you work for me. Now get some sleep."

"I'm going to bed right now," she promised him, and that wasn't a lie, she thought as she clicked her phone off. Though there'd be little sleep involved.

She washed up and then slipped into the ridiculously sexy nightgown she'd bought at the lingerie shop in town. It was the color of antique gold and looked fantastic on her. She'd probably bought it because it reminded her of the décor.

Since she'd freeze on the way down that passage, she threw on her cotton robe.

Half an hour had passed since she'd come upstairs. She sure as hell hoped the Wiggins business was taken care of.

She turned the acorn knob with the ease of practice, and entered the dark passageway. She'd pushed the flashlight into her pocket, but she didn't switch it on. She sort of liked the secrecy and the sense of adventure of going through a dark, secret passageway to meet her lover.

Of course, she'd checked it out pretty carefully the first couple of times she'd come through here, and there were no bugs or signs of rodents or anything disgusting. She even thought, with a sense of sadness, that it was cleaned period- ically. There were no cobwebs as thick as carpet, no myste- rious casks or strongboxes. The air was musty and a little dusty, the corridor was narrow and not very high, and there was no light. Otherwise, it could have been any corridor.

But even though she suspected Wiggins came through here once a quarter with the DustBuster—she was sure he wouldn't let any of the staff in on the secret—she still got a thrill every time she came through here.

Naturally, knowing what was at the other end of the tun- nel was part of the thrill. The tunnel of lust, the corridor of sexual power, the—Abruptly her clever musings were cut off when she bumped into a body.

Chapter Eleven

Warm, solid, and breathing, but the man struck her so suddenly that she screamed and would have jumped a mile if shock hadn't frozen her in place.

"Max, it's me."

"Oh, God, George. You scared me."

"I thought you must be able to hear me. I could hear you coming down that tunnel like the three o'clock train from Croydon."

"I was thinking."

"Ah. Thinking about me, I hope."

He reached for her and pulled her against him, so her robe fell open and she pressed against him in nothing but a tiny slip of silk and lace that had cost about ten British pounds per inch. He wasn't wearing much more. His torso was bare, and he had on nothing but cotton pajama bottoms that were warm from his body.

"I like the feel of this," he said, running his fingertips over the lace and silk scraps that crisscrossed her breasts.

"It's new," she whispered, feeling a little breathless as he teased her.

"What color is it?"

"Antique gold. Here, I've got a flashlight. You could see it."

"No. Put your torch away. I rather like it in here. It's very private, isn't it?"

"So are our rooms," she said, but she didn't urge him back to hers or onward to his.

"I don't know. I'm terrified that Simon will come barging into your bedroom banging on about some sodding production problem or Wiggins will burst into my room because desperate criminals are destroying the estate."

"Desperate criminals? Is that what he wanted?"

"Oh, yes. Three ten-year-olds and a twelve-year-old. They were caught trying to pinch the trampoline from the adventure playground."

"Oh, no." She knew it was serious, and criminal tendencies in kids that young weren't a good sign, but she still had to stifle a snicker. "What happened to them?"

"The gardener caught them, and instead of letting me deal with it, as he should have, the bloody fool called the local constable."

"But—"

"The trouble is that the parents of two of the boys work on the estate. It's hideously embarrassing for them, excruciatingly so for me."

"But what would you have done?"

"Oh, I expect I'd have had the gardener haul each of them home to his parents and have worked out a fitting punishment. Make them pick up all the litter from the public grounds for a few weekends or something. Officially, I'd have known nothing about the incident. Now, there'll be all the awkwardness. Ah, well," he sighed, and leaned in, kissing her hair. "Can't be helped."

"I think," she said, rubbing her nose against his sternum, "that you make a very good earl."

"I'm still so new at it. I wish my father were here so I could ask him. Though, of course, if he was here, there'd be no need. He'd be the earl and doing a far better job of it."

"You miss him."

"At times like this, I do. And . . ." He stopped.

"And?"

"I'd have liked him to meet you. He'd have adored you."

She was touched. "I'd have liked it, too."

They stood quietly for a moment. The darkness was blanket-thick, both cover and comfort. When he touched her it came as a surprise.

"Your skin feels so smooth, so soft," he said, running his hands over her shoulders and down her arms. Then he skimmed her waist until his hands rested on her hips, orienting himself to her. Anchoring her.

Oh, how she would miss this, not just the sex, but the way he brushed her skin with his fingertips, as though it was a fresh experience every time. The way he'd talk to her. Those charming little compliments that slipped from between his lips like sighs.

Waiting to be together tonight had been dragged out so long, and they were both so desperate, and yet, still, he took things slowly.

She felt the slight friction of his fingertips against the silk, felt the warmth of his skin through the sheer fabric, and wanted more.

She reached for him, finding his shoulders, putting her arms around his neck and pulling his head down until she could kiss him. She tasted toothpaste and a hint of scotch. As his mouth moved against hers and their chins brushed, she could tell that he was freshly shaven.

How thoughtful. All the parts of her that wouldn't be getting chafed through close contact with his stubble tingled in anticipation. She opened her mouth to him, tasting him, nipping his lower lip. And all the time his hands were stroking her, exciting her through the silk. He traced the long muscles of her back. "Your muscles are tight. You seem really tense."

"It's been a long day. And that last hour was hell. I thought I'd have to drug Simon's drink to get away."

She moaned softly as he began kneading the knots in her shoulder. "Then my boss in L.A. wanted to chat. It's late afternoon there and he wants to talk about new ideas for programming. While all I can think about is finding you and getting naked." She kissed him. "All I can think about is this."

"I know," he said, his slow, soothing hands in odd contrast to the barely restrained need she recognized in his voice.

Even though her belly was growing heavy with desire and she ached to have him inside her, it felt so good to have him massaging away the day's tensions that she leaned into his hands, like a cat being stroked. He spent a long time on her shoulders and her back, and then he moved—very sneakily in the dark—and she felt his hands at her stomach, so warm and sudden that she gasped. He stroked her belly as he had her back, long, soothing strokes that left her quivering and wanting. It was like the Kama Sutra of massage therapy.

It was so quiet here, so still and so dark that her senses were abnormally heightened. Without sight, she was aware of subtle sensations. The sound of their breathing, the slight rustle as her gown brushed her skin, the smell of George's shaving cream on his freshly razored face, the feel of the ancient wooden wall at her back, and the firm warmth of George at her front.

When his questing fingers reached her naked thighs, he said, "You're trembling."

"I want you so much."

"It's different now, isn't it? Now that I've declared myself."

She smiled in the darkness. Such an old-fashioned expression, but it suited him.

"It's partly knowing how we feel, I think, and also knowing we won't see each other for a while. We have to make enough memories to last us a while."

"How long?" he asked, running his lips along her jawline.

"A few weeks." She clutched at him. "Shorter if I can manage it."

"I don't think I can bear to be away from you. We've barely begun to know each other." His hands were urgent on her, tracing her thighs, squeezing her buttocks.

"I know." She was so empty, so hot for him, waiting.

"Maybe I can come up and you can sneak me into your hotel room at the next location."

She could barely take in his words. If she didn't have him inside her soon, she'd explode. But the meaning finally sank in. "You'd do that? You'd drive all that way for one night?"

"I'd drive twice as far. You haven't even gone yet and I miss you already."

She smiled against his chest. "I know. I feel it, too."

His hand was moving higher, and she parted her legs to give him ready access to where she wanted him most.

"Your skin is so soft here. I don't think I've ever felt anything so soft."

"It's arousal," she panted. "Blood's rushing to the capillaries."

"Really?" His fingers paused, no doubt in surprise.

"I produced a documentary on sexual arousal one time. It's amazing the facts you pick up." She laughed softly.

"Let's see if we can find any more signs of arousal," he said in a low, teasing tone, letting his hand sweep higher.

She wanted to open up for him but her legs were shaking and she thought she might topple. He seemed to understand her dilemma, for he raised her knee and draped her leg over his elbow. She felt the air wafting across her privates and was so sensitive that even the slight movement of air felt like a caress.

Then he touched her and she let out a moan of pleasure. His fingers explored her with a deft, light touch, making her squirm.

"You're so wet," he whispered.

"I'm so desperately horny, you have no idea."

"Oh, yes I do," he said, and pushed a finger inside her.

"I want you," she cried. "Can't wait."

He didn't say anything, but she heard the rustle and tear of the condom package, then he grabbed her hips and hoisted her up. She opened her legs, wrapping them around his waist, and he pushed up and into her, shoving her against the cold wall. The shock of the cold wood paneling against her back was in sharp contrast to the heat coming off George. He took her fast and hard, and she took him right back, spread so wide that she felt the shock of impact right through her with every thrust.

Shudders rocked her. She felt that she was floating, with only the solid walls of the historic mansion and the solid arms of George holding her to earth.

When he came it was like an explosion inside her.

He staggered a little, and she clutched at his shoulders, wondering if they'd topple to the ground, but he recovered enough to let her down slowly.

They stood there, panting, leaning against each other until she whispered, "Your place or mine?"

"Let's start in your bed and end up in mine."

"Good plan," she said, and led him back the way she'd come.

Her room seemed overbright when she flicked on a lamp. Her nearly packed suitcase sat by the door, a reminder, if they needed one, that this was good-bye for a while.

Sure, they'd be able to visit, but it wasn't going to be the same. The fairy tale quality of living in his house and creeping to his room via secret passageway each night was over tomorrow. The next stage wouldn't happen because of circumstance and convenience; they'd have to make a deliberate and extraordinary effort to keep seeing each other.

Would they? She wondered. As strong as her feelings

were, she wondered if she'd get to the next site, throw herself into the next program, or series, or concept, and discover sooner than she could imagine that George was a sweet and erotic memory.

Then she felt his arms come around her, leaned against the solid warmth of him, and knew it wasn't ever going to be like that.

"I'm in love with you." The words, spoken aloud, surprised her even as she said them.

"I know," he said. When she turned and gazed at him, she found all the understanding she could have wished for in his face. He did know.

He kissed her softly, and the last of her barriers fell. She loved him. She'd owned up to the feeling she'd hoped would disappear, or at least turn out to be false. But it wasn't. She'd lived long enough, known enough men, to recognize that this was the real, till-death-us-do-part thing.

This time when they made love it was in the light. With gazes fixed and the passion slower, but deeper. With the truth out, their bodies could express the love they'd finally admitted.

She wanted to imprint this moment and carry it around her neck in a locket forever, so she could take it out and look at it every once in a while, when she was lonely or far away or simply irritated with life.

When he entered her, she felt herself open as she never had before. Love was scary, she realized. It made you utterly vulnerable. Except this didn't feel scary, it felt right.

His skin was warm and smooth against hers. There was a smatter of freckles on his shoulder that she'd never noticed before and which filled her with such tenderness she wanted to weep. She didn't. She kissed them, those pale, almost unnoticeable sun freckles. And she kissed the place where she felt his heart beating, and then she kissed his lips and was lost.

Chapter Twelve

They lay with their hands clasped, heads close together on one pillow, legs entwined.

"This situation, as you Brits would say, is bloody inconvenient."

"It is."

She sighed, and gazed at the gorgeous room, with enough antiques to remind her of where she was and who he was. "If you could change your circumstances, would you?"

"As you Americans would say, in a New York minute."

"Really?"

He traced her nose with a finger. "I was an architect in London, as you know. And a pretty bloody good one, if I do say so. I could have met you at a club in Soho, or maybe your firm would have done a bit on Britain's sexiest architects."

She made gagging noises, but he merely grinned and carried on.

"And we'd have met. I'd have fallen all over myself trying to impress you."

"You'd have succeeded," she offered.

"And we'd have gone to dinner. Walked around Hyde Park, gone to the theatre. And when you went home, I could have followed you."

"Would you really? What about your job?"

"A job you can get anywhere. A woman like you comes along once in a lifetime."

She glanced at him sharply. Was he making a point? That she should quit her job and move to England to be with him? But he didn't seem to be hinting. She thought he really was contemplating his own life. He was right, though. This kind of love didn't hang around on street corners waiting for you to bump into it.

"And then your father died."

"Yes. I'd always known he would, of course. And I've always known this would one day be my life. My duty."

"Duty. Such an old-fashioned word. An important one, though."

"I could hire somebody and then leave the place for a good portion of every year."

"But you won't," she realized. "And maybe I wouldn't love you if you were the kind of man who could. The estate needs you. I can see how much good it does for you to be here, a part of it, trying to bring it back to prosperity."

"Yes. I suppose so. It's ironic really, isn't it? I'm a sort of Robin Hood in reverse. We charge the tourists money in order to hang onto a symbol of ancient wealth." He shook his head. "It's a funny old world."

"There's so much potential here, too. You could expand the wedding business and add more holiday options."

"We rent two of the former laborer's cottages," he said. "We've got them fixed up for self-catering holidays." He looked at her apologetically. "But this is still a private home. I don't want to live in a hotel, or operate a caravan park or something."

"No, of course not." But there were ways. She could see there were things that could be done to improve the bottom line. What this place needed was someone with some fresh ideas. Someone who had ties to the United States. Someone, in fact, like her. If she wasn't already employed.

She'd imagined they'd make love most of the night, but as it was they talked. Silly, intimate stuff. What scared you when you were a kid. (Him, the dark. Her, the fear of getting lost.)

"What scares you now?" she asked.

"I would have said losing Hart House. But now, I very much fear it's losing you."

Oh, how her heart leapt at those words. "We'll work this out," she promised. "I'm not sure how, but we'll work it out."

He nodded. Maybe a little sadly. Well, it wasn't like he could do much. She was the one who had to make a decision to change her life—or not. They both knew that.

"What about you?" he asked. "What's your biggest fear?"

She took a deep breath. "Failure."

"But you're amazingly successful."

"Yeah, well, now you know why. I'm terrified of failing. I think that's why I'm so driven."

"I suppose, then, that a lot hinges on your definition of success."

"And failure."

Sometime in the night they fell asleep.

George woke to the ominous sound of a zipper. He wasn't certain why it was ominous until he opened his eyes and realized that it was the zipper on Maxine's travel case. And that it meant she was leaving.

He flopped to his back and watched her. He didn't know what to say, only no. Please, no. Please don't go. But of course he didn't. Instead, he watched her gather her things together and then turn. She started slightly when she saw his eyes were open and on her, and the expression of longing he'd caught was quickly zipped away along with her makeup bag.

But he'd seen it. Recognized it. Inside herself, he knew she was saying no to their parting, too.

He had to say something, but they appeared to have run out of words. Good morning wouldn't do it. It was a shit morning. She was leaving. Have a nice trip? He hoped she had such a rotten trip she was back here within a fortnight.

I love you? She knew it. Repeating the words would only make him sound like a pathetic wanker.

She came forward, leaned down, and kissed him quickly on the lips. Soon she'd be gone and not a word spoken.

"Wait," he said.

She turned. Her brows rose slightly.

"I want to give you something." Oh, bloody hell. What? He was naked but for . . .

"My ring. I want you to take my ring. It's not a proper engagement ring, obviously. Well, for that you'd have to be engaged." He managed a bit of a grin. "And you haven't said yes, yet." He tugged at the ring on his pinkie finger until it gave way, scraping over his knuckle. "It's just something to remember me by."

He held it out and she looked at the thing shining dully on his palm. "In the States we have something called a promise ring."

He shook his head. "No promises. Call this an answer ring. If you decide you can bear to marry me, we'll get you a proper ring. If not, then keep this one. With my love."

She touched it with a fingertip, as though scared. "It's not a priceless heirloom that ought to be on display with the crown jewels, is it?"

"No. It's my school ring. I'm fond of it, that's all."

She nodded slowly. She pushed it onto the ring finger of her right hand, and it fit pretty well. "Thanks."

There was a pause, so thick with meaning that there was nothing left to say.

"I have to go."

"Yes."

And she was gone.

Failure. What did that mean exactly? Max mused as Simon's rented Land Rover lumbered up to the next grand manor on the list. Simon was morose this morning. He wasn't a morning person and she had a strong inkling that the beer followed by the scotch last night had left him less talkative this morning.

Green hills and fields dotted with sheep made restful, almost hypnotic viewing as they headed north. She'd already visited the location and knew that the industrious owners were selling a lot of Olde English jams, jellies, fruit cakes, condiments, and candies over the Internet.

The estate was family-run, and the baronet she'd be interviewing had three pink-cheeked English children, so perfect they looked like a politician's Christmas card.

For some reason, going to that perfect family depressed her a little.

Failure.

Would she be more of a failure if she quit her job and became the wife of an estate-bound earl? Or would true failure involve passing on the only man she'd ever loved?

She'd received an e-mail from her mom with the news that her sister Rachel's divorce was final. Somehow, if the universe had the time to send her signs, that seemed a clear one that true love wasn't all it was cracked up to be.

Although Rachel's choice of husbands sucked big-time, which had to be a factor. Rachel hadn't given up her career, though. She was a chef with a growing reputation in one of L.A.'s hottest restaurants. Even with her marriage breaking up, she'd have her life. Her identity. Her work.

All the things that Max would have to give up.

But she could still marry George and be herself, for God's

sake. And there was always work. She could take over the marketing of the estate, for instance. She could produce a short film for the visitors to see that would add value to their experience.

She could maybe even get some TV work over here.

She ran her thumb over the bumpy ring on her finger. He'd looked so sweet when he'd given her the ring, still warm from where he'd slept with it on his finger. She missed him so much already.

George tried not to be a whiner. He liked to think he was a chap who got on with things. But it wasn't easy when everywhere he looked, he saw Maxine or remembered something she'd said.

Two weeks passed and they managed one snatched night at an inn near York. Enough time to freshen their longing for each other, and make him more miserable when he returned home.

Two more weeks passed and the phone calls were getting longer, the sadness when they hung up deeper. She'd be finished in another few days and they were going to meet in London for a weekend before she took a flight back to L.A. for postproduction. Then how long until they could manage to see each other?

He was embarrassed at his own state of peevish lovesickness and, determined to rid himself of it, headed down to the pub for his regular Wednesday night darts game.

Arthur greeted him with a nod, and already had George's pint on the counter before he'd reached it.

"Cheers," he said, as he lifted the heavy mug and sipped.

"You look like a bag of shite," Arthur said.

"Thanks very much."

"You've got it bad."

George contemplated asking what Arthur was referring to, but decided he'd look like more of a git. "Yeah."

"I didn't think I'd live to see the day that you got that lovesick look about you."

"If you don't mind, I came here to have a few drinks with the lads and throw darts. I did not come to discuss my love life."

"Then you shouldn't come into my pub looking like a wet weekend."

"Sorry. You're right." George sipped again. "I thought I'd be able to forget about her for five minutes down at the pub, but I was remembering the scene they filmed here."

"Aye. I remember. That's the day she told me she loves you."

George set down his mug with a thump, feeling foolish and eager. "She did?"

"Clear as a bell. We were watching you. Well, I wasn't, but that girl couldn't tear her eyes off you. She had it as bad as you."

"I wish I knew what to do."

"Don't worry. She'll come back."

"And if she doesn't?"

"Then it wasn't meant to be. And a year from now you'll be falling all over yourself for some new bird."

He wouldn't, but he appreciated that Arthur was trying to cheer him up.

"You ever been in love?"

"Funny, Maxine asked me the same thing."

"She did?"

"Yeah."

"What did you tell her?"

"Same as I'll tell you. Lots of times."

George shook his head. "Wasn't real love. Believe me. When it hits you, you'll know."

"Well, if it makes me look as sick as you, I think I'll stick to the kind I know, thanks."

"You're the smart one. This kind hurts like hell."

Arthur glanced up as the door opened. It was Wednesday; with the darts they were always busy Wednesdays.

"What would you tell Maxine if she walked through the door right now?"

A tiny shaft of pain pricked him. God, if only.

"I'd tell her I love her. Which she already knows." He rubbed a hand over his face and realized he'd forgotten to shave. Which wasn't like him. Arthur was right. He was turning into a wet weekend.

"What else?"

"I'd tell her I've already set up three interviews for estate managers. I want to tell her I'll chuck the place entirely." Arthur looked startled until George shook his head. "But I can't chuck it. All I can do is work it out so I don't have to be here as often, I suppose. I'd tell her I can live without her, because there's nothing more nauseating than somebody pretending they'll die if they don't get the woman they want. But I won't live as happily, you see."

"That's not a bad declaration," Arthur said, a tiny grin playing around his mouth.

"Yeah. Maybe you should tape it and send it to her. She likes things that go on telly."

"He doesn't have to. I already heard it," a voice said from behind him. A female voice, one he heard in his mind all the time and hadn't imagined he'd hear again in person, not so soon.

He turned so fast he damned near fell on his arse. "Maxine."

He couldn't quite take it in. So he stared at her for another full minute. "You're here."

How had she grown more beautiful? She hadn't, of course, merely more precious. "God, I missed you," he said, pulling her forward and kissing her, not caring that everybody in the pub was staring. Let them stare.

Max didn't seem to mind, either. She kissed him back, clinging to him so tightly he could feel her heart hammering.

He pulled back, trying to keep some measure of cool. Remembering that one wretched snatched night, he asked, "How long are you staying?"

"I'm not sure."

"Right." Disappointment whacked him, but he tried not to let it show. "You've got more filming to do?"

"No. I need to give you this back," she said, and tugged his ring from her finger, placing it on the bar, where it made a tiny tap.

He stared at it. He felt every man, woman, and minor who'd snuck in with fake ID stare at that ring.

"It doesn't fit very well," she explained. "It was kind of big and I was afraid of losing it."

Didn't she remember? Didn't she know what he'd meant when he gave her the bloody thing? "I don't care if you lose it. It doesn't matter."

"I want to trade it in on a different ring," she said.

As the haze of his own rank stupidity cleared, he jerked his head to look at her and this time he could see what Arthur had obviously recognized the second she'd walked in, given that the man was popping the cork on a bottle of champagne.

"You don't mean . . . ?"

She nodded, the smile on her face widening. "The answer to your question is yes, unless you've changed your mind."

"No. God, no. I haven't changed my mind." He laughed shakily and pushed the hair off his forehead. "You mean it? You'll marry me?"

"I tend to be pretty decisive. Once I make up my mind, I move. That's something you should know about me."

He couldn't keep his eyes off her, or the grin off his face. "I'll keep it in mind." He glanced at Arthur. "You'd better keep opening those bottles. Champagne for everyone. I have an announcement to make."

"Right you are," Arthur said. He nodded to Maxine. "Good to see you back, love."

"Thanks. It's good to be back."

While corks were popping and the wait staff were delivering drinks, he said, "But what about your job?"

"I phoned my boss in L.A. to tell him I'd met someone and was staying here. I phoned to quit. Toughest decision I've ever made, by the way." She reached for his hand. "He said he's going to keep me on a contract basis. I won't work as much, or travel as often. But I'll still be able to do what I love."

"Maxine, that's fantastic."

"And while I've been away, I've been thinking that I could take over the marketing for Hart House. I've got connections, enthusiasm, I know how to get Americans interested. We're going to have corporate retreats, management seminars, wine tastings, and a lot more weddings."

"We are?"

"I'll have us in the black if it kills us."

He found glasses of champagne pushed toward him. He handed one to Maxine, gave her a quick kiss, and looked out at the people who lived and worked here, in this quaint, anachronistic village.

Some of their families, like his, had lived here for five hundred years. He was about to add a line to the family history.

"Friends," he said, "I have the pleasure of announcing that Maxine has agreed to be my wife. I ask you to raise your glasses to the future countess of Ponsford. Maxine."

A chorus of voices echoed, "To the countess!" Or simply, "Maxine!"

"I love you," he whispered so only she could hear, and then sipped.

"When are you getting married?" Arthur asked as the three of them sat together, drinking champagne with pub fish and chips.

"Well," George said, "what do you think about the spring?"

"George," she said, fixing him with the determined expression that had so unnerved him when he first met her. "Do you have any idea what a wedding costs?"

"Well, but darling . . ."

"Once we get things on a better footing financially, then we can think about a wedding."

He sipped more champagne. "What exactly do you mean, a better footing?" God, she didn't know the size of the debt. Or did she? He remembered hazily that he'd told her when they were having one of their intimate middle-of-the-night chats.

"I mean," she said, "that I will marry you when we are in the black. When the debt's paid off."

"But—"

"It's important to me. I've got so many ideas for getting the estate into the black they keep me awake at night. I've got spreadsheets and a report already written."

"Spreadsheets?"

She nodded vigorously. "By my calculations, and if you like all my ideas, I figure we can have the debt paid off in six months."

"Darling, you're not—"

She stopped him with a kiss. "Trust me. You have no idea how good I am at this stuff."

"But I want to get married now," he said, feeling a bit put out.

She only shook her head with a look that said, *Why buy the earl when you can get the family jewels for free?*

George looked at Arthur and shrugged. "Terrible, these American girls. All they want is the sex."

"I pity you, George," said Arthur, with a laugh. "I really do."

"In fact," Maxine said, as the chuckling Arthur moved away, "I'm wearing your school ring as an engagement ring. We can't afford—"

He put his hand over hers, stopping her from taking back the ring.

"I've already got you a proper ring."

"Oh, George."

"If you don't mind a family heirloom. The countesses of Ponsford have all worn it."

Who would have thought that this bossy, annoying dragon of a woman from across the sea would sweep into his life and steal his heart? But she smiled at him with tears in her eyes, and his world felt utterly right.

"I'd be proud to wear it," she said, and leaned in to kiss him in a way that made him think he'd be missing his weekly darts game.

"And there's one more thing," he said, putting his arm around her and leading her to the door, and home.

"What?" she asked, after they'd made it through all the congratulations and to the door.

"You'll have to sit for an official portrait."

She turned, her expression startled. "You don't mean . . . ?"

"I'm afraid so. Your portrait will hang in the long gallery. Five hundred years from now some nosy young journalist will come by spaceship to study you."

She leaned her head against his shoulder. "Can we have our picture painted together?"

"Anything is possible."

"But not until we're out of debt."

"God, no." He had a feeling he'd be scrounging pennies like a bloody miser, anything to get closer to the day he'd finally make her his, permanently.

He thought of her here, every day, warming his bed every night, and decided he could put up with the wait.

NIGHTS ROUND ARTHUR'S TABLE

Chapter One

Meg Stanton loved the smell of an English pub. That mixture of old blackened wooden beams and the centuries of beer spilled, drunk, and giggled over. If there was a moment that shouted, *Yes, you're in England*, it wasn't the glimpses of the Thames and London Bridge as she'd flown into Heathrow, it wasn't Big Ben, the Parliament Buildings, or the London Eye, or even the views of the countryside she'd caught through the window of the train. No. It was walking into this quintessential scene of English life: the pub, with its quintessentially English name, The Royal Oak.

The bar itself was a long stretch of ancient, scarred oak that looked far from royal. Tables were scattered on the dark wooden floor as though tossed there. A handful of older men played darts in a corner and an Inglenook fireplace gaped from one end of the big room, a cozy size for roasting an ox in.

A lone bartender was speaking to somebody through a doorway that led, she assumed, to a kitchen, his broad back turned her way. She was no expert on the complexity of the English accent, but he sounded like he was from up north somewhere.

He turned and she caught sight of his face. And felt a

rush of recognition flood her. *Oh, my God,* she thought. *I've found him.*

Uncompromising. That was the first word that sprang to mind when she saw him full on. His jaw was strong, the nose pugnacious, his brow smooth as though he didn't spend a lot of time with it wrinkled in indecision. His eyes were straight on and clear. For a woman constantly racked with indecision, Meg was immediately drawn to his strength. His eyes were pale, but in this light and from this distance it was impossible to tell the color. Blue maybe, or gray. He looked rough and capable. A working man who could build things with his hands, or use them to defend his village from attack.

"With you in a mo'," he said, and she nodded.

She stepped closer. While she waited, she continued to gaze about herself. There weren't many patrons at three o'clock on a Thursday. Apart from the darts players, she noted a couple in the corner lingering over the remains of lunch. An older man in a cap read a newspaper and nursed a beer, and a lone younger man worked on a printed document of some kind.

Stenciled quotations adorned the plaster walls. She couldn't pass words without reading them.

Work is the curse of the drinking class, Oscar Wilde.

Appropriately, that was stenciled above the dartboard. On the wall over the fireplace was: *I drink no more than a sponge, Rabelais.*

She spotted another, but it was hard to read because the lighting in that corner was dim. She squinted. *Eat, drink, and be merry, for tomorrow we die.*

A padded bench was attached to the wall and rectangular tables, perfect for one or two patrons, lined up in front of it. The vision came to her suddenly. A man's death, there in the corner. She could see it as clearly as though she were witnessing the murder. She stood, entranced, and stared into that corner of dark deeds . . .

Eat, drink, and be merry, for tomorrow we die . . .

"Are you all right?" A deep voice pulled her back to the present. Meg realized that the gorgeous bartender was speaking to her, and the way he spoke made her realize he'd addressed her several times before wresting her attention.

"Sorry," she said, the vision still so strong her fingers itched for a keyboard. "It was the blood."

His slightly irritated expression vanished. He blinked. Looked past her to where she'd been staring, then back again. "Blood?"

"That table there in the corner. A patron sitting, dead, but no one notices in the din of a Friday night at the pub, not until blood drips." She nodded. "Yes, that's it exactly. Not a bullet wound, of course, too noisy. A knife. It must have been a knife." She raised her hand, mimicking the motion of the murderer's fisted hand wrapped around the knife hilt, up and under the ribs and then a sudden twist to make sure death was quick and silent enough that no one would notice in a busy pub. The flash of red on her own fingers distracted her for a second until she remembered she'd treated herself to a mani and pedi before setting out on her adventure.

Every writer had her superstitions, her tricks for kick-starting a recalcitrant muse. One of Meg's—and she'd tried them all recently—was a manicure. There was something about perfectly manicured fingernails dancing across a keyboard that appealed to her. She loved doing a job properly, believed in keeping her tools in good working order. Her brain she fed with good food, books, and poetry. Her writing computer was not hooked up to the Internet, keeping it virus free and unpolluted by promises of a larger penis or a lottery win in Nigeria.

And her hands she pampered because they did the yeoman's work of writing. She had a special set of exercises to keep them supple and ward off the dreaded carpal tunnel syndrome, she bought wonderful almond-scented hand lotion to keep the skin soft, and she kept her nails polished and buffed, the way a race car driver might polish his car. Her brain was the engine, but it was her hands doing the work.

The pedicure she'd had simply for indulgence. Meg believed in small indulgences. She worked hard, and in the last few years she'd been able to enjoy quite a few of the fruits of her labors, so she could afford a little pampering.

Maybe a lot of pampering.

The dark-haired man behind the bar had given the table she motioned to a quick glance and then transferred his gaze back to her face. He didn't look at her as though she were a lunatic. He seemed more . . . intrigued. Up close she noticed the shadow of beard stubble and a single chicken pox scar at the corner of his right eye. Black eyelashes a woman would kill for, eyes that were keen, intelligent.

"What does he look like, the man?"

Meg glanced at the gorgeous bartender—no, she thought they called them publicans here—with approval. Excellent question. She closed her eyes for a moment and then saw him. The victim. "Salt and pepper hair, close cropped. A tiny moustache, kept well-trimmed, discreet. He's vain, but tidy with it. His clothing is somber but expensive. Yes, expensive."

"You've got the sight then, have you?"

No, she realized now, his accent wasn't from the north of England but from Ireland. Softened to a slight lilt, she guessed, by years in this country. And that's where he'd come by the extraordinary combination of that black hair with the blue eyes, for she was close enough now to see that they were a wonderful cross between bright blue and slate gray.

"I have a kind of sight," she admitted.

"I'm sure there's many a ghost around here. The pub's been here half a millennium."

He could have said five hundred years. But half a millennium sounded so poetic. Especially the way he rolled the words with that soft, deep voice. He was so perfect she wanted to kiss him. She dug into her bag for the paper and pen she carried everywhere. Her hands were tingling with the need to get this down while it was fresh.

"Do you mind if I sit down and take a few notes?"

"Not at all."

She walked to the table where the murder had happened, sat across from where the victim had enjoyed his last pint. Yes, she thought, a pint of Guinness. No, he was too fussy for that. She suspected he watched his weight.

"What do you call the half-pints of Guinness?" she asked the barman.

"A glass? Do you fancy one?"

"Hmmm?" She glanced at him vaguely, his question intruding on the words she needed to set down. "Oh, no, thank you." But she couldn't sit here and have nothing. "But I'd like a pot of tea, please."

Then she began to write.

And write. When she had the scene down and the heat of inspiration had cooled, she found she'd filled half a dozen pages of her notebook and her hand was pleasantly tired. She flexed her fingers.

She glanced around, realizing that time had passed. The lunch couple were gone, and a few more patrons had arrived. She was aware of a couple of curious glances, but whether they were due to the fact that she was a stranger or because she'd been scribbling madly, she had no idea.

The bartender caught her gaze and walked over.

"You've not touched your tea. I'll fetch you a fresh pot."

"Oh, thank you," she said, lifting her head and smiling at him. She hadn't even noticed the tea. She'd been in her own world, or at least that of the story. She felt dizzy with delight. Six handwritten pages wasn't much, but it was the first six decent pages she'd managed in months. She wasn't one to tempt fate, but she began to feel hopeful that her unexpected drought was over.

She was reading over what she'd written, scratching out a line here, adding a sharper adjective there, when he returned with a fresh pot of tea.

"Thanks," she said, adding milk and sugar and then pouring.

"When do you think he lived, the poor murdered man?" he asked her, nodding his head toward the chair where Manfred Waxman had breathed his last.

"Oh, he's contemporary," she said.

The dark brows rose. "How contemporary?"

She laughed suddenly. "I am so sorry. You must think I'm nuts. I'm not psychic." She paused. "At least, not very. I'm a writer. Fiction. I made him up. I saw him sitting there, and the blood, and I knew I had the victim for my next novel."

"Ah," he said, seeming a little disappointed. "I was hoping for a ghost."

"You like ghosts?"

"Well, it would make the quiet times more interesting."

She looked at him and found him even more attractive than the last time she'd seen his face. The angles were so strong. His skin was swarthy; she bet it would be tough and leathery to the touch. He wasn't even handsome in the acknowledged movie star way. What he had was magnetism. Amazing animal magnetism, the kind that would lead a woman to do very foolish things.

"You write murder mysteries, then?"

"Yes." She sighed with pure bliss and sipped her tea, strong and hot as only the English could make it. "I can't tell you what a relief it was to find my victim."

"Is that the hardest part? The victim?"

"No. The hardest part is the villain." This probably wasn't the moment to tell him that she thought she'd found her villain in this out-of-the-way country pub, too.

"Really?"

He appeared more than politely interested and the pub was nearly empty, so she told him. "A villain is the crux of a murder mystery. Especially one like mine. A maniacal, cruel, serial killer. He or she has to be attractive, subtle, devious, and deadly. You want the readers to identify with him enough that they become truly gripped."

"The reader identifies with the people trying to catch the killer, surely?"

"Who's the most interesting character in *The Silence of the Lambs*? For me it's Hannibal." She shrugged. "When I'm writing, the villain is the key." And as she stared into that deeply magnetic face with those stunning eyes, she began to be very glad she'd come into the pub. There was something tough, uncompromising, and somehow dangerous about this man. She had not only discovered her victim, but she had a strong sense that her villain was gazing at her now. A tiny shiver of excitement, apprehension—hell, maybe it was glee—traveled across her skin. "When I figure out who he is, I'll be able to really get going."

"Are you staying in the neighborhood?"

"Yes." She put a hand to her forehead. "I'm staying at Stag Cottage. I came in here to pick up the keys."

"And found a bloody corpse."

She started to laugh. "I'm so glad I came here."

"So'm I." And he sent her a glittering half smile that made her thankful she was sitting down so he wouldn't notice that he'd made her knees tremble. Dark, brooding, intense. There was something about him that made her vision of murder fade and something equally visual take its place. She envisioned hot, sweaty, high-octane sex, arms and legs tangled. His skin tawny, his hair so black against her own pale skin and light brown hair.

His eyes were staring into hers and she felt that he shared the intense awareness. She forced herself to break eye contact and take refuge in her tea.

"You must be Ms. Stanton?"

"Meg Stanton, that's right."

"Arthur Denby. Welcome to Ponsford." He held out his hand and she shook it. Arthur, she thought. Noble, resourceful, a warrior king. It fit him, though she wasn't sure the sexually predatory Lancelot wouldn't have suited the man better.

He strode back behind the bar and returned with a set of keys on a disappointingly modern-looking key ring. "Come on, then. If you're ready, I'll take you over."

"Oh. I'm sure I can manage." She didn't want him in her living space until that insistent picture of them together could be excised from her mind. For all she knew, the guy had a wife and six kids living upstairs, the kids washing glasses and the missus ironing his shirts while he lorded it over his domain down here.

"There are a few things I need to show you."

"Okay." She glanced around. He was the only bartender. "Do you want me to wait until it's more convenient?"

"Now's fine." He turned to the young guy with the printout. "Joe, I'm going to show this lady to Stag Cottage. Can you watch things for half an hour?"

"Yeah. Sure."

"Cheers."

They walked out together and Arthur said, "Have you got a car?"

"No. I thought about renting one, but I'm here to work, not sightsee."

"Where's your luggage?"

"At the train station. I walked over."

"Right. Come on then, Stag Cottage is across the way."

The sun was sudden and warm after the dim light in the pub. The stone walls glowed golden and the great estate on which her cottage was located was as elegant as a dream. Hart House, seen in context, looked even better than the pictures she'd viewed on the Internet.

There was no traffic on the narrow road, so they crossed it together. She liked the way Arthur walked, his long limbs swinging with confidence. He wore jeans and a long-sleeved black T-shirt that advertised no band, no cause, no brand-name clothes maker. She got the feeling that this man was nobody's billboard.

She tucked that notion away as an excellent detail to give her villain.

"How long are you staying?" he asked as they reached the road's dusty shoulder.

"Three months."

"To write your book?"

"Yes. I really hope to have a first draft written by then." A complete first draft. Not bits and pieces of chapters that went nowhere.

"This is the short way, across the fields. If you'd a car we'd have gone around by the road." As he spoke he gestured to a stile. An honest-to-goodness stile. She felt like a heroine out of Jane Austen as she stepped up and over and into the public footpath on the other side. Late-summer sunshine spread like butter across the fields.

And the tiny stone house sat there like a perfect retreat from the world.

"And there's Stag Cottage."

Her heart flipped over. She actually felt it somersault in her chest. The cottage was so perfect—exactly what a cottage should be, built of warm stone, with a thatched roof. She wanted to hug the place. Her senses were stirring and the mild panic that had traveled across the ocean with her relaxed. Maybe, just maybe, her crazy idea was going to work.

Chapter Two

Arthur Denby opened the door for her with the key, and she stepped inside. And she knew. If she hadn't already had a pretty big hint in the pub, she knew that she'd find her story here.

"This is so perfect," she breathed.

"Ever set a book in England before?"

She turned to stare at him. "No," she said slowly. "This is the first time." How stupid—it wasn't until he'd asked the question that she'd realized her book was going to be set in England.

She wanted to walk right up to Arthur and kiss him. Not because he was gorgeous and sexy and about to be written into her book as an irresistible villain, but because he'd saved her wasting any more time in the wrong setting. She'd come to England thinking her book would take place in the Puget Sound.

Nope. Britain all the way. She must have known. Somewhere inside her she must have known the solution, so she was receptive that day she was idling on the Internet looking for inspiration, and she'd come across the Web site that featured Hart House and its visitors' accommodation in Stag Cottage.

She put down her bag, containing her laptop, passport,

and wallet. The essentials. Everything else, including her toothbrush, was at the train station, but she already felt at home. In fact, she couldn't wait to get started.

"I'll show you how to use the cooker," he said, pointing to the oven in the small galley kitchen. She tried to follow what he was saying, but instead she found herself watching his hands when he lit the pilot light. Such capable hands. Such sensual hands. Oh, he'd know his way around a woman's body, this one. He exuded sexual power.

They could kill, too, those hands. Somehow she knew that. He wouldn't waste time on moral dithering. If someone he loved was threatened, if he felt he had no choice, he'd kill.

He'd have even less compunction making his interest in a woman clear. She doubted he'd often been told no.

"I'll take you upstairs now," he said, and she thought he'd listened in on her thoughts. She almost said "It's a little soon" before she realized he was still playing tour guide.

"Sure, okay."

Up they went. She followed him and felt the quiver of awareness. Oh, he filled out a pair of jeans nicely. She told herself to stop ogling the guy's butt, but where else was she supposed to look? Besides, she was a woman who believed in life's little luxuries, and this was surely one of them.

Just because she looked didn't mean she had to touch. And until this book was written, she reminded herself, looking was all she'd be doing.

The staircase was narrow, the walls rough plaster, wonderfully old and atmospheric.

There were two bedrooms upstairs, and a bathroom. The largest bedroom contained a big, comfy bed with a chintz-covered duvet in lavenders and greens. The walls were palest yellow, the ceiling sloped, and a dormer window overlooked the fields and the immense grandeur of Hart House.

When Arthur stood in her bedroom and explained about

the heat register, she could barely concentrate. He was looking at her, talking about the electric heat, but there was an
entirely different heat stirring the air. She felt it coming off
his body, from the eyes that looked at her so keenly.

She felt such an intense physical reaction to this man who
was a complete stranger that she took refuge in looking out
of the window. There was a river on the other side of the big
house and she could imagine herself tramping all over the
area on the many footpaths as she wrestled with her story.
In the distance she could see sheep moving slowly, like scattered clouds.

"It's a lovely part of the country," he said from behind
her.

"Yes, yes it is. But I'm here to work," she reminded both
of them.

They clomped back down the stairs and he handed her
the keys. "The number of the pub is by the phone. My home
number is there as well, if you need anything."

Was it her imagination or had he put the slightest emphasis on the last bit?

He was the most appealing man she'd met in a long time,
but she didn't have the time, not while her deadline was
breathing down her neck. So she sent him her blandest
smile.

"There are a few staples in the cupboards, but if you plan
to cook tonight, you'll need to get to the shops. The ones
in town close at five. There's a Sainsbury's—that's an
American-style supermarket. It's open until seven, but it's a
drive."

"Any chance of home delivery or takeout meals?"

"Not in the village. There's the King George Café—does
a nice breakfast, lunch and cream tea, but it's not open for
dinner—or there's the pub."

"Right. I guess I'll see you for dinner, then."

"You'll see me before that."

Her brows rose.

"I'll fetch your bags from the station."

"Oh, there's no need, I can—"

"It's all part of the service."

She took the keys he held out. "Thanks."

She allowed herself the luxury of watching him walk back across the fields, watching the long gait, the easy stride of a man at home in the country. She told herself it wasn't lust gluing her gaze to his retreating back, but research. When he got to the stile, he turned and lifted a hand. As though he'd known she'd be watching him. Which she had, damn it, she thought, waving back.

Okay, lady, she said to herself, *time to write.* The tingling in her fingertips that had never quite gone away since she'd had her vision in the pub now warred with a slight queasiness in her stomach that she knew was nerves.

She unzipped her bag and pulled out her laptop, placing it on the sturdy oak kitchen table. The kitchen chairs were also oak, though they appeared to be a later vintage than the table. They were also hard.

At home she had an ergonomic desk and a chair with about seventeen levers and knobs to adjust height, angle, and amount of lumbar support. She shook her head at herself as she found a cushion on the sofa in the lounge area, as Arthur had called it, and placed the flattish square cushion covered in green brocade on the kitchen chair. She faced the window and the view of the fields with the big house in the background.

A bit of crawling around on her hands and knees and a minor amount of swearing later, and she had her adapter plugged into the English socket. The computer seemed perfectly happy with the new system, powering up with a reassuring whir.

She sat down. Opened a new file, flexed her fingers as

though she were a pianist about to perform at Carnegie Hall. Typed *Chapter One.*

Then she sat against the hard wooden back of the kitchen chair and pondered the murder in the pub.

She pulled out the six pages and typed in what she'd written, adding details as she went.

The pub was busy. It was a Friday night. She imagined a lot of laughing, the thunk of darts hitting the dartboard, the end-of-the-workweek letting loose as the place filled up and the pints went down. The restaurant would be kept busy. Patrons as thick around the long bar as seagulls around a fishing boat. And, in the dim corner, the man in the expensive dark suit drinking his beer slowly. Was he waiting for someone? Or was it a surprise when the tall figure sank down beside him on the long upholstered bench?

A surprise, she decided. Her victim did not know his killer. She described the knife briefly. It wasn't elegant or showy. It was an unadorned stiletto: a tool of death. Nothing more. It was the hand holding the knife that fascinated her. The long, sensual fingers curled round the hilt. It was a man's hand. He wore no ring, but the fingernail of the thumb was ridged as though it had been smashed and had regrown in a strange manner.

Meg felt the moment that the knife moved. It wasn't a simple matter to stab a man to death in a public place. He needed strength, her villain, as well as guile and an amazing self-confidence. She saw all three come together in the way he watched for his moment, then took it, muscles bunching in his arm, the suppressed grunt of effort, the gasp of shock from the victim, and the quiet sigh as his last breath was expelled.

By the time Manfred Waxman slumped to the table, stabbed through the heart, the villain had pocketed his knife and was making his way to the door before the first drop of blood hit the floor.

She heard the pub door open, and shut. Then the villain sauntered down the village high street as though he were a man on his way home after a couple of pints. She felt the knife in his pocket, as though her own fingers touched the blade, still wet with a dead man's blood.

When a hand touched her shoulder she jumped a mile. She'd have screamed if her heart hadn't jammed in her throat, preventing her from making a sound. She swung around to find Arthur looking down at her in some amusement.

"I've never seen anyone go into a trance the way you do. I knocked on the door, and then I called. I could see you in here through the window so finally I let myself in. Sorry I startled you."

She put a hand to her chest, feeling her heart pound. She needed a minute before she could speak.

"I really frightened you," he said in a concerned tone. "You're trembling."

He touched her hand and she jerked back instinctively. His thumbnail was ridged. "What happened to your thumb?"

He took his hand back and looked down at the misshapen nail. "I banged it with a hammer a couple of months back. Terrible looking thing, I know."

"It's weird because my murderer has a thumbnail exactly like that." Of course, his misshapen thumbnail didn't make Arthur a murderer. It meant she'd noticed his nail and it hadn't registered consciously.

She shook her head. "Sorry. I scare myself when I'm writing. You crept up on me when the murderer was leaving the scene."

Amusement flickered in his eyes. "Writing your books frightens you?"

"Of course. If I didn't scare myself I'd be worried. It would be like a comedy writer not getting her own jokes, or a cookbook writer not feeling hungry when she dreamed up recipes."

He nodded, looking down at her with a thoughtful expression. "Better to end up laughing or eating a fine meal than trembling with fright, though."

"You're right, of course. Sometimes I get so scared when I'm writing that I can't sleep."

"What do you do then?"

"Keep writing. With every light burning and all the doors locked."

"Well, I can assure you it's safe round here, but if you're ever bothered by anything, you can call me." He gave her a rueful grin. "For a chat. I'm a light sleeper, myself. I live alone, so you'd not be disturbing anyone."

"Thanks," she said, hoping that she'd be strong enough to resist. Or at least strong enough not to phone him unless she was really, really scared. She wasn't happy with herself for being so pleased that he'd casually let her know he slept alone.

"Shall I take your bags upstairs, then?"

"That would be great. I found some tea bags and everlasting milk. Do you want a cup?"

He hoisted her three bags with such ease she felt jealous, knowing her arms and shoulders would be sore tomorrow from hauling them on and off the train. "Better not. I've got a few things to do."

"Okay." She was relieved, of course, since she didn't want to be interrupted now that the heat of the story was upon her, and she'd only asked out of politeness. But now that he'd turned her down, she wished he was staying, instead of abandoning her with no one but a murderer for company.

Hunger pangs, eye strain, and jet lag finally dragged her out of her story. A glance at the watch she'd already set to local time told her it was seven.

She prepared to head back to the scene of the murder.

Chapter Three

Arthur didn't admit to himself he'd been watching for the new tenant of Stag Cottage until the door opened and in she walked, the eccentric author who seemed to spend a great deal of time in her own world, deaf and blind to real life being lived under her nose.

Her hair flowed over her shoulders, glorious, the color of wheat right before harvest. Rich with gold and biscuity browns. She'd changed into a dark green sleeveless jumper, a black skirt that showed off a very nice pair of legs, and leather sandals. She'd applied makeup, he noticed, since he last saw her. She glanced around as she walked in, not shy exactly, but unsure.

He waved to get her attention and she sent him a smile that might be all about relief at seeing a familiar face, but which nevertheless got his blood up. She was much too pretty for her own good. Or his.

"How's the writing going?" he asked, loud enough to be heard over the din.

"Fantastic. I have a very good feeling about writing here." She'd done more than change her clothes, he noted. Her hair was shiny and slightly damp at the ends. Her eyes were hazel. Big and round and thoughtful. She had a glossy magazine smile, fine skin, and a few freckles.

"What can I get you?"

"Red wine, please."

He poured it for her and set her glass in front of her. "Everybody comes up here eventually. I'll introduce you round, if you like. Or are you here for absolute peace and quiet?"

She laughed. "I wouldn't have come here if I was. I'd have stayed home with the cans of soup and crackers in the cupboard."

"I shouldn't think anyone in town will be a nuisance. We get plenty of toffs—George's friends—coming through. And film and telly stars, of course, since the castle's been used for everything from toothpaste commercials to costume dramas."

"Well, that's a big relief." She held up her glass in a silent toast and sipped. He served a few more drinks, keeping half an eye on her. He could have sworn she was off in her own world again, but when he had time to mop up a spill, he found her chatting happily to Edgar Nolan, who ran the tobacconist's shop across the way. Edgar was an old widower, harmless, but he could bore the eyebrows off a beetle given half the chance.

George and Maxine wandered up to the bar. "Bugger me, if you don't get uglier every time I see you," the lord of the manor said to him.

"You can sit yourself outside with the rest of the lager louts," Arthur responded. Having proven their mutual respect and esteem, Arthur turned to Max. "Hallo, gorgeous. When are you going to give him the shove and run away with me?"

"How's Friday for you?" Max asked. But her hand never left George's. If he'd ever seen two people crazier about each other, he couldn't remember it.

He grinned at her. "What can I get you, luv?"

"Do you have those little bottles of champagne?"

"Of course," he said, hauling one out. He didn't bother asking George, just pulled him a pint. Probably because he'd been ribbed so mercilessly as a teenager, Lord Ponsford had learned early to prefer beer to anything posh. Knowing they'd soon find friends and disappear into the crowd, Arthur said, "Come and meet the new tenant of Stag Cottage. Another Yank."

George cocked an eyebrow.

Maxine was predictably thrilled to find that their temporary tenant was American. George did his charming lord-of-the-manor routine, then sent Arthur a glance that conveyed definite approval. *Yeah, keep away, dirty dog,* was what he telegraphed back.

Already, Maxine was catching up on news from home. Politics and celebrity gossip seemed equally fascinating. While they were at it, he and George discussed how they were going to annihilate their opponents next Saturday on the football pitch, in their local over-thirty league.

"I'm starving," Maxine said. "Meg, will you join us for dinner?"

"Oh, that's okay. I don't want to intrude."

"No, really, I insist. I want to know what the Supreme Court is up to. Not to mention the latest on Jennifer Aniston. *Hello!* is great if you need to know about Liz Hurley or the Beckhams, but I feel like I'm losing touch with home."

"You were in Los Angeles two months ago," George reminded her.

"You don't understand, honey."

Maxine turned to Arthur, as he'd half known she would. Maxine already knew him too well and took as keen an interest in his affairs as his sister did. "Come and take a dinner break," she ordered him.

If he didn't want to eat dinner with Meg as much as Maxine knew he did, he'd be annoyed. But Maxine was right—he did. So he shrugged and said, "I'll see." Which, of course, Max being Max, she took as a yes.

"Great." She turned to Meg. "We order off the board here. I can recommend everything, but my favorites are the shepherd's pie and the lasagna—meat or vegetarian."

Meg, who he suspected was feeling the effects of international travel followed by a good few hours spent murdering people, looked a little dazed. "Vegetarian lasagna sounds good to me."

When they'd ordered, George took them away to settle at a table. She fit right in with them, Arthur thought. Already Meg and Maxine were on the friendliest terms. A lot of people were intimidated by George's title and all the pomp that surrounded him, at least until they got to know him. But he could tell Meg wasn't like that. He suspected every man would have to prove himself in her eyes. Prince or pauper.

He waited until the food was up to take his break, reasoning that Meg hadn't asked for his company and she'd made it fairly clear she wasn't looking for any action. At least, not on her first day here. Give her a week or so to acclimatize and he might see if he could interest his temporary neighbor in a possible holiday fling.

The dinner rush was ending and Joe was on with a couple of waitresses, so Arthur picked up the tray of food and delivered it, serving himself today's special: chicken Kiev.

"Oh, my God," Maxine squealed as soon as he sat down. "I can't believe you're Meg Stanton." She looked at Arthur and George in turn. "I love her books." She shook a carrot stick at Meg. "You have kept me awake way too many nights."

He could tell from the pleased and rather smug look on her face that Meg thought a sleepless reader was a high compliment.

"So you're famous?" He'd accepted that she was a writer without ever thinking she might be well known. Well, he'd never heard of her, but that didn't mean much.

"No—"

"Yes," Max interrupted. "She's totally famous in the States. Maybe not so much here. But I'm sure that will change. I thought your last book was your best yet."

"Is it a chick read?" George wanted to know.

Maxine rolled her eyes. "Lots of men read her novels. My dad is a huge fan."

Arthur had wondered the same thing, whether the lady was writing for her own kind, but he wasn't going to have his nose snapped off. "I'll have to track down one of your books."

"I can lend you one. I think I've got them all," Maxine said with pride. "In fact, while you're here, maybe you could sign them for me?"

"I'd be delighted," Meg replied.

"I can't believe this. I know, I'm gushing. But I am such a fan. I've read every one of your books."

"Really? Which is your favorite?" Meg paused and put her fork down, obviously taking this seriously.

"I have two favorites. I can never decide whether I like the one about the wife who murders her adulterous husband, and then decides to rid her city of all cheating men—oh, and those guys totally got what they deserved. It was so deliciously gory. Or the woman who was abandoned by her father, and after she tracks him down and kills him—well, I don't want to give any more away."

"Men don't do so well in your novels," Arthur commented.

"I've had lots of different kinds of killers," Meg told him. "And victims." She sent him an odd look. "My current killer is definitely male."

"Mmm." Maxine nodded with enthusiasm. "Those two are my favorites, Arthur. But you can come up to the house and choose whichever you like."

He was fascinated. He'd had a glimpse of how this woman worked; it would be interesting to see what her books were like. And if he could see her in them.

Maxine was enough of a fan, and she missed her home enough, that he and George didn't say much. Fine with him. He wanted to know more about Meg, and he enjoyed watching her. He liked her quick intelligence and the thoughtful way she answered questions she must have been asked hundreds of times.

When Joe appeared a little overwhelmed, he excused himself.

George soon found an excuse to sidle up to the bar. "I haven't seen you that smitten since Keira Knightley came into the pub."

"Do me a favor, George?"

"Drop dead? Mind my own business? Do something vulgar to myself that will no doubt involve my bottom?"

"Walk Meg home."

"Pardon?"

"She's new here and I think a little scared of the dark. I'd appreciate it if you and Maxine would walk her right to her door on your way home."

George stared at him as though he'd gone mad. "Wouldn't you rather walk her home yourself?"

Of course he would, but the woman had jet lag and he wasn't in the mood to make a fool of himself.

"Too busy. And she's exhausted, can't you see it?" Her eyes had that smudged look and her smiling response to what was obviously Maxine's continued gushing was becoming mechanical.

"Yes, of course. Should have seen it myself. Can't have

the tenants dropping dead of fatigue. At least, not before they've paid the rent. Right. I'll try and get her away from her most enthusiastic fan."

"Cheers."

With George's usual social dexterity, he had the women on their feet and headed out the door before Maxine had quite realized she was leaving.

Arthur was gratified to see Meg turn as they reached the door and search him out. Across the noise and bodies, their gazes met and held for one of those timeless moments. *When you've had a good sleep,* he promised her silently, *you'll be hearing from me.*

In an instant she was gone.

Chapter Four

The banging on the door pulled Meg out of an intricate scene. It was like a chess game, keeping so many things in her head and trying to see several moves ahead. She felt almost as murderous as her villain when she stomped to the door and yanked it open.

"What?" Then the scowl dropped off her face. "Oh, Maxine. I'm sorry, I—"

"Sorry to bother you like this, but your phone's not working."

"Yes, it is. I unplugged it. I always do when I'm working."

"God, I'm sorry. I've disturbed you."

Well, that was the truth, but there was something about Maxine that made her impossible not to like. Besides, she had purchased all of Meg's books. In hardcover, Meg was sure. So she forced a smile to her face and pushed her hair out of the way. "It's good to see you. Do you want some tea?"

"No. But you look like you could use some. In fact," her new friend said with devastating frankness, "you look like hell."

"I probably do." Meg was pretty sure she'd showered this morning, but she had no idea what she was wearing, if or what she'd eaten today, or even what day it was. She grinned. "The book's going really well."

"Then I'd hate to see you when it's not. Look. Have you eaten lunch?"

"I'm not sure." She glanced at the kitchen, looking for hints. There was a cup with a tag hanging out—that was the herbal green tea from breakfast. Whatever else she'd eaten was a mystery. She'd cleaned up after herself.

"Tell you what. I'll come in and make you lunch and a cup of tea. I'm not staying, but you really look like you could use a meal."

Meg blinked. She felt disoriented, as though she'd been ill or in solitary confinement, which, come to think of it, she had. Self-imposed solitary confinement. She followed Maxine into the kitchen.

"So I came to invite you to watch the boys play soccer tomorrow," Maxine said, "and come to dinner at our place after."

"Boys? I didn't know you had kids."

Maxine laughed. A good, rich sound. "Big boys. George and Arthur, among others. They play soccer two Saturdays a month. Overgrown schoolboys who still like to run around in shorts and push each other into the mud. I thought we'd have a few people back for dinner."

"By your place, I assume you mean the castle?"

"Not a castle, honey. A house. And if you ever figure out how a five-hundred-year-old pile of stone with hundreds of rooms doesn't count as a castle, you let me know." While she talked, she bustled about the small kitchen and Meg was still too stunned to stop her. She realized she'd become a little obsessed, so driven to work while the writing was going well that she'd lost touch with the world.

"So? Can you tear yourself away?" Maxine was opening the tiny fridge and poking in cupboards.

"I don't know. Is amateur soccer something I'd enjoy watching?"

Maxine glanced up from her position crouched on the floor. "Between us? They look hot as hell."

"I'm not sure—"

Maxine rose. "You have no food in this place and the milk's sour. I am staging an intervention. Come on."

"Where are we going?"

"To get you some lunch."

"The café?"

"The castle."

"I thought it wasn't a castle."

"Quit stalling. Come on."

"I need to back up my files. And comb my hair." She glanced down at herself. "And change my clothes."

"I'll wait."

Meg glanced longingly at her computer. What if she left and the muse took off, too? Could she take that chance? "If I paid you fifty bucks would you leave?"

"Not a chance. Guests who work themselves to death don't give the place the right ambience."

"Okay." She sighed heavily but there wasn't much heat behind the gesture. She had to back up her files first on the device she kept on her key chain. It went everywhere with her, in case her house burned down when she was out. She had a secondary backup system, of course.

When she sat down to back up, she noticed she'd left a sentence half finished. She hated doing that, so she finished the sentence. And then she was worried that she'd forget where the scene was going. Maybe she could get in a couple of paragraphs before Maxine noticed . . .

The hand waving in front of her face startled her. "Whaa . . . ?"

She turned to find Maxine staring at her and shaking her

head. "You were somewhere completely different. It's the weirdest thing I've ever seen."

"Oh, I'm sorry. I'm so scared I'll lose the momentum. You don't know how long it's been since the writing's flowed like this." She inhaled and noticed a wonderful aroma of food. Real, cooked food that hadn't come out of a can or box. She looked around and noticed a tray sitting on the low table in front of the couch. "How did you . . . ? I thought we were going to the castle for lunch."

"I lost you. After I called your name twice and you didn't answer, I figured you were going to be a dud for lunch company. And you seemed so happy typing away that I walked over to the pub. It's today's lunch special. Vegetable soup, a Cornish pasty and salad. Now you sit down and eat while I make some tea."

"What about you?"

"I'm not staying. I've got some things to do. I really only came over to invite you for tomorrow. And I'm picking you up, by the way, so you don't end up forgetting."

Meg knew she should feel guilty, and in fact she did, but she decided to simply be grateful for the food delivery instead. The soup was incredible. The Cornish pasty, a pastry-wrapped meat dish, was delicious and filling. By the time the tea was ready, she'd forked down the last of the salad and was feeling all the contentment of enjoying her first decent meal in days.

"Please stay and have some tea with me. I could use the company."

"Won't I interrupt your work?"

"No. I was getting a little crazy there."

"Okay," Maxine said, looking pleased.

Meg blinked a few times and rubbed her eyes.

"Is it always like this for you? Writing nonstop for days?" Maxine asked, pouring tea and passing it.

"Almost never. That's why I'm scared to quit. It's a case

of whatever's working . . ." She sipped her tea. "I'm a pretty organized person, and I have a fully equipped office in my home in Seattle with a wonderful reference library. I've written thirteen books there without a hitch. Inspiration comes to me when I'm already at work. Sure, I'll get a spell where I can't type fast enough to keep up with the story. Oh, those days are the best. And I have been known to write all night when the mood is on me. But with this book"—she nodded toward the computer, where the cursor winked at her coyly—"nothing was working. This trip was really desperation. And almost from the first day I got here, I've had that sense of urgency. The story's suddenly bursting to be told. It's amazing."

She sipped more tea.

"Did you know you'd write better in England?"

"No. That's the scary thing. I was so desperate. I had no idea I'd write here at all. I wanted to get away for personal reasons."

"How did you find us?" Maxine asked.

"Your Web site."

A cat's-got-the-cream smile curled her new friend's lips. "The Web site was my idea. I'm working all the time on new markets and profit centers for this place."

"It's wonderful. I'll certainly recommend it to my friends and acquaintances."

"Excellent. So." Maxine settled back and tucked her feet under her. "Tell me about this guy?"

Meg laughed. "How did you know it was a guy?"

Maxine sighed. "Isn't it always? Who was he?"

Did she want to talk about this? Strangely enough, for the first time in months, Meg found she did. "He was another writer. A good writer, too, but not very successful. It's not easy to find interesting, attractive men who are also literate."

Maxine snorted. "Been there."

"I was fooled by the packaging, I guess, and saw what I wanted to see. He taught college English and wore tweedy coats with elbow patches. He smoked a pipe. You know the type."

"I fell in love with an art prof exactly like that."

"Well, I was a fool. I didn't realize he was jealous of me until I let him start critiquing my work. He'd be so helpful, showing me all my weaknesses, pulling my scenes to shreds, poking holes in my plots, questioning my character motivations. I never realized he was destroying my confidence until I found myself struggling in a way I hadn't struggled before."

"Pompous-assed little weasel."

"Yep." She stared down into her tea, frowning. This part was hard. "I finally called him on it. I told him I wasn't going to let him read my work anymore. It was interfering with my confidence. He called me spoiled and manipulative. That made me mad, so I yelled at him that he was jealous." She shook her head. "Big mistake. Then he really let me have it. And the trouble with truly literate men is that they can destroy you with such beautiful, big words. We broke up, of course, and then these vicious reviews started appearing online. All with false names, or maybe he was getting his students to write them. Who knows? I couldn't stand it anymore. I couldn't concentrate, couldn't write." She made a face. "I ran away."

"And what a good thing you did. That asshole is history and you can write here."

"That's true." Meg leaned back and let her gaze roam the comfy cottage, take in the fields outside. A rabbit hopped across the grass in front of the French doors. "I feel free again. I'm having more fun writing than I've had in a couple of years."

"Excellent." Maxine beamed at her. "Maybe we can ad-

vertise a resident writer's muse among the many other benefits of a holiday at Stag Cottage."

Meg laughed. "I'm not sure muses work that way, but
what do I know? This is a magic spot for me, though, that's
certain."

"I'm glad you're here. It's great to have somebody from
home to talk to."

Somehow, Maxine's visit broke the spell of urgency she'd
been operating under. Meg had written more in the last
week than she'd managed in months. And now that she'd
been pulled out of her writing cave she felt stir crazy. When
Maxine told her she was going into town if she needed anything, Meg begged a ride and had the fun of shopping in a
British supermarket, looking at biscuits instead of cookies,
crisps instead of potato chips, and discovering there were
kinds of apples she'd never heard of. Her senses seemed
starved after too many days indoors, so she spent time hovering over the Cox's Red Pippins and the black currants, the
grapes and melons and figs. She loaded up on fruit. And she
bought cheese and fresh bread, veggies and chicken. Two
bottles of French wine. And fresh flowers for the table, because she deserved them.

She discovered an Internet café, and while Maxine was at
the post office she checked her e-mail, finding nothing urgent. A note from her agent about a book sale to Poland, a
few fan letters, some chatty e-mails from friends, an invitation to join a panel in the fall at the Elliot Bay Book
Company. Suddenly, she felt so far away from her regular
life. But in a good way. She'd needed this break.

Once home, she put away the food and decided that a
tramp around the countryside would do her good. The tray
and the few dishes from the pub lunch were still on the
table. She washed them and decided to begin her walk by
dropping them off.

As she clambered over the stile and headed for the pub, she noticed her pulse was kicking up. She'd see her villain, her gorgeous/scary villain.

As it was, she saw Arthur sooner than she'd expected, nearly colliding with him as she rounded the corner. Only by amazing dexterity—and him having the sense to grab the soup bowl before it crashed to the ground—was disaster averted.

He looked even more dangerous somehow, when he wasn't inside the pub. As though the lion had been let out of his cage. He'd be unpredictable. Unfettered.

Every time she saw him she experienced the shiver of attraction and the hint of danger. She'd assumed it was because she'd used him as the model for her villain.

But now she wasn't so sure. There was something about him that made her very wary. She might write about dangerous men but in her life she preferred safe ones. The kind she could control. This man was not safe or controllable.

And she was far too glad to see him.

"I was starting to think you'd gone home," he said, his voice as rich and rough as the Liffey River.

"No. I've been working." She glanced up at him and admitted, "Maxine dragged me out today, and now I can't seem to go back inside." It was the weather, too, she decided. One of those days that was still warm, but with a hint of the coolness to come. There'd been some rain, she thought, in the last few days, but now it was clear and sunny. "I'm going to take a walk."

"Well, that's a good thing. Too much work isn't good for a body. I'm taking a break myself."

"Care to join me?" She said the words before she'd thought them through, before she realized she was thinking them.

There was the tiniest instant of silence, as though he were surprised, too, and then he said, "Yeah, all right. I'll run these things inside." He relieved her of the tray and dishes and was back, leaving her just enough time to beat herself up for asking him along.

They walked along the river, where there were miles and miles of footpath. "I hear from Max that you're coming to watch the football tomorrow."

"Yes. Maxine isn't easy to say no to. She says she's coming to pick me up so I don't forget."

"You don't want to come?"

Was it her imagination or did he sound a little hurt? Oh, dear. She didn't want him to think she was avoiding him. "No, of course I want to come." But that sounded a bit too eager, didn't it?

She made a grunty-groany sound she hoped indicated frustration. "It's this book. It's finally going well. I'm terrified to stop in case I can't start again."

"Lots of murder and horror?"

"I'm really getting to the good stuff now."

He looked down at her, an expression almost of challenge on his face. "You haven't called me in the middle of the night."

Her stomach curled over, as though she were on the downhill rush of a roller coaster. She returned his gaze, feeling breathless. "I haven't been scared enough." Her gaze dropped to his lips, and she wondered how such a tough face could have such a sensuous mouth. "Yet."

"I know a wonderful technique for chasing away fear," he said softly, turning to face her. The river lapped quietly behind them, and a breeze ruffled the trees.

"You do?"

"Yes," he said, and grasping her shoulders, he put his mouth on hers, soft and slow, but determined. She'd known it would happen, of course. She supposed she'd known it from the first second she'd seen him. His mouth was warm, so warm, his lips strong and agile. Her hands ended up on his shoulders, though she had no conscious thought of putting them there, so she felt the play of muscle, the warmth of his body.

He pulled away slowly, looking down at her as though he knew the single kiss had rocked her to her pedicured toenails.

"Desire," he said. "That'll keep your fear at bay."

Oh, how wrong he was. Now she began to fear that this very inconvenient and impossible-to-stop attraction was going to totally screw up her work.

The author of a book couldn't have sex with its villain.

Chapter Five

Meg was finger-combing the last dampness from her hair. She hadn't been able to decide what to wear for dinner at the big house, and finally settled on a simple coffee-colored linen dress with chunky amber beads and earrings. Her heels were never going to make the tramp all ten miles or whatever it was up to the house, so she stuck on her walking shoes and carried her ridiculously high-heeled sandals in a shopping bag.

After days being cooped up with her muse, she was pretty excited to be going out.

A butler opened the heavy oak door to her. A real, honest-to-God butler. Oh, and wasn't he straight out of central casting with his beaky nose, long face, and air of gentility.

She gave her name, and he looked discreetly off into the distance when she hastily changed her shoes, then relieved her of her shopping bag.

He trod with stately slowness down the flagstone hall. She almost expected him to announce her, like at a ball, but he merely opened a door and said, "You'll find his lordship and Miss Maxine in here."

"Thank you."

She entered and saw not Maxine or George, or anyone except the tall, dark man standing beside the fireplace, one elbow on the mantel and a crystal glass winking amber in his hand. Arthur's eyes warmed when he looked at her and she suddenly felt as breathless as she had in that moment right before he'd kissed her.

Then Maxine rose from her chair and came forward, breaking the spell.

"I'm so glad you could come," she said. "George needs cheering up."

Meg smiled at the poor earl, sitting with his bare foot wrapped in a tensor bandage and resting on a low footstool that had to have been embroidered by the Normans shortly after the conquest. Other than the bare foot, which showed a certain purple aspect, he looked movie star handsome.

"How's your ankle?" she asked him as she walked over and gave him her hand.

"It bloody hurts," he complained. "If that great oaf hadn't trodden on me, I'd be standing up and greeting you properly."

Since the wicked way he was grinning at her had her thinking that Maxine was going to have her hands full, she shook her head at him. "It looked to me like you were both playing like you were ten years old." The soccer players were all in their thirties, with a few who looked to be in their forties, but they'd played their football, as they insisted on calling it, as though they were kids, running and shoving and getting filthy. Max was right, though—they were all men in their prime and they looked totally hot.

"Nonsense. You don't understand the complexities of the game," he told her.

"You are such a wally," Arthur told him. "And if you can't greet your guests properly, I can." Then he walked forward, said "Hello," and gave her a quick kiss. Just a brush of his lips over hers, really, but the thrill danced all the way down her spine.

"Hello," she said, telling herself there was no need to

blush. He was only winding up their host. Still, the tingle remained.

Arthur, who was standing in for George as host, it seemed, in anything that required standing, asked her what she wanted to drink. "Um, I don't know."

He lowered his voice. "Mrs. Brimacombe, the cook and housekeeper, tends to solid British fare. I recommend a good stiff belt of something."

"Surprise me," she said, knowing that one way or another, he was going to do exactly that.

There were two other couples. Old friends of George's who'd also played today and their wives. Meg fell into the evening feeling almost like a spectator at a play. These people had known each other forever and the back-and-forth banter, the in-jokes, and the shared history were laid out before her. Of course, they were polite, well-mannered people, and they included her. The discussion was general, but every once in a while there'd be a line or a joke that had to be explained.

Since she was now writing a book set in England, with a British villain and a lot of characters much like these, she was only too happy to watch them live their very English lives in front of her, while she absorbed.

The perfect butler announced dinner and a single waitress served it, a come-down, she suspected, from earlier days when there would have been a full staff. The meal was fine. Roast beef and Yorkshire pudding with peas and green beans and roast potatoes. Maybe a little overcooked for her taste, but not so dire that she really needed the martini in her system. She wondered if Arthur had ulterior motives for getting her drinking and one glance at him convinced her that he did.

The conversation flowed with the wine. From British-American relations to books to new plays in London's West End.

She discovered that George and Maxine were at the stage in their relationship where they couldn't seem to keep their hands off each other. A touch here, a steamy glance there. Obviously, those two were deep-down crazy for each other.

And Meg discovered that Arthur had a sneaky sense of humor and that he was a local chess champ.

"Do you play?" he asked her.

"Sometimes. But I'm not very good."

"We'll have to have a game," he said, and the way he looked at her made her wonder if chess was the game he had in mind.

And then Maxine brought up the subject of Meg's writing. "You know, I've always fancied writing a book," said Charles, one the men.

"Then you should do it," she said. She heard this all the time and always wondered why, if they wanted to do it, people didn't sit down and try. It was like saying, "Oh, I've always wanted to speak German," without ever taking a lesson.

"Meg writes the most incredible murder mysteries," Maxine said. "I can never sleep when I've got one on the go. Honestly, they're terrifying."

"Don't you find it difficult to imagine the mind of a killer?" asked Charles's wife, Nora.

"Well, yes and no. The thing to remember is that in his or her mind, the killer has no other choice, no option but to kill. He may be insane, but in his mind, it's the right thing to do. He or she is the hero in their own mind. If I can find a compelling enough reason for what they do, then my villain comes to life."

"You sound like you approve of your villains."

"Not approve. But they are my favorite characters." She glanced at Arthur and found him rapt.

"But a killer? Someone like that would be so evil."

Arthur spoke from across the table. "I think every man has it in him to kill."

Yes. She'd known he would see it that way, of course.

"Could you kill a man?" Maxine asked him, her eyes wide. She reached for George's hand.

"I have done," he said matter-of-factly, and Maxine gasped. Meg looked at him and saw the lines harden in his face. His eyes grew suddenly stony.

"Arthur was in the army," George said. "That's different."

"Is it?" Arthur asked.

"Well, of course it is," George insisted. "You were fighting for your country."

"That's what I was saying. It's all a question of motive. Am I not right, Meg?"

"Yes. I think so. People kill for many reasons. Duty to your country, of course, but also revenge, greed, obsessive love."

"I don't think I could kill anybody," George said, making a face. "All that blood. It would put me off."

"What if your home were threatened?" Arthur challenged. "Or Maxine? You'd kill to protect them."

The glance Maxine and George shared was intimate and powerful. Oh, yes, she thought. George could act the upper class English twit, but he had a great deal of strength.

She knew from Max that he'd pretty much given up his career as an architect when his father died suddenly, and he was forced to come home and manage a cash-draining estate decades before he'd anticipated stepping into the earldom. He didn't complain, though. He was managing to hold everything together, run a huge estate, and build it into a business. That took guts. And drive. Yes, she thought, he was one you could rely on in a tough corner.

When the evening broke up, Wiggins, as she'd discovered

the butler was called, appeared with her bag of shoes. She changed into her flats even as Maxine said, "Why don't I run you home in the car?"

The other couples were staying the night, since they lived in different villages quite far away and the wine had been flowing.

"No. It only took me ten minutes to walk here. I need the air." She'd understood what Arthur had meant about the cooking when the dessert turned out to be bread pudding.

"I'll walk you home," Arthur said, as she'd somehow known he would. A quiver went through her.

"It's not far."

"No. But it is dark. Don't want you tripping on a rabbit hole and ending up like George there."

"I don't know," George said, having hobbled into the hall with the aid of a cane and Maxine's arm. "You could come round and keep me company in my infirmity."

"Good night, George," she said, leaning forward to kiss his cheek. She hugged Maxine. "Thanks. This was just what I needed."

"Come anytime."

Arthur and Meg set off in the direction of her cottage.

It was surprisingly dark. Well, duh. What had she expected? Streetlights? As though he'd read her mind, Arthur said, "I've got a penlight. Let me know if you want me to switch it on. I always find my eyes adjust in a minute or two."

"No. It's fine. There's some light from the moon."

The night was quiet and still. She liked the dark, though she was intensely aware of the man beside her. Once she stumbled over a rock she hadn't seen and he grabbed her hand to steady her.

He didn't let go. She could have pulled away, but she liked the feel of him, the sturdy, capable hand, the warmth of his skin.

"I bought one of your books today, when I was in town."

"You did? I thought Max was going to lend you one."

"I decided I'd like to have my own."

"Well, thank you. Which book did you choose?"

"*Tying Up Loose Ends*, I think it's called."

The book that first put her on the *Times* list, but she didn't tell him that. "Well, let me know what you think of it."

"I will."

After that, they didn't talk much.

When they reached her cottage, he still didn't talk, merely turned her to him and took her mouth.

Okay, so she'd guessed it was coming, had spent most of the short walk wondering how she felt about it and whether she'd stop him if he tried to kiss her. Now she knew that he wouldn't give her time to stop him and how she felt about it was indescribable. It was even better this time. He was so warm, so strong, his mouth both taking and giving.

Drugging pleasure began to overtake her senses. It had been so long since she'd felt like this. Excited at the possibilities of a man, wanting, with quiet desperation, to be with him. Held by him, taken by him. She began to shiver and he moved closer, so her back was against the stone wall and his warm body pressed against her.

Her hands were in his hair, wonderful, thick, luxurious hair. Her mouth open on his, wanting, giving, taking. She felt him hard against her belly and experienced a purring sense of her own power. And also a stabbing sense of regret.

She couldn't do this, she reminded herself. Her book. Her book was her priority. If and when she finished the novel, then she could think about indulging herself like this. Not until then.

So she tipped her head back out of kissing range and looked up into that dark, intent face. "What was that about?" She'd meant to sound sophisticated and slightly amused. A woman who got hit on all the time on every continent. Instead she sounded husky and, even to her own ears, like a total goner.

"I'm interested. I'm letting you know."

"Telling me with words would be too mundane?"

"Words are your world. I'm more a man of action." Oh, man of action. Oh, aphrodisiac to her senses. She'd always gone for the cerebral types, but there was something about a man who tackled the world in a physical way that appealed to her on the most basic level. His words from dinner came back to her. He'd kill to protect those he loved. Every other man she'd been with had been of the pen-is-mightier-than-the-sword persuasion, mostly, she suspected, because their swordplay was so minimal.

Arthur was a man who would make her feel safe. When she crawled into bed, terrified of the fruits of her own imagination, she could see herself burrowing against his warm skin, his arms coming round her in comfort.

Then she gave herself a mental slap. What was she doing? Always imagining things. Arthur ran a pub. Was obviously single and probably took a fancy to every unattached woman who rented the cottage. How convenient.

She shook her head with mingled irritation and regret. "I'm here to work. I really don't have time for . . . anything personal."

"That's a shame." He ran his warm, leathery palm down the side of her neck so she wanted to press against it. Rub at him like a kitten.

"I have to finish this book. I can't afford any distractions."

"I'm glad I distract you," he said, a thread of amusement running through his voice.

"You are?"

"I wouldn't want to think I was the only one feeling . . . distracted."

"Well, it was a very nice evening," she said, easing away.

"Did you not want me to come in, then, and check under the bed for monsters?"

"No, thank you."

"I'll tell you what. You see that lighted window, across the way there?"

"Yes." There was only one lighted window. It wasn't that tough to spot.

"That's my house."

"You don't live over the pub?" For some reason, she was surprised.

"No. I live in that house there. And anytime you see my light, you can call me."

"I told you—"

"I know. But even a hard-working writer needs a distraction now and then."

Before she could respond, he was kissing her again, fast and addicting, like a shot of heroin before he headed away, so sure she'd soon be pining for more that he didn't bother to say good-bye or even glance back.

Well. If he thought she was going to run after him, he was going to be seriously disappointed.

He was a dark shadow, and then he was gone, blending into the night, so only the odd scuffling sound allowed her to chart his progress.

"Go on in, now," he said from the direction of the stile, and she was annoyed with herself that she'd so obviously been staring after him in the blackness.

She didn't say a word but opened the door and slipped inside.

Right. For two days now she'd played. It was time to get back to work. She licked her lips, tasting his kisses, and was flooded suddenly with a wanting so sharp she closed her eyes against it.

Chapter Six

Arthur felt his heart pound and his innards clench. When he turned the page he noticed his fingertip was damp with sweat. No wonder Meg Stanton was afraid of her own books. She wasn't the only one.

Knowing the author herself was a stone's throw away, as needful of him as he was of her, made him half crazy with the wanting. Reading her book was a poor substitute for going to bed with her, but he'd thought it might at least lull him to sleep. Instead, she'd not only left him aroused and unsatisfied, but now she was scaring the wits out of him.

One more chapter, and then he'd put the damn thing down, he promised himself.

When the phone rang he jumped, jarred out of his terrified skin. Fool, he admonished himself, glancing at the clock. Two A.M. Who'd be calling at . . .

He glanced out the window on his way to pick up the ringing phone and noted that his wasn't the only light on in the area. Meg's upstairs light was glowing like a beacon.

A grin tugged at his mouth as he identified himself on the phone.

"I didn't wake you, did I?" It was Meg, as he'd known it would be, but still, the sound of her voice acted like stroking fingers on his skin.

"Wake me? You kept me awake, woman."

"You were thinking about me?"

"Aye, I was. But worse, I started reading your book. Bloodcurdling stuff."

"I know," she said with smug pride.

"Are you working this late, then?" He rubbed a hand across his chest. Hoping that she wanted more than a chat.

"I was. Now"—she blew out a breath—"I'm too scared to sleep."

"Well, that's two of us." He grinned broadly and settled back on the bed. "What do you think we might do about that?"

"Do?" She sounded startled. "I don't want to do anything. I mean, I wanted to explain. I was kind of abrupt earlier."

The stiff paper of the book jacket crinkled as he opened the cover, revealing a photo of the author. It was a professional photo of Meg looking full on at the camera, in a black dress, smiling slightly. She wore pearl earrings and her hair was suitably restrained. Looking at that photo acted on him the way graphic nude photos in a men's magazine might.

"You were telling me you don't have time for me, with your book to write. I understood."

"Yes, but I think I was a bit arrogant."

Not arrogant, he thought, but hasty. They could have been tangling the sheets and enjoying each other at this moment instead of talking on the phone. Obviously, she was feeling as aroused and deeply unsatisfied as he.

She sighed. "In the daytime it's so peaceful here. But at night, it's so black out there. Not a light for miles."

"It's perfectly safe." He soothed her automatically, hearing the trace of nerves.

"Oh, I know. It's not that. It just feels . . . well, kind of lonely."

"It can be."

"How do you stand it?"

"It was peace I was after when I came here. The army is never peaceful. And believe me, you are never lonely."

"I'm sure that's not true," she said softly.

"Well, never alone at any rate." He shifted. "What are you doing at this moment?"

"I'm trying to get comfortable in bed."

"Ah." He looked at the formal publicity photo and smiled to himself, imagining her in bed. In what? Flannel nightie? A sexy scrap of lace and silk?

"What are you wearing?"

There was a pause. He heard her uncertain intake of breath. "You're not planning on having phone sex with me, are you?"

It wasn't easy to keep his laugh inside his chest. She was adorable. "I hadn't thought about it. Would you like to have phone sex?

A longer pause. He could tell she was thinking about it as clearly as he knew what her answer would be. "No. I don't think so."

"Of course not. That won't keep the monsters under the bed."

"No," she said softly, "it won't."

He let the silence lengthen just long enough. "Do you want me to come over, then?"

"I thought you were scared, too."

"Terrified. I'll run all the way."

She laughed. He loved the sound of her laugh. It was so unexpected. For all her ladylike ways, the laugh was low and sexy.

"I'm not sure I'm ready for this."

"I'm not sure I am, either." And he found it was true.

"I could make you some coffee if you came over," she said.

"But that would keep us awake."

"Warm milk?"

"That's a long way to run in the dark for a bit of milk."

"Maybe there will be something to go with it."

"Like what?"

"A chocolate cookie. I mean biscuit."

He laughed aloud at that. Well, there were biscuits and there were cookies. "I'm on my way."

He didn't run. He savored the night air and the quiet sounds of the countryside asleep. The big house slept. The flats and houses of the village slept. He looked about himself and saw no light but hers. And it drew him the way a fire draws a cold man.

When he got to the door she was waiting for him. With her face scrubbed free of makeup and her hair down around her shoulders, she looked young. She wore a pale blue terry cloth robe and a pair of sheepskin slippers. All very practical, not a bit sexy. And he found himself growing frantic for the taste of her skin, anxious to ease her out of the robe and toss the slippers across the room.

However, he wasn't the sort of man to begin ravishing a woman in the wee hours when she was alone in her house, unless he was certain she wanted him to ravish her.

Her breath shuddered slightly as she drew it in. Her eyes were wide and alluring. Her lips were slightly parted.

"Lead the way, then," he said, his voice a husky whisper of sound.

She took his hand, turned and led him, not to the kitchen, but up the stairs. Her palm was so warm it was almost feverish, and he felt the fine trembling within her. As she walked up ahead of him, he knew her body was unfettered by underwear, and he was as aroused as though she wore nothing at all.

Soon, he thought, she would.

He would tease her about her warm milk later. For now the atmosphere was serious.

He knew the room well, of course, had helped the delivery men bring in the new bed at the end of the summer season. But with her things scattered about, it seemed mysterious, very feminine, and all hers. He smelled the subtle scent of her skin and her powders and women's lotions and things. There were some bottles neatly lined up on top of the bookcase, her clothes hanging regimented in the wardrobe where the door was ajar.

"I'm glad you rang," he said.

"I don't want to be alone tonight."

So he held her. First he simply held her, feeling the shape of her press against him, the smell of her hair as he buried his face in it.

"You smell so good," he murmured.

She wrapped her arms around him and pulled him even closer. "Thank you for coming."

Then he took her mouth, because he couldn't help himself. She clung to him, kissing him the way she had earlier, like a drowning woman.

She made tiny purring sounds in her throat. He doubted she was even aware of them but they drove him half mad. He wanted to rip away her clothing and throw himself onto her, into her, and the effort at civilized control had sweat breaking out on his forehead.

He skimmed his hands over her breasts, smiling against her lips when she quivered with reaction. Over her belly, and then he found the cord of her robe. It came undone with one pull, but instead of pushing it off her shoulders and letting it fall, he traced the opening, followed the lines of the open robe, so he touched silk, warmed by her skin, and felt the resilience of her flesh beneath. He cupped her breasts through the sheer fabric and felt them jump to life under his palms, the nipples teasing him. He continued up, over her shoulders, this time knocking the robe free, so it fell in defeat to the floor.

There was a lamp burning in the corner of the room, giving a soft, golden light to the proceedings. When he eased back from kissing her, he saw that her face was softly tinged with the pink of arousal, her lips swollen, her breathing ragged.

Need and want warred with care and consideration, so he was strung tight with conflicting desires as she began undoing the buttons of his shirt with fingers that quivered. Damn, he wished he'd sprinted over here in nothing but a robe. Would have saved him an agony, an eternity told out in buttonholes.

After an eon, she got the last one undone and smoothed the shirt over his shoulders and down his arms, as though she were afraid of wrinkling it. But her touch was soft and sure. And she did the maximum touching of his bare skin.

He reached for the hem of her nightgown—silk and lace, not flannel—and brought it slowly up, unwrapping her like a gift. Her skin was post-summer golden. She was long, a little curvier than her clothes had led him to believe, her breasts small and high. "Beautiful," he murmured as he kissed her again.

She undid his belt, opened his fly, and then surprised the hell out of him when she reached inside and cupped him with her long-fingered, capable writer's hands.

He heard his breath draw in on a sharp hiss, felt the curve of her lips beneath his own. She was pleased with herself for shocking him, he could tell. He nudged against her hand a little, letting her explore to her heart's content until he felt things getting a little too warm, then he backed away, toed off his trainers, stripped off his jeans and socks, and came back against her, rubbing her naked body with his.

She was so soft, her skin fine and paler, even with her

light tan, than his darker, hairier body. He probably looked like some great hairy beast to her. He must take extra care to go slowly, gently.

Oh, she liked them hairy, she thought. Loved the rasp of his hair-roughened chest against her sensitive breasts. Loved his darkness against her paler skin.

His mouth was everywhere, it seemed, nipping at her, eating her up.

The bed was a mess from where she'd tossed and turned in it for hours, trying fruitlessly to convince herself she wasn't scared. That the villain she'd so brilliantly created was in fact that, a product of her feverish and far too fertile imagination. That he wasn't at this moment creeping up the stairs to stab her in the heart as he had his last victim. But it was no good. As she'd written the victim, she'd become her. Of course, only through feeling terror could she portray it for the reader. But imagining herself murdered took its toll. Why couldn't she have found her niche writing fairy tales for toddlers?

When Arthur wrapped his arms around her she felt comforted, not confined; when he pushed her to her back on the rumpled bed her skin trembled with excitement, not fear.

He spread her legs and she felt herself burn with need. Oh, God. He was so big and gorgeous and it had been so long. He played with her, kissing her all over, touching her with hands that were as tough and leathery as she'd guessed, but that were surprisingly gently and sure.

He'd brought condoms, thank God, since she hadn't packed any.

When he fitted himself to her, she felt that moment, that eternal moment, when he hovered on the brink. Not yet lovers, soon to be, and then, impatient of waiting, she grabbed his hips and pulled him into her.

He spread her, filled her. And when their passion grew, he

stabbed into her, her gorgeous, sexy villain, thrusting again and again. Even though she cried out, it wasn't a dreadful end she experienced, but something new and very exciting.

When at last they slept, the night was at its thickest and darkest, but she felt warm, comforted, and very, very safe.

Chapter Seven

The sound of rain drumming softly on the roof woke her. Meg's eyes opened slowly and her whole body reveled in the luxury of a good, deep sleep. And she was warm, so warm.

Gradually, she came to full consciousness and became aware of the naked body pressed against hers, the soft puff of Arthur's breath against her hair, and that his big, working-man's hand was curled possessively round her breast.

She needed to pee, she needed coffee, she wondered what time it was. But still she didn't move. She remembered the way they'd made love last night, learning each other, exploring, touching, tasting.

The wind kicked up, and the rain drumming on the roof was joined in chorus by the drops slashing against the windowpane. What a great day to stay in bed and be lazy. They could make love all day, eat the food she'd bought—thank heavens—only two days ago. He could build them a fire. They'd be as cozy as alpine skiers nestled up at the lodge after a hard day on the slopes, with their roaring fire and their *glühwein*. Did Arthur ski? She knew so little about him. Except that he was the most exciting lover she'd ever known.

She turned to look at him, his dangerous face softened by sleep. A coarse black beard already shadowed his jaw.

She'd make him breakfast, she decided. And she'd give herself a whole day off. Sliding out carefully, she padded to the bathroom. She'd shower, get the coffee on, and make her new lover breakfast. How long had it been since she'd been this excited about a man? She pondered the question as she stepped into the shower and decided that she'd never in her life been this excited about a man.

Arthur woke to the sound of water. At first he thought it was rain, then realized it was the shower. He glanced over at Meg's spot, but of course it was empty.

He blinked at the clock. Ten. They'd had a good lie-in, then. But after the night they'd spent, their bodies had needed the rest. He stretched, enjoying the pull in all his muscles, and the slight scent of Meg that clung to the bed-clothes.

He didn't really need to be at the pub until evening. Joe was covering the lunch shift. Maybe he'd take Meg out for a good old English fry-up. Bangers and beans, eggs, fried tomato and fried bread, with lashings of hot tea. Then he'd bring her back here or take her to his place . . .

Except that she'd been very frank about her need to work. Sure, she'd been the one to ring him up in the wee hours, but still, if he wanted to see her more than when she was shit-scared in the middle of the night, he'd have to show her he was sensitive to her need to work.

Reluctantly, he rolled out of bed, yawning, and shoved himself back into his clothes.

He was dying for a pee, but he'd wait until he got home, not sure how she'd feel about him barging into her bath-room to relieve himself on such short acquaintance. Of course, he'd been inside her body and knew the taste of her intimate juices, but women were incomprehensible about the bathroom.

She seemed like a closed-door type. The shower had stopped, so he banged on the door in passing.

"I'll be off then, love," he said. He wished he could join her in the shower, or take her back to bed all damp and smelling of soap, but she'd likely have his hide if he distracted her from her precious book.

Her voice sounded odd. "You're going?"

"Yeah. Hope the work goes well today."

"Thank you." She didn't open the door, so he'd likely been right.

"Well, cheerio."

"Yes. 'Bye."

He whistled as he ran down the stairs. He ought to do some tidying up at home, and maybe some shopping. And he'd definitely change his sheets. After all, nobody could work all day and night every day. Not even Meg.

Because he was preoccupied he did a very stupid thing. He walked right out of Meg's front door without having the bloody sense to have a doss out the window first, which is how he all but bashed straight into Maxine.

He recoiled at the sight of her, feeling as stupid as though he'd been caught by his nanny doing something naughty. Her knowing smile didn't help.

"Well, hello, Arthur," she purred. She wore wellies, a yellow mac, and a striped umbrella, and managed to look like a runway model.

Fuck, fuck, fuckety fuck. "Hi, Max. I was just . . . um . . . changing a lightbulb for Meg. Bloody things keep burning out. I'll have to have a look at the electrical when I get a minute."

"Good idea." Her amusement circled him like smoke. "And next time you come to change a lightbulb, lover, make sure you fasten the buttons on your shirt in the right order."

He didn't say another word, simply barged past her and plunged into the rain.

When Meg heard the knocking on her door she thought Arthur must be back. Hopefully for breakfast. But then why didn't he let himself in? Had he locked the door behind himself? But when she ran lightly down the stairs, in jeans and her favorite blue cotton sweater, it wasn't Arthur standing there, but Maxine.

"Oh," she said, wondering why on earth she should feel embarrassed and whether Maxine could tell she was blushing.

"Hey, neighbor. I just passed Arthur coming out of your place."

"Did you?"

"Yes. I wonder what he was doing here so early."

"He was looking at the faucet in the upstairs bathroom. It sticks." Luckily, the faucet did stick, and she'd been thinking of mentioning it or she never would have invented such a smooth lie. Not that she even wanted to lie to Maxine, but the relationship was too new. Anyway, she wasn't even sure it was a relationship, especially not the way Arthur had sprinted out the door this morning without so much as a cup of coffee or a kiss good-bye.

"Would you like some coffee?" she asked Max, who was still standing, dripping on her doorstep.

"No. I'm not staying. You left one of your earrings last night. It must have fallen off at dinner." She dug into her pocket and emerged with a dangle of amber.

"Thanks. I didn't even notice. The catch must be loose." She took the earring and played with it like worry beads. "I haven't started work yet. I'm going to make some coffee for myself. I wish you'd stay." Maxine did not strike Meg as a woman who would slog through mud to return an earring. Something was on her mind, and even if it was no more than nosiness about Arthur and her, she wouldn't mind the distraction of another woman's company.

"Well, okay." Maxine stepped inside, removing her damp outer clothes and stepping out of her boots.

She wore thick woollen socks that someone had knit by hand. Meg had a feeling the socks were a new part of her wardrobe since she'd moved here.

"What?" Maxine said, following her gaze. "Did I put two different socks on? I do sometimes."

"No. I was thinking you probably didn't bring those socks from L.A."

A snort of laughter greeted her. "You're right. I pretty much had to abandon my L.A. wardrobe." She sighed softly. "There are days I really miss Rodeo Drive."

"So? What's the deal with you and George?"

She shook her head and looked helpless. "Bliss. Pure bliss. I cannot help myself. I'm crazy about that man."

"You know, it doesn't take a genius to see that he's crazy about you, too."

"All I wanted was documentary footage of the earl. Who'd have thought I'd end up with the earl himself?"

"Will you stay?"

"I think so. I'm in negotiation for a series that would be a joint production of the company I work for and the BBC. But"—she shrugged—"if it doesn't work out, I think I can keep myself busy on the estate."

"Wow. Isn't it hard to leave your home?"

"It's hard to leave the people you love. I have a sister who needs me right now. She just got divorced and her job is probably going to end. I feel a long way away. But"—she looked out of the window in the direction of the manor house—"you make your home, too. I think mine is here."

Meg couldn't imagine moving across an ocean for a man, but she'd seen the way George and Maxine were together. For love like that? Maybe.

She poured coffee and served it.

"I'm glad Arthur fixed the faucet for you."

"It was really no big deal," she said, wishing Maxine would shut up already about the faucet.

"It's funny. When I bumped into him, he told me he was here replacing a lightbulb."

Their gazes met. Maxine raised one eyebrow. "And his shirt was buttoned all wrong."

Meg put her coffee down, the ceramic mug making a sharp click against the table. She slumped back and looked at the ceiling, feeling like her mom had just caught her sneaking in past curfew and she was about to be grounded. "Okay, so I slept with him. And I'm not apologizing for lying to you about it. It's so new. Last night was our first time and it was—oh, God, I'm babbling."

"You're cute when you babble. Hey, I think it's great, and don't think I'm trying to pry into your private life. But it's hard. You know? I've been a journalist and researcher for a long time. And this is my first stint as a matchmaker. I got curious. Can't help it."

Meg sat forward, thinking that journalists were also pretty good at spreading news. "You tell anybody anything and I'll make you the murder victim in my next book. Got it?"

"Absolutely. I won't tell a soul." Maxine's eyes were dancing, and Meg was suddenly glad she had a female friend here. Even though they'd only recently met, she had a good feeling that she and Maxine were destined to be friends.

"And, since you're obviously dying to know, it was fantastic."

"Hah. I knew it. I always figured he had to be good in bed. Some guys, you can just tell. I thought last night that there was something happening between you two."

"Hey, it's nothing really," Meg said, thinking of how he'd

disappeared so fast this morning. "Only a casual holiday thing."

"Arthur's not the casual type," Maxine informed her. "Since I've been here, I haven't seen him fixing anybody else's faucet or replacing her lightbulbs."

"Really?" Her heart bumped and she wasn't sure whether the knowledge that she wasn't one in a string of women made her feel better or worse.

"I'm not saying he's a saint, don't get me wrong. I'm sure he has women, but he's not a player, if you know what I mean."

Maxine didn't stay long. After a little more of the female bonding of a good gossip over a cup of coffee, she left.

Meg slapped peanut butter on whole wheat toast, because it was a healthy breakfast, and ate it with a banana for potassium. She did not think about what she would have eaten had Arthur stayed.

Then she cleaned up her small kitchen, poured another cup of coffee, turned the phone off and the computer on, and sat at her desk, while her coffee grew cold and the cursor blinked at her, teasing.

She thought about Arthur and what she'd learned of him last night. A man who could kill. A man who had killed. That's why she'd seen him so clearly as her villain, that first day. It wasn't merely his rugged, dark good looks and the hint of danger. It was something deeper that she'd glimpsed without understanding what it was. That dark place inside him.

Many men and women went to war. Many had come home, and how many carried that dark shadow within them?

A man of many parts, of darkness and of light.

When she began typing, she followed her villain as he went home, having stabbed his victim through the heart, which was his individual signature. She entered with him into his home in the suburbs, where he climbed into bed and made slow, tender love to his wife.

She shivered when she wrote the next scene, where he arrived at his appointment the next morning with her novel's protagonist, his psychiatrist. Meg knew what the psychiatrist didn't. She was his next intended victim.

She finished her work for the day, feeling excited. For some reason, this book that had been so stubborn to begin was now flowing. She packed up her computer and walked up to Hart House, where Maxine had told her she could use the Internet connection. After checking her e-mail and finding an amusing story from one of her writing pals, and some routine messages from various friends and relatives, she felt as though she'd never left home.

If she lifted her head, she'd see her own office wall, with her calendar, her inspirational framed quotes, her own book covers which her father always had framed for her. She'd look out her window to waving cedar trees and the bird feeder where the chickadees played.

She'd spent a lot of time in the last few months watching the chickadees, so much so that she could identify a few of them. And there was the crow who liked to give them a bad time, and the cat from next door who would watch from the ground, tail flicking.

Now, when she raised her head she saw a small Vermeer. Behind her left shoulder was an honest-to-God suit of armor, and on the walls of the office were various family photos: the weddings, picnics, usual fare, except that some of these family snaps included members of the royal family.

And that's when she knew she was miles from home. Some days it seemed like centuries from home.

She e-mailed the first few chapters of her book to her agent, knowing her rejuvenated muse was going to make one man in New York very happy.

When she'd sent the chapters, she packed up her laptop once more and emerged to find Maxine pacing the grand entrance hall with a cell phone glued to her ear, giving rapid-fire instructions to some poor lackey. She held up a hand to Meg indicating she should wait.

Wiggins walked in his slow, stately way across the flag-stone entry hall, his very blank expression giving away his disapproval of Maxine's conversation. Did he disapprove of her doing business in the front hall? Ignoring a guest? The very notion of the cell phone? Probably a bit of all three, Meg decided, responding to his greeting of "Good after-noon, miss" with "Good afternoon, Wiggins."

Maxine wrapped up with an order to "overnight me the script." Then she clicked her phone shut and turned her at-tention to Meg. "Had a great idea," she said.

Somehow, when Meg looked at that very determined, very businesslike face, she had a bad feeling she wasn't going to love the idea.

"Writers' holidays," Max said, grinning broadly.

Yep, Meg thought. Her instincts hadn't led her astray. "What about them?"

"Don't be dense. Here. With you to lead them. We'll fill the place with novice writers and you can teach them all how to be best sellers. Isn't it a great idea? And, of course, we'll make a documentary of the process."

"If there were a course that taught people how to be a best seller, believe me, there'd be a lot more best sellers."

"Oh, you know what I mean. You can teach writing. Hey, I could do a section on filmmaking. We could bring in a few more people and a few more pounds. God knows we could use them."

"I'm not—"

"Come on, think about it. We'll have a meeting sometime before you go home. I think it would be great, but if you hate the idea I'll—"

"Give it up?"

"No." Maxine sent her a *duh* expression, then grinned with devilry in the curve of her lips. "I'll find out who your greatest competition among suspense writers is and ask them."

Meg immediately envisioned Constantin Fishbourn staying in her cottage, lecturing with appalling pomposity, telling students how to write badly, plot sloppily, and drink heavily. The very notion infuriated her. She narrowed her eyes. "You are a very devious woman."

"I know. And I wouldn't do it unless you absolutely turned us down."

"I'll think about it," Meg said loftily.

"It's all I ask. And, not to put pressure on you or anything, but I told George I wouldn't marry him until this place was in the black. You know, every pound counts. So, you coming tonight?"

Meg could not believe she was being blackmailed like this. She shook her head, half aggravated, half amused. "Am I coming where?"

"I keep forgetting you don't live here. Isn't it weird? It feels like you've been here for years instead of weeks. Darts. We play every week at the pub."

"I'm not very good at darts."

"You can be on my team, then. I'm killer."

The pub equaled Arthur, who had so casually drifted out of her door this morning as though the night of searing intimacy meant nothing to him. Casual? What could be more casual than a game of darts? She'd show Arthur Denby casual, all right.

"I'd love to come."

"Excellent. We meet at seven. Want us to pick you up on the way?"

"No. I can get there on my own."

So she found herself, at precisely seven, outside the pub door. She was wearing her favorite Seven low-rider jeans, a gossamer soft cashmere sweater in her preferred shade of green, Italian leather boots, and some chunky jade jewelry she'd picked up at a Seattle craft fair. Her hair shone, her makeup was fresh. She was as hot as she had it in her to be.

With a deep breath, she opened the door.

Her gaze went straight to the bar. And there was Arthur, pulling the cork out of a bottle of bordeaux. The corkscrew drilled into the cork with efficient precision, and then his arm muscles flexed and he pulled the cork out with the same ease with which she'd take an egg out of an egg carton. She remembered the way those arms had felt around her last night, the way his hands could arouse her. He'd brought her so much pleasure with hands and mouth and driving cock last night that she was momentarily light-headed with the pleasure of seeing him again.

For a long second she couldn't move, could only stand there inside the door watching him. Then his gaze lifted and stared unerringly directly at her, as though he'd known she was there.

It was the kind of moment she'd write about, the kind she didn't believe happened in real life, a moment of absolute intimacy across a crowded room.

His blue-gray eyes darkened and burned into hers. She felt branded, marked, compelled. She couldn't look away or move. Then his gaze traveled her body, and she decided the ridiculously priced jeans were worth every penny.

Casual, she reminded herself, as she walked slowly forward, fighting the urge to sprint, to pound across the floor so fast her boots would catch fire. To launch herself over the ancient, scarred wood of the bar and into his arms. To take his mouth with her own, drag him down to the floor behind the bar where neither of them would emerge for several days.

Instead she walked slowly. And said, "Hi," as though she hadn't come in his mouth last night.

And he said, "Good to see you," as though he hadn't buried himself inside her body and called out her name as he exploded.

Casual, she reminded herself as her pulse kicked up and she curled her fingers against each other to keep from reaching for him.

God alone knew how long she might have stood there staring at the man like a publican's groupie, when she heard herself hailed.

"Hey, Meg."

She turned. "Maxine. Hi. Hello, George. Is your ankle better?" They'd come in behind her and she hadn't even noticed.

"Yes, thanks. Sorry, we're a couple of minutes late. We got held up." She glanced at the pair of them and saw the heightened color in Maxine's cheeks, the wild hair, and a red mark on her lip that looked like a bite mark. George might be limping slightly, but it obviously hadn't slowed him down in bed.

He wore a similarly blissful, just-fucked expression. He held onto Maxine, but not only for support for his injured leg.

Instinctively, she glanced at Arthur to find him meeting her gaze with a broad grin on his face. *Yep*, he seemed to be saying to her privately, *freshly shagged*.

Chapter Eight

"Right, then," George said, as though calling a meeting to order. "What will you have to drink?"

Meg was certain she must have played darts sometime in her life. There were vaguely related family members and old friends of her parents who'd been into British pub style rec rooms, and the odd bar she'd visited that included a dartboard among its attractions. But if she'd ever thrown a dart at a dartboard, it hadn't made much of an impression.

Maxine hadn't lied. The woman was a menace. George was too busy making jokes and being charming to bother aiming. Still, he did a great job. Played the game with the same focus as Meg's Aunt Martha and Uncle Bert gave to their weekly bowling team.

She was the odd one out. The only player who tossed darts the way she might throw a penny into a fountain.

"It might help if you opened your eyes next time, Meg," George offered.

"Right."

"Honey, it's not a paper airplane," Maxine reminded her after her next round. It seemed Max didn't like to lose, and her new teammate was pretty much making losing inevitable.

"Arthur," Maxine finally wailed. "We need you."

He was there in a gratifyingly short amount of time. "What seems to be the problem?" His voice was low, rough, and sexy. She felt it rumble through her like an earth tremor.

"Meg's never played darts in her life."

"I told you I'm terrible," she reminded Max.

"I thought you were being modest. Arthur, can you help her?"

Meg shot her new friend a fierce glare. It must have been obvious to everyone that Maxine could have given her some coaching. She was the best player of the bunch.

As though having read the annoyance in her eyes, Maxine said, "I can't teach things. Arthur's good at that."

Warm hands settled on her shoulders, sending heat and sexual awareness flooding through her. "Relax," he said in her ear.

"Are you kidding? Maxine will have me clapped in the dungeon if we lose."

"I'll come and rescue you if she does," he said into her ear so only she could hear. "Though it might take me a while. The thought of you tied up and helpless gives me ideas."

He wrapped his hand around hers, the one holding the dart, and showed her how to aim, how to throw. With his help, her dart actually hit the outer rim of the actual dartboard. She was delighted.

"Arthur, you have to be on my team. We're losing."

"All right." And like that, they had a new team member and she had Arthur sitting so near her their thighs touched. Under the table he placed his hand on her knee and then trailed his fingers higher, bringing her to aching life.

When it was her turn to throw he turned, looked deeply into her eyes, and said, "Think of something you really want, and aim for the center."

What she really wanted was to be naked in his arms, his body deeply and completely connected to her own. Her desire was reflected in his eyes. She rose, brushed past him. Picked up the dart.

She thought about the way she'd focused last night, the way Arthur had of giving her his absolute attention. She stared at the board, saw the center, imagined. Dart equals penis, bull's-eye equals—she started to feel warm. Well, focusing on sex couldn't make her a worse dart player and might in fact make her a better one. She squinted, imagining the moment of perfect union between dart and bull's-eye, pulled her wrist back, and launched.

Then she closed her eyes.

"Good God," said George.

"I don't believe it," cried Maxine.

"Bull's-eye," said Arthur.

She opened her eyes and sure enough, her dart was dead center on the board. She checked around to see if in fact someone else had thrown a dart that accidentally landed in the center of their dartboard, but no. That blue one was definitely hers.

Maxine hugged her, squealing in excitement, and she looked over her friend's shoulder, finding Arthur's gaze on her. He knew, of course. He knew.

Well, whatever it took to fit in during the weekly darts game, she was willing to do. In fact, she felt like she was beginning to belong here, finding the rhythms of Ponsford. While she didn't know many people, she recognized faces from the village. She imagined their lives, the predictable rhythms of a week. All the ties of a small community, the binding of family, friendships. She felt a mild ache and realized it was sadness that this wasn't hers. Not really. Not beyond three months.

The dart players left, all but George and Maxine and her.

George was politely listening to an extremely boring man explain at great length something to do with soil drainage.

She glanced at Maxine, who pulled a face. "This whole lord-of-the-manor crap isn't half as fun as it seems."

"Yeah. I can see how much you hate your life."

Maxine chuckled. "I wish you weren't going home. You're the only person around here who gets me, and who will come to my July Fourth party next year."

Finally, George was able to extract himself. Putting an arm around Maxine, he said, "Ready?"

Meg started to rise.

Arthur put a hand on her arm. "Don't leave."

She was trying to think of a reasonable excuse to stay when she found that Maxine was already dragging poor, limp-jogging George toward the exit and bundling him out the door.

"They didn't even say good-bye," Arthur said.

"I think they're on to us."

"Do you mind?"

She was surprised, and probably showed it. "No, of course not. I thought you'd mind. You'll have to live here long after I'm gone."

His eyes flashed. "I don't mind. Closing time's in half an hour. Wait for me and I'll walk you home."

There was such a world of meaning in *walk you home* that her knees turned to mush. "Okay."

"Joe," he called to the kid who helped him. "Tell them it's last call."

"All right."

An hour later, the last customer said good-bye, and the bartenders and servers weren't far behind them.

She was alone in the pub with Arthur.

"Well?" she said, when he began turning out the lights. "Are you going to walk me home?"

He turned and gazed at her, cold fire in his eyes. She shivered. "I've got a better idea," he said. He walked up to her, put his hands around her waist. He kissed her, mouth open, so hungry there was no room for finesse, and then hoisted her onto the bar. She gasped in surprise and then laughed. He perched her on the big bar and stepped between her open legs.

"I thought about you all day," he said, pressing his mouth to her belly, breathing warmth through the cashmere.

"You did?"

"Mmm. I was hoping you'd come for the darts tonight."

His hands slid under the wool, warm and tough and leathery.

"And if I hadn't?"

"I'd have come to you."

That was something, she thought as he opened her jeans.

After the pair of them had managed to wriggle off—her—and unpeel—him—her skintight jeans, and then the ice blue silk panties beneath, he resumed his former position, standing between her legs.

He put his big hands on her thighs and pushed them gently apart, spreading her, exposing her. Heat settled in the very spot where his gaze was raptly centered. She leaned back on her hands, feeling as though she were on a stage. If she looked out, there were the dim shapes of tables, the room fading to blackness as she looked farther into the pub. The surface of the bar was hard under her. When she breathed she smelled the yeasty beer, and a hint of the steak and kidney pie that had been tonight's dinner special.

He pressed kisses to her open thighs, warm, soft, fleeting kisses. Desire pooled heavy inside her, which he could probably see for himself since he'd managed to place her in the beam of one of the overhead pot lights. If she leaned back on her elbows, her upper body disappeared into darkness, but the way she was positioned, the way he held her, there was no way to avoid the light that beamed on the area from her belly to her thighs.

Arthur slipped one finger inside the gorgeous woman spread before him. "You're so wet. So hot," he murmured, his dark head bent over her. He curled his finger toward her pubic bone, finding her G-spot and pressing lightly. Her gasp told him he'd hit his own bull's-eye. He slipped a second finger inside her. Already her clit was swelling, flowering under his gaze. Her torso was still mostly covered by the soft wool sweater, and with her head thrown back he couldn't see her face, but he'd spent enough time watching her last night that he could imagine her expression.

Her eyes would be closed, her lips smiling slightly. She was so damn polite, even in bed, that she smiled with closed lips as her pleasure began. But when it mounted, she lost all her manners and bucked and moaned like a wild woman.

He was looking forward to taking her to that place. Just the thought had his prick feeling as hard as the oak she was sitting on.

He leaned forward and touched her with his tongue. She must have been expecting it, but maybe not quite yet, so he felt her hips jerk forward, pressing her more deeply against his mouth. He took her up, following her rhythm when she began thrusting her hips against his mouth and fingers, licking, teasing, and finally sucking on her as her passion grew hotter. Her lips swelled until they were as hard as his cock, her honey was flowing, and the sounds she was making were wild.

"I'm going to . . . I'm going to . . ."

"I know," he said against her damp flesh.

And then she did. He held her hips and licked her from the outside, rubbed her from the inside until she exploded in his arms, against his mouth. And then, with a final cry, she slumped, limp and pulsing against him.

Her legs were draped over his shoulders, her thighs trembling with reaction. He kissed them, so white, the skin so soft, even softer now that she'd come.

She pushed herself up to sitting, her eyes still unfocused, her mouth swollen and moist. "I want you inside me," she said, her voice passion-rough.

Not something he needed to be told twice.

He'd stuffed a couple of rubbers in his pocket before closing time, so he unzipped, dropped his drawers, and was ready in seconds.

There was nothing elegant about the pose, but he didn't care and he doubted she did, either. He lifted her carefully down, keeping his hands on her ass and her thighs still splayed. She put her arms around his neck and he slid her, soft and open and hot, right onto his burning cock.

She opened her mouth on his, kissing him deeply as they started to move. Her legs wrapped around his waist and he buried himself deeper, driving up and into her while she clutched him, the echoing pulses of her orgasm stroking him like damp fingers.

He wanted her to climax again before he let go, but he was so hot, so horny, so absolutely desperate that he wasn't certain he could make it. She surrounded him, her scent, her taste, the feel of her, so hot and eager and agile, and the little sounds she was making against his mouth were the last straw.

He pulled her away, giving them both a second of anticipation, then let go so she slid down the length of him, deep and hard.

Once more, twice, and the climax built, uncontrollable, unstoppable within him. As he groaned into her mouth, he felt her own wild tremors and let go completely.

It seemed like days later when he could see again. His chest burned as though he'd run a bloody marathon. She was on her feet, but they clung together still, leaning against the bar and panting. His legs were trembling, his trousers were around his ankles. He must look a right fool, but at the moment, he couldn't have cared less.

She straightened and began looking down at the floor. When she spotted her knickers in a dainty heap, she bent down, giving him a view of the nicest ass he'd ever been privileged to see.

He reached out and rubbed the gorgeous, fleshy curve. "Come back to my place," he said.

She stepped into her panties and then dragged on her jeans.

When she turned back to him, her face still wore the glow of recent pleasure.

"If I leave your home in the morning, won't people be suspicious?"

"I hate to tell you this, but when I left Stag Cottage this morning I bashed straight into Max. I told her I'd been changing that bloody lightbulb in the lounge that keeps burning out, but I'm not sure she believed me."

Meg bit her lip, her face reddening.

"I'm sorry, love, I should have had a doss out the window before I blundered out the front door at ten in the morning."

But instead of consternation or embarrassment, which he was expecting, Meg burst out laughing. "I told her you were over fixing the faucet in the bathroom, the one that sticks."

"And when I got home, my buttons were done up all wrong."

She laughed louder, holding onto the bar for support. Suddenly, he found himself joining her. "So," he said at last, "do you think she's guessed anything's up?"

"Totally, she called me on it. But, you know, she's really excited. She thinks she made the match."

"Do you mind very much?"

"Of course not. I'll be leaving in a couple of months. It doesn't matter to me."

She'd be leaving, of course, but not for a good while yet, so he put the notion of loss out of his mind. "I want you to come to my house. I want to make love to you in my bed and sleep beside you all night."

"Will we get any sleep?"

"Only enough to get us ready to go again. What do you think?"

"I think it's the best offer I've had all night."

Chapter Nine

They walked out of the pub and down a village road lined with the low stone walls that were so prevalent in this part of England.

He held her hand in a loose, warm grip and they didn't speak. She was still savoring the amazing sex; she suspected he was, too.

She hadn't slept with a ton of men, but with enough to know that what happened between her and Arthur was special. There was something about him that inspired her trust and that left her free to let herself go.

The night was cool, but after the heat of their passion, not unpleasantly so. There were few lights still burning in the village, and other than a cat skulking under a bush doing whatever it is that cats do at night, they were alone. Their footsteps shushed along the road. They turned again and she saw a pair of carriage lamps burning in a wonderful two-story stone house. She was surprised when that was the house he led her to. Inside, her astonishment grew. Had she expected some slovenly bachelor flat in a basement? She supposed she had.

"Oh, how beautiful," she cried when he flipped on the lights inside and she saw that the place had been furnished with antiques and paintings on the walls that, even to her inexpert eye, were obviously the real thing. "How old is the house?"

"Late seventeen hundreds. It was the parsonage. It fell into disrepair so I was able to pick it up quite cheaply a few years ago. It's been my hobby ever since, fixing it up and furnishing it to period."

His pride was evident and she found that endearing.

When he led her upstairs, her steps were quick, knowing that pleasure awaited her.

"I've got two rooms up here that I haven't got to yet, and then I'll be done."

She walked into the master bedroom and fell in love. With the window seat that needed a woman's touch. A pretty cushion, she thought, so you could sit in there and read a novel with a cup of tea. She loved the angles of the ceiling, the slight unevenness of the floorboards. He'd kept the room masculine, but she thought a few more touches of the feminine would make the room perfect.

A few more things like the vase of roses on the mahogany drum table would give the room more balance. She had a suspicion that the roses were there for her, and that made her heart skitter.

"The bathroom's through there," he said. "I converted one of the bedrooms."

"I take it this isn't authentic to period?" she teased as she took in the marble shower enclosure, the huge tub, and the gleaming sinks.

She walked back into the bedroom, losing herself in imagining, as she'd done since she was a child.

"Tell me you're not picturing a grisly murder in my bedroom," he said, watching her in some amusement.

"No." She shook her head. "I was picturing this house with the vicar and his wife and several children reading, or sewing. Taking tea in that lovely room downstairs. You know, I get the feeling that this house has held a great deal of happiness, don't you?"

He didn't look at her as though she were crazy, but as though he finally had found someone who got it. "First time I walked into this house it felt . . . content. I bought it soon after."

It was too big a house for one guy. She felt that it must be waiting for him to settle down and have some kids so the sounds of laughter and young voices would fill the house once again.

But, long before that, she suspected the walls were going to echo the sounds of their passion when she saw him advance on her with that look in his eyes she was beginning to know well.

His predatory look.

She'd already had two orgasms tonight, and now she was firing up like a woman who hadn't seen action in months. How did he do that to her?

Then he put his mouth on hers and she knew exactly how he did it.

Chapter Ten

When they woke the next morning, the sun was shining. In the daylight, the old parsonage was as perfect as it had been the night before. The gardens needed work. He kept the lawn mowed and the hedges trimmed, but she could see that the rosebushes needed pruning and the beds were empty of color.

She'd put a wrought-iron table and chairs right there, she thought, looking at a flat patch of grass that would make a perfect place for a stone patio. Mentally, she added a rose arbor, a small stone fountain, or maybe a birdbath in that corner under the mock orange.

Whoa. What was she doing? Inserting herself into the scene?

Bad idea. Bad, bad, bad. This wasn't her house, even her country, and this man certainly wasn't hers. Well, not in the long term.

With regret, she turned away from the window to find him watching her with an odd expression on his face.

"What?"

"You look good in my house. Right."

How bizarre that they should both be thinking the same thing at the same time. On such a subject.

She smiled and tried to lighten the mood. "I was planting a flower garden in my head."

"That's another thing I haven't had much time for."

He came up and touched her shoulder. He was always doing that, dropping little touches as he passed. It was like this second conversation going on between them on a much deeper and unspoken level that had nothing to do with the superficial words.

It felt like he was saying, *You're special, I care*, as though he needed that briefest physical connection between the major ones.

If she'd thought about it before, she'd have said that some guy touching her all the time would irritate the hell out of her; but it wasn't true, and she found she was starting to do it, too. For such a new relationship, they already had patterns of behavior that were astonishingly intimate.

"Coffee?" he asked.

"Mmm. Please." He poured a cup and added a drop of skim milk and half a spoonful of sugar into the china mug before handing it to her. She stared at him. "You know how I like my coffee?"

"Bartender's trick. Memorize your best customers' drinks. Brings them back."

"Am I one of your best customers?"

"The best."

"You make good coffee."

"Thanks. I'm also handy with a fry-up. I can make you breakfast or I can let you scamper back to Stag Cottage to get to work. Which is it?"

She blinked at him, comprehension dawning. "Is that why you rushed out of my place yesterday morning? So I could work?"

"Of course. You made such a bloody production about

not having the time for a bloke that I reckoned my only hope of another shag was to make myself scarce."

"Oh." She felt foolish, and was fairly certain her cheeks were pinkening. "I thought you were racing off out of there to keep things casual."

He came up to her, up and up until they were pressed hip to hip, and he glared down into her eyes. "Then you are a very silly woman."

She'd been called a few things in her life, but silly, in that utterly endearing way, had never been one of them.

She felt silly. Deliciously so. "Well," she said, nudging him with her hips until she got a gratifyingly firm response, "I'm not so silly that I'd turn down breakfast."

On top of her earlier surprises, she discovered that the man could cook. No bangers and beans and chips this morning, but an omelet with spinach and feta cheese. She squeezed oranges for juice, and they ate at the round table by the window.

Of course, the sailcloth table mats would have to go. The round table begged for a linen cloth, in a pink toile, perhaps.

She could see them sitting here, sharing the paper years from now. But she could also see him in her modern West Coast house. He'd never been there, but she could see him as clearly as though in memory. It was the spookiest damn thing she'd ever experienced.

After breakfast, she wasn't ready to leave him. She said, "I need to drive into town to the Internet café. Could I beg a ride?"

"Absolutely. It's my day off. I'm at your service."

When they got to town she felt good walking by his side. He told her a few stories about the shopkeepers and some of the people they passed, nearly all of whom knew him and then glanced at her curiously.

She had an e-mail from her agent, which she'd half thought

might be there. She clicked on it. No matter how many books she wrote, she worried over each one. She thought this book was good, but what if she'd been fooling herself? What if her writer's block had become so bad she'd completely lost her judgment?

Before she could come up with any more what-ifs, she opened the damn thing.

Hi Meg, This is the best thing you've ever written. The villain is delicious. Much love, Herbert.

Relief washed over her. And a sense of absolute satisfaction took its place. Herbert had no idea. Oh, yeah. The villain is very delicious, she thought to herself. Her great fear, that somehow she'd lost her own judgment, that after her uncharacteristic dry spell, she was writing dreck and unable to distinguish it, was relieved.

She even had the secret satisfaction of knowing that her sneaking suspicion that this was her strongest book yet was shared by someone whose opinion she trusted.

Today was a very good day.

"What's put that smile on your face?" Arthur asked her when they met outside once more. "Apart from me, of course."

"My villain is delicious," she informed him.

"I hope that means he's less terrifying than the awful bugger in the book I'm reading."

She chuckled in delight. "No, it means he's much, much worse."

"How can someone so young and full of light write such evil?"

She shrugged. "I have my nightmares on the page."

"I'd best get you home so you can get a few more written down."

And so their days fell into a pattern. They slept together

every night, either at Stag Cottage or at the parsonage, though increasingly, it seemed, she found herself in the parsonage. The place comforted her almost as much as Arthur's arms wrapped around her in sleep comforted her.

She went to the darts nights, and improved enough that she could usually hit the board, or not stray too far, though after that first one, the bull's-eye continued to elude her. She and Maxine had lunch or coffee, or simply walked the estate. The days grew cooler, more rain fell. Fall progressed and an early frost reminded her that winter, and the end of her time here, was approaching.

Her work was going well. Too well. The book that wouldn't start now raced to its end, long before she was ready.

She had two weeks until her time was up. Then a week. Arthur took her to London, where Christmas decorations were another reminder of how little time was left. They shopped in Soho and Carnaby Street, Oxford Street, and Knightsbridge. She bought gifts for home, and in Liberty of London saw the toile tablecloth she'd pictured on Arthur's kitchen table. She bought it, and napkins and a pottery jug in a matching shade of dusky rose, where a person could put a couple of tulips from the garden, early roses, or a handful of wildflowers.

They had afternoon tea at the Ritz, something she'd dreamed of since she was a little girl.

"How's the book coming, then?" he asked her over tea and scones and tiny, delicious cakes. He hadn't asked her for a while. She knew they both marked the progress of her book as the journey to the end of her time in England, and their time together.

"It's going well. Frighteningly well, in some respects." He didn't ask her what she meant. "I've got my big climax between the villain and the heroine still to write. Heart-pounding suspense, terror, and then the conclusion."

"He's the delicious one?"

"That's right."

"Hmm. What happens to him?"

She drew a finger across her throat.

Arthur bit into a scone with strong white teeth. "Shame, if he's delicious."

"He has to die," she said, gazing across at Arthur and wishing it weren't so. "To release the heroine. That's how it ends."

They were no longer speaking of some fictitious villain and they both knew it. Somehow, he'd become as central to her as the villain was to her story, and soon both would be gone.

"No hope of saving him?" His eyes were sad and serious. She looked at his handsome, rugged face and knew she'd fallen in love with him.

"How?" she asked him.

When they returned home they were uncharacteristically somber. He made love to her as though it were the last time, and when their cries echoed around them, her eyes stung.

It was a long time before she slept. Arthur was silent and still in the bed beside her, with his arm around her, his hand curled around her breast, but she was fairly certain he wasn't asleep either.

Of course, they'd never exchanged words of love. It hadn't mattered. She knew he loved her as much as she knew she loved him. But what was the point of getting any deeper into a relationship that had been limited from the start?

Sometime in the middle of the night she turned to him, and found his eyes open and on her. She reached for him, climbing onto him and riding him with desperation, as though she could cram an entire lifetime into this last week.

There was no finesse to her loving; she was greedy and desperate, grabbing at his skin, scratching, riding hard, until they were both sweat-drenched and panting.

"I love you," she cried, as though the words had been yanked out of her.

"I know, love. I know."

When she slumped down onto his still-heaving chest, her cheeks were wet. He kissed her slowly and then held her until at last she slept.

She awoke determined to make their last few days good ones. She could mope and whine and snivel at home. She'd have lots of time.

Arthur was still sleeping when she woke, heavy-eyed and a little sore.

Well, she could make him coffee. And breakfast. She slipped into the spare bedroom where she'd stowed all her bags from their shopping trip and found the toile cloth, the napkins, and the jug.

When he came into the kitchen half an hour later, she thought she'd never seen anything so good as this scratching, shirtless man with his black hair sticking out in tufts and his boxers riding low. "Smells good," he said. She gave him a bright smile, one that suggested *No, I didn't cry all over you and tell you I loved you last night*, and handed him his coffee.

And, as he turned to sit at the table, he stopped.

"Don't say it's too girlish," she begged as she saw him staring at the pretty cloth, the neatly folded napkins, and the jug containing a scatter of rose hips since that was all she could find in the garden.

"It's perfect," he said. "I wouldn't have chosen it, mind, but it's exactly right."

"I saw them at Liberty's and knew it would look great."

"I think this house is better with you in it," he said, still staring at the cloth. "It's been waiting for you for a long time." He turned to her slowly. "So have I."

"Don't say it, please don't say it," she begged.

She saw a flash of impatience along with the sadness.

"How can I not say it? You know it's true as well as I do. You belong here. You work well, you've made friends, we've found each other. Why can't you cancel your ticket home and stay?"

"You make it sound so easy, but it's not you being asked to give up your life. It's me. Would you give up this? The pub? Your house? Your friends? Come home with me if I asked you?"

He regarded her. "Are you asking me?"

Her heart felt like a moth flapping around a hot light-bulb. Stupid, foolish, and determined to be incinerated.

"I don't know. Love hasn't worked out that well for me in the past."

"Of course it hasn't," he said with contempt. "Any more than it has for me. You think you're going to find what we have again? This"—he gestured back and forth between them—"this happens once in a lifetime if you are very, very lucky."

"I wish I knew what to do," she said softly.

"You'd best tend to whatever you've got burning on the stove."

She gasped and turned to find the fancy oatmeal she'd made from *Woman's Weekly* was scorched. Perfect.

Just perfect.

She left after breakfast but when she got to Stag Cottage she was too restless to write. Arthur had broken the unspoken agreement between them. Well, she supposed she had first when she'd blurted out her love, but surely some allowances could be made for a woman in midclimax.

He'd asked her in the cold light of day, however, bringing up not only love, but a future. A family, meals stretching for their lifetime around that toile-covered table in the parsonage kitchen. Or around the sleek glass and steel table in her

Seattle kitchen with the granite counters and the stainless appliances.

Two homes. Why not?

It was such an appealing image, and so terrifying she couldn't even bear to consider it seriously.

She stopped at Stag Cottage only long enough to drop her bags and change into walking clothes, then she headed out, needing to think.

Her path took her, as it often did, beside the river. The walking path was a favorite. There was a pair of swans that hung around, and she took out the whole wheat bread she'd brought specially and tossed them a few pieces.

Behind her was Hart House, as elegant and grand every time she looked at it. The village had to be the prettiest in England.

She and Arthur and Maxine and George would be best friends all their lives and have children together. She'd write part of the time in England, and of course give in to Maxine's demands that she run a writers' retreat here.

And they'd live part of the time on her side of the pond. She could certainly be as flexible as she wanted to be and Arthur had intimated he could be, too. Although she hadn't put him to the test by asking him.

But the solution was perfect. Frighteningly so. Joe, the other bartender, would likely be thrilled to take over the pub part of the year.

And perfect scared the hell out of her. Life was messy and fraught with disaster. In her books, the minute things were going too well was the time her characters should be looking over their shoulder because terror, disaster, and death were creeping up behind them as sure as it was chapter four.

She didn't hear herself hailed until a hand grasped her shoulder. She swung round to find Maxine, out of breath and half laughing. "I had to chase you miles, yelling your name. What's up?" Then the smile faded. "Oh, honey. What's wrong? You look like shit."

"I feel like shit."

"Is it Arthur?"

"Of course it's Arthur. Who else can wreck a perfectly good day like the man you're in love with?"

"Don't tell me he doesn't love you back, because if you tell me that then one of you is lying."

"Oh,"—Meg flapped her hands—"of course he loves me. It would be so much easier if he didn't. Or I didn't."

She kicked a stone out of her path and into the water, *plop*. Bringing the greedy-assed swans floating back.

"Ah," Maxine said, in the tone of a woman who had been there. "It's the go or stay dilemma, isn't it?"

"No. There's no dilemma. My life is in Seattle. Arthur's is here."

"So what are you going to do? Walk away from a guy who makes you glow?"

"No . . ." She glanced up. "I glow?"

"Like Rudolph's nose."

"Oh."

"If it's any consolation, Arthur's glowing, too."

"I left a man who was controlling. Who made me lose confidence in myself. It was so bad I stopped being able to write. I can't go through that again."

"I've sure seen how much your confidence has been suffering since you got here. And the writing's definitely not going well."

"Gaaaggggh!" Meg yelled, so the swans, who were still hanging around the bank, floated off with their beaks in the air. "Weren't you scared?"

"Of course I was. I still am when I realize that no one in this country understands the concept of the Super Bowl. And these people fry bread. In bacon fat. I'm telling you, you look at an English breakfast and your arteries clog."

Meg smiled. "I can't move to a foreign country for a man. I can't."

"Have you asked him to move to the States?"

She thought about how he'd dared her to do exactly that this morning and panic washed over her anew. "How can I ask that of him? His whole life is here."

"Seems to me that he has the right to decide for himself what's important."

"I wish I hadn't come here. There was a darling stone cottage in Wales."

Maxine laughed at her. "No, you don't. You're a big girl, Meg. Act like one."

And finally, in despair, she stalked back to Stag Cottage and did exactly that. She acted like a big girl. She wrote the final chapter that she'd been putting off because it seemed symbolic that when her story ended, when the villain she'd recognized the moment she saw Arthur, was no more, then her romance would as effectively be over.

And Arthur was a villain. He'd stabbed her in the heart as effectively as her murderous psycho.

Her computer hummed and the words danced in front of her eyes for a few minutes. She felt like a drowning woman with her life flashing before her eyes as she wrote herself to *The End*.

Meg wasn't one to plot her books ahead. She knew writers who had systems, with color-coded charts and diaries for their characters. She admired that kind of organization and knew she would never write a book if she charted the whole thing out first, and already knew her characters intimately.

For her, that was the point of writing the book. It was the voyage of discovery as she came to know these people and their story. Sure, she was the one creating the world and the people in it, but she discovered that world by writing it.

So she typed her villain to his justly deserved doom.

And never had she killed off a villain more unwillingly.

But there he was, as she'd always imagined the last chapter. He had the heroine with her back, literally and figuratively, to the wall. He'd toy with her a little. Because he had the luxury of time and privacy, and because he believed that she of all people would appreciate his brilliance, his subtlety, his daring.

He'd been her patient. He'd had her attention, her clinical diagnoses, occasionally her smile. But he'd never had her respect. He wanted it, ferociously.

And when he didn't get it, he grew angry, exactly as the psychiatrist had hoped. Her only chance to get out alive was to use her knowledge of his diseased mind against him. So she taunted him, shamed him, ridiculed him. It was a dangerous tactic, but she didn't have any other weapon.

Finally, he snapped. She'd been watching his eyes, so she knew the second he lost control. When he rushed at her, he was no longer the cool madman, but an overgrown boy in a vicious tantrum. She kneed him hard in the balls as he came at her.

It wasn't enough to save her from the knife, but the move saved her life. By the time the police arrived, she had her attacker at gunpoint, having retrieved her handgun from her purse, and called the cops from the cell in her purse while she staunched her bleeding arm with her Hermes scarf.

When the detective with whom she was having an on-again, off-again affair arrived on the scene, there was some catchy banter about women and their purses. He offered her a lift to the hospital. She said only if he hung around to see her home.

Behind them, the villain was carted away, raving and furious.

But he wasn't dead.

Chapter Eleven

Meg stared at the page, the final page of her novel. It wasn't often that the ending surprised her. Not like this. How could the villain not be dead? All along, she'd envisioned that final desperate fight. The psychiatrist would get to her bag, she'd reach in it for her gun, which she shouldn't even have in her purse, but the detective had warned her to be extra careful and so she'd tucked it in there that morning.

Of course, the weapon had fallen to the bottom under the lipsticks and the pack of tissue. Oh, there it was—no, shit, that was her sunglasses case.

And the madman would be almost upon her when she'd grab the gun, fumbling for the safety, and boom, she'd shoot him through the bottom of her Fendi bag. Shot through the heart, they'd discover in the autopsy, in a nice bit of irony.

How could it not have ended that way?

Meg read the final scene again, her hands shaking, from too much coffee probably.

Had she cheated? This new final scene, was it some manipulation by her own psyche?

She reread the entire chapter. And then she saw what

she'd missed with her clever bit of shot-through-the-heart irony. The quick, clean death wasn't enough of a punishment for this guy. No. Prison. Lack of control. No privacy. Being looked down on, ordered, insulted. Forced to perform menial tasks. Oh, how her villain would suffer. It was a much more fitting punishment.

Her new ending was the perfect one.

In every way.

She stretched back in her chair, reached her arms up to the ceiling, and stretched.

Done. She was done. Of course, she needed to read and polish it a few times, but her story was told.

She walked to the tiny village, humming under her breath. She stopped in at the newsagent's. The shop carried a couple of international papers, always a day or two late, but she limited herself to the Sunday *New York Times*.

Tramping back across the fields with her paper, a pint of milk, and a loaf of fresh bread, she stopped for a moment and took a slow, luxurious turn. It took no imagination at all to picture this as it had been a hundred years ago, two, three hundred years. Block out the cars and trucks and the telephone poles, and the scenery would have looked almost precisely the same. Sun glinted off the fields while sheep munched quietly, barely bothering to lift their heads as she walked by on the common footpath.

The village at her back was postcard quaint with its old stone houses scattered with thatched roofs. Hart House rose like a fairy tale, and behind the lawns, at the edge of the wooded section, sat her little house. Built from the same pale stone.

It was so peaceful. A perfect place to work. She'd never felt so content. Perhaps it was a perfect place to live. At least, part of the year.

She wouldn't give up her house on Bainbridge Island. Why should she? And Arthur wouldn't give up the parsonage. Or the pub. They'd simply enjoy two homes.

She opened the thick oak door and walked in. The fresh flowers she'd bought herself yesterday were a cheerful sight on the kitchen table where she'd written. She opened the French doors to connect herself with the outdoors.

"Still at your murder and mayhem?"

She glanced up to find Arthur walking toward her. She couldn't have written a better timed entrance.

"No," she said. "I'm finished." She reached for the bottle of bordeaux on the counter. "Care to celebrate with me?"

"Yes." He walked in, looking much less happy than she felt, and kissed her. "Congratulations."

"Thanks. I know there's a corkscrew here somewhere." She opened the cutlery drawer and he reached over her shoulder. "I'll do it."

While he opened and poured the wine, she watched him, feeling ridiculously pleased with herself.

He handed her a glass and raised his. "Here's to my favorite author," he said.

"And here's to my favorite villain."

"You drink to your villains?"

"Well, I have a small secret. Something I've been keeping from you. I never, ever write characters who are in any way like people I know. Never ever."

"I see. Makes good sense, that."

"Except this time." She looked up at him, at that strong face, the sharp cheekbones, the blue-gray eyes, and the black hair. He gazed at her in the same magnetic way he'd stared at her that first day. "I saw you and you were the perfect model for my sadistic killer."

He blinked. "Well, cheers."

She laughed. Oh, she was so high on this moment she

might never come down. "You know what? I always fall in love with my villain."

"You do?"

She nodded. "Especially this time."

He put his glass down as though he'd forgotten about it. "What happens to this one? In the end. You said you were going to kill him off. Was it very gruesome?"

She put her own glass down beside Arthur's and walked up until they were almost touching. "I thought he was going to die. All along, I knew his death. But when I wrote it, I found out I was wrong. He doesn't die."

"Don't tell me the rotten bugger gets away?"

"Oh, no. He gets caught, of course."

"Does he now? What's his punishment?"

She kissed the man she loved more than all her villains combined. "He gets the perfect punishment."

"And that is?"

"A life sentence."

He reached out and traced her jaw with one finger, his blue-gray eyes glinting at her. "To be served where?"

"Does it matter?"

Maxine was right, she realized, gazing at Arthur—he did glow. Or maybe it was her own glow of happiness reflecting back. He smiled at her. "Not particularly, no."

He moved, letting his finger trail lazily down the side of her neck to follow the curve of her collarbone. She shivered as ribbons of pleasure played over her skin. They were going to make love, right here in the kitchen, maybe on that sturdy table where she'd typed her novel, always with his dark, sexy image before her.

"Come with me to Seattle?"

He pulled her to him and kissed her, a long, perfect kiss. "I thought you'd never ask."

UNION JACK

Chapter One

To: chefgal@hotmail.com
From: Maxinelarraby@Harthouse.org

Subject: I know you're there!

Message: Hey, sis. We're worried about you.
Mom says she hasn't seen you for weeks, and you
sound weird on the phone. Yeah, yeah, I know,
but nobody else has seen you either. Possibilities.
1. You're seeing a hot new guy and you haven't
crawled out of bed in weeks. 2. You're depressed.
Which makes perfect sense given that your divorce became final and they closed the restaurant
a couple of weeks later. Pissy timing, huh?

Let me know what's up. Miss you.

TTFN, Max

To: Maxinelarraby@harthouse.org
From: chefgal@hotmail.com
Subject: I'm fine

Rachel Larraby paused and looked at her subject line. Should she add an exclamation mark after fine? Or would snarky punctuation make her older sister suspicious?

She looked down at herself and was glad she'd never invested in one of those Internet cameras. She really didn't want designer Max to see her like this. Her comfy sweatshirt was a pretty accurate food diary for the last couple of weeks. There was a Thai noodle, desiccated and lonely, rather like Rachel herself; there was the tea stain from where she'd fallen asleep watching an *I Love Lucy* episode. There a blob of chocolate from where she'd laughed so hard at a *Seinfeld* rerun she'd dropped the chocolate out of her mouth. Not one of her finest moments. Day-Glo orange Doritos dust, butter smears from popcorn, an unidentifiable foodstuff she suspected had once adorned a pizza. The old UCLA sweatpants that had been Cal's weren't in much better shape. Still, she was showering daily and brushing her teeth regularly. She even took her vitamins every morning. She was fine.

Mostly.

> *Don't worry about me. I'm catching up on my sleep and hanging out at the beach.*
> *How's England?*
> *Luv, Rach*

Maxine Larraby cried out, "I knew it!"

"Knew what, darling?" George asked, coming up behind her at the computer and kissing the nape of her neck.

"My sister is a mental case."

"Every family has one. My uncle Cecil takes my aunt Winifred everywhere with him."

Maxine stared at the screen as though she could see all the way to L.A. and her sister. "So?"

"She was cremated. In 1966. He has a lovely box for

her—Georgian silver, I believe, with her favorite poem engraved on the lid. A Shakespearean sonnet, but it's a bit disconcerting to people who aren't used to the pair of them, such as the staff of restaurants. And the family. I once sat on poor old Aunt Winnie at Christmas dinner. Caused a fearful row and put me right off my roast goose."

"Rachel's not that kind of mental case. She's depressed."

George read over her shoulder, leaning in so she smelled his skin and felt the warmth of him. "She says she's hanging out at the beach. That doesn't sound very depressed."

"Rachel hates the beach and she gets hives if she sits in the sun. That's what worries me the most. If she had to lie, couldn't she make up something I might believe? No," she said, rising. "This has gone on long enough. That e-mail is a cry for help. We'll have to stage an intervention."

George blinked at her, his sexy blue eyes wary. "But what are you going to do? We're in England, love. She's in America."

He had a point. What were they going to do?

"She'd be okay if it was only the divorce, but losing the restaurant at the same time has taken away her natural outlet for stress."

George nodded. "I feel for her. I remember how awful it was losing my father and then having to give up my job in London to come down here and run this place with all its responsibilities and debts."

"Still, at least you had Hart House. You had a purpose. That's what Rachel needs. She's passionate about her work," she said, pacing. "She needs to cook, she needs a change of scene, a new start." She snapped her fingers. "She needs to come here, George. I'm sure Arthur would give her a job at the pub. She's a brilliant chef."

"You can't have an American cooking English pub food," George argued.

"Why not?"

"It's not seemly."

"She'll be in the kitchen. Who'll know?"

"You must be joking. Everyone in the village will find out. No, really, Max."

She swung around. "Cal's been gone a whole year and she's not moving on. At all. At least she had her work. Now, the restaurant's closed. Every time I talk to her she has a harder time faking that she's fine. She is not fine. Traveling here would do her good, and besides, I miss her."

"Fair enough. Have her to stay. We've got loads of bedrooms. She won't be in the way."

"She needs work, a sense of purpose. She needs to cook."

"Well." He spread his hands in a reasonable way. "She can cook for us."

"Rachel needs a real job that earns real money." She turned to him. "Come on. It would only be for a few months. Please?"

"Stop looking at me with those melting eyes. It's not working."

But his mouth was having trouble remaining serious and she knew she had him. In the months she'd known George, she'd yet to find an argument that couldn't be resolved between them. She walked up to him and put her arms around his neck. "You know, for an earl you're pretty damn sexy."

"I'll speak to Arthur. That's all I can promise." Then he bent her back over the desk, and had begun showing her exactly how sexy he could be when the phone rang.

"Ignore it," George mumbled against her skin. His lips and tongue were seducing her whole body by kissing the spot where her neck met her shoulder. His hand was already sneaking under her shirt, headed north for her breasts. Knowing the service would pick up, she ignored the ringing until it stopped, putting her arms around George's neck and kissing him until they were both breathing hard.

Wiggins's heavy tread could be heard crossing the foyer, so George slipped his hand out of her shirt, took a step back, and said, "My friend Jack's sister Chloe wants to have her wedding here."

George was so smooth it was obvious he'd been used to having servants around all his life. She was still having trouble adapting. But she was learning. She hauled herself upright and pushed a hand through her hair. When Wiggins walked past the open door of the office, she said in a voice that was only the tiniest bit husky, "Fantastic. Will it be a big, expensive wedding?"

"Should be. She's marrying an Italian ski racer. His family owns half the Italian Alps. Pots of money."

"Perfect," she said, forgetting sex at the prospect of making more of the money they needed to pay off the bank debt. "Oh, but if we're doing a wedding for people like that, we're going to have to do something about the catering. We can't have those clowns we hired the last time. That mother-and-son duo from the next village. We'll have to—" She stopped midsentence and smacked herself in the forehead. "Rachel!"

Rachel's intercom buzzed, waking her up from her second nap of the afternoon. Soon, this laziness would really have to stop. One more week, she promised herself. Then she'd go out, start assimilating back into society. Think about another job.

She dragged herself off the couch. Must be the groceries she'd ordered by phone.

The thing was, she'd already had offers to work again. By e-mail, by phone message, by mail. All so far unanswered. She didn't want to work for someone else and risk losing another restaurant. If only one of those calls, letters, or e-mails said, "Here's a couple million bucks. Open your own place. Pay us back when you can." That message she'd have answered.

She let the delivery guy up, and when he got to her door she peeked through the peephole. She didn't recognize him, but he wore a uniform. She opened the door with the chain on it. "Yes?"

Now she recognized the uniform. It was a courier holding not groceries but an envelope. He was cute, with sun-streaked hair and a fresh scrape on his knee. Surfer boy/courier guy. "Is that a check for two million?"

"If it is," he said, "can I get your number?"

She managed a laugh, unhooked the chain, and took the envelope. Checked the address and wished she could reverse time far enough to ignore the door. Max + special delivery package = bad news.

She considered throwing the envelope away unopened, but with her bossy, tenacious sister, avoidance was pointless.

Inside the package was a plane ticket to London and a letter. There wasn't much in the way of chitchat.

> *Dear Rachel,*
> *I miss you, and need a favor. I'll tell you when you get here. Don't even think about not coming. Mom and Dick are going to drive you to the airport.*
> *If you're not packed when they get there, Mom will pack for you. You don't want that to happen.*
> *There is no escape.*
> *Love, Max.*

Rachel fingered the ticket.

She could be bitchy about the fact that her big sister was interfering—again. Or she could appreciate that Max had gone to a lot of trouble for her, and she missed her.

Besides, she could use a holiday. The first spark of excitement she'd felt in weeks flashed through her. Oh, what the hell? Maybe it was time to get off the couch.

A carefree vacation in an English mansion was exactly what she needed.

Chapter Two

"You didn't tell me you were marrying Hugh Grant." Rachel and Maxine were having tea served in dainty china cups while they sat curled up on an overstuffed couch in a bright sunny room of Hart House and munched the Oreos that Rachel had brought from home, since they were Maxine's favorite cookie in the world and she doubted Maxine could buy them in England.

"He does look sort of like Hugh Grant, doesn't he? It's the eyes, I think."

Rachel narrowed her own eyes. "So you *are* marrying him. I knew it."

"We haven't decided anything yet," Max said, trying unsuccessfully to look nonchalant, but her heightened color and extra sparkle gave her away. Then she dropped the airy pretense and complained, "Anyway, you could at least sound happy about the possibility of your sister getting married."

"Marriage is a patriarchal institution designed to enslave women."

But Max had known her longer and better than anyone on the planet, and she wasn't buying it. "You picked the wrong guy, Rach. You made a mistake. It happens."

"I guess." She shrugged. "Getting divorced and losing the restaurant was a lot of failure for one year."

"I know. And we don't take failure well." Max hugged her, something they hadn't done much of since they'd both grown up. It was nice, Rachel thought, hugging her back. "So," her sister said, all girlish and un-Max, "do you like him?"

"Hugh Grant? I adored him in *Love, Actually*."

Her sister's glare sent her back to childhood. "George, moron."

Somehow discussing a distant movie star was a lot easier than talking about a man who could become part of her family. "He seems very nice," she said slowly. *Seems* being the important word there. It was the character lurking underneath the charming veneer that counted, as she knew from bitter experience.

Rachel had been looking forward to a relaxing vacation, but now it seemed she was also here to check out Max's prospective husband. Right now, that seemed like too big a job. Okay, so she hadn't worked in two months. Hadn't done much of anything but catch up on soaps she hadn't seen since college. It was amazing how you could pick up the story lines again. She'd watched and rewatched classic movies and sitcoms, reread her entire collection of Sherlock Holmes, *Anne of Green Gables*, and the Harry Potter series which she'd somehow missed. With cable TV, online bill paying, and a grocery store and restaurants that delivered, she'd hunkered down in her apartment for weeks. The final divorce papers were in her filing cabinet under *D*, for disaster.

She'd still be in her pajamas surrounded by junk food and watching the classic movie channel if it weren't for Max.

Bossy, pushy, never-give-an-inch Max.

"George *is* nice, but I want you to get to know him better." She pulled another cookie out of the bag. "I'm so glad you're here."

"Don't be. I'm a mess. Your butler wanted to send me round to the servants' entrance when he saw me."

"Wiggins doesn't approve of trousers on women," Max said in a stern British accent, pointing to Rachel's jeans.

Rachel snorted. "You're kidding me."

"No. He's a sweetie when you get to know him, though."

"It's not only the jeans," she said, looking down at herself. "I'm a total wreck."

"Maybe you're a little pale, and your hair, it's so . . ."

"I look like shit. I know," Rachel said, pushing the tangle of dark brown over her shoulder, as though she might be able to minimize the disaster if she hid it from sight.

Her sister didn't argue with her about her looks. "I'm not used to it being so long. When did you last have a haircut?"

"When I had a regular paycheck."

They'd always been different, she and Max. She was the one who worked summers at the deep fryer at Kentucky Fried Chicken while Max worked in the showroom of their uncle Wilf's car dealership. When they got older, they stayed different. While she was in chef school learning how to remove the intestines from scampi, debone a chicken, and make stock from the bones and yucky parts, Max was taking the communications program at Berkley, after which she slid right into the glamorous world of television.

Now Max was a respected producer with a great wardrobe living in a castle with a guy who was in spitting distance of being an honest-to-God prince.

And she, Rachel, was unemployed, divorced, and suffering from a bad hair millennium.

"Well," her sister said, in a brisk voice Rachel knew from experience would be full of plans, "now you're here, we'll get you all fixed."

Listening to her made Rachel tired. She stifled a yawn.

"We'll get your hair done. I found a fantastic place in London."

"London. You go to London to get your hair cut?"

"It's not that far. A couple of hours on the train. There's nowhere nearer. Trust me."

"Maybe I'll be okay with my hair. I'm thinking of growing it," she lied. Mostly, she'd been avoiding anything more strenuous than pressing the remote with her thumb and crawling to the freezer for more ice cream.

As though she'd read her thoughts, Max said, "Your skin looks sort of pasty. Have you been eating properly?"

And, out of nowhere, irritation spurted. "No, I haven't been eating properly. I've been holed up in my apartment scarfing junk food. I'm a chef, and I can't even be bothered to cook for myself. I cry at commercials—and not the long distance phone ones everybody cries at. I found myself in tears when the woman with her first job bought herself a Saturn. I feel like my skin is breakable." She leaned back into the couch until she was staring up at the ancient ceiling. "I think I'm having some kind of breakdown."

"We'll get that fixed, too." Max reached over and patted Rachel's knee briskly. "You're going to be a lot happier when you start work."

"If anybody still remembers me when I get back home." She thought of the now-defunct restaurant where she'd invested so much of herself and let a scowl settle on her face.

"I was thinking you might do some cooking while you're here."

Rachel had known that I-know-what's-best-for-you expression too long to be fooled by it. "I'd be happy to cook dinner for you and George."

"I was thinking more along the lines of a professional gig."

"I came here for a rest."

"Mom says you've been 'resting' since the restaurant closed."

"Mom should mind her own business."

"Rach, we're worried about you."

"Well, don't. Apart from the small breakdown, I'm fine. I'm free. Free of that phony bastard I married, and free of eighteen-hour shifts."

"The restaurant closing wasn't your fault," Max said gently.

"No. I know. Bad luck, bad management. Owners who didn't have the same commitment." But if it wasn't her fault, then why did she feel like such an abject failure?

Max took the last Oreo and offered it to Rachel, who shook her head. Around the cookie, Max said, "Your reviews were fantastic, your food is amazing."

"Thanks."

Of course, despite having grilled her about her professional life, Max wasn't nearly done torturing her. After finishing the cookie she said, "Are you seeing anyone?"

"You mean like a man?" The entire notion revolted her. She didn't think she'd go out with a guy for a couple of years, at least. And as for weddings! She'd developed a severe allergy to tulle, cakes with pillars between the layers, and vellum stationary. Max, with the chorus of *Ave Maria* playing in her head, was not good company.

"I meant like a therapist."

"I'm not crazy." Though secretly she thought she must have been to marry Cal, and throw her heart and soul into a restaurant that wasn't hers.

"I know you're not crazy. I think you're depressed."

Rachel picked at the end of her thumbnail. "You'd be depressed, too."

"I know. That's why I have a therapist on speed dial."

"You lived in L.A. too long." But, amazingly, Rachel was smiling. It must have been a while since she'd tried it because her smile muscles felt lax and out of shape. Kind of like the rest of her.

"Anyway, now that you're here, we'll have fun, you'll

rest, but George is trying so hard to make this estate pay for itself that he takes in catering jobs. It would be so great if you could help out—"

That was fair. If her possible future brother-in-law and host needed catering help, it wouldn't kill her. "I'll do anything but weddings."

If Maxine's dominant quality was persuasiveness, Rachel's was stubbornness, and she glared at her sister.

Outside, two volunteer docents walked by sharing an umbrella.

"The catering job I'm thinking of is to celebrate a merger," Max said.

Max had been in TV long enough for Rachel to be suspicious. "What kind of merger?"

"Look, it's a dinner reception for a hundred people. You worry about the food. You can do something absolutely amazing. They won't believe your food."

"What kind of merger?"

"Two separate entities becoming one."

"Will there be champagne involved?"

"I think champagne is very likely."

"A multilayered cake with two tiny people perched on top, perhaps?"

Max made a face. "I hope they have more imagination."

"It's a wedding." Rachel shot to her feet. "I don't do weddings!"

"Honey, you've got to get back on the horse."

"Get on a horse? I'm supposed to get on a horse? What the hell's that supposed to mean?"

"It means that your marriage is over, and I'm really, really sorry Cal turned out to have loose morals even by L.A. standards. But you can't give up on all weddings."

"Getting back on the horse after Cal left would be having sex again, not catering weddings. And for your information I have already done that."

Max was staring at her. "You had sex and didn't tell me?"

She flapped a hand. "Completely forgettable. I just needed to ride a different horse."

"Who was he?"

"Friend of a friend. Like I said, no big deal."

"Huh."

"What?"

Max was suddenly grinning like a fool. "England has excellent horses."

Rachel spent three days getting the kitchen cleaned, organized, and stocked exactly as she wanted it. She'd been in England two weeks, and amazingly she was starting to feel better. The smell of crisp apples ready to be picked stirred her senses when she walked around the estate. The scents of lavender, rosemary, and thyme lay heavy in the autumn sunshine bathing the kitchen garden, and her hands itched to cook.

If Max was going to make her cater events then she was going to have the kitchen as efficient as possible. She'd brought her favorite chef's knife with her, the one tool she hated to be without. Vaguely, she'd imagined cooking a few meals for Maxine and Earl George, never that she'd be catering a wedding. But holding out against Max at the best of times was tough. When she was emotionally pathetic, it was hopeless. In fact, there were lots of catering jobs large and small she could do while she was here, and after she'd heard about the mother-and-son catering disaster, she knew she had to step in and help her sister. On some level she even understood she needed to do this for her own healing.

The knife was lightweight Japanese steel and fit her hand so well it was like an extension of her fingers. The rest of the knives at Hart House were German, and so dull she'd made Max drive her into town this morning to get them sharpened.

A mistake she wouldn't be making again anytime soon. How had she forgotten that Maxine couldn't talk and drive at the same time in the States, never mind while driving on the opposite side of the road?

She shuddered in memory. She was hot, frazzled, had seen her life pass before her eyes too many times today, and had discovered something called a roundabout, a traffic circle of hell. She wished she hadn't picked today to offer to cook for Maxine and George because Maxine had trilled her excitement and run off to invite a few friends.

The produce she'd discovered at a local greengrocer's lay before her, along with the perfectly ripe soft cheese from the cheese shop. Marinating in the fridge was lamb so local she didn't want to think about it too closely.

Somebody who'd cooked here recently had let the big orange cat who paraded around the place make a nuisance of itself. Rachel did not allow cats in her kitchen, but this old tabby was acting like the kitchen was his and if she fed him enough tidbits, he might consider letting her stay.

It was hot, too hot to close the door that led to a small yard and then the kitchen garden.

Still, she was cooking again. The knife felt like a forgotten lover back in her arms, the vegetables and fruits and fresh herbs scattered before her were like paints ready to be mixed and, by her hands, turned into art.

Some of her black mood drained and she found herself falling into the rhythms that gave her life work and made her work pleasure. While she prepared a sauce for the lamb, she mentally worked out the timeline for table service and made a list of the wines she'd need.

That done, she moved to the homelier task of peeling veggies. When she thought about how many aspiring chefs had fought for the sous chef jobs in her restaurant, she smiled to herself. How far the mighty had fallen. She didn't really mind, though. The rhythm of the movements, the scrape of peeler on carrot, the smell of vegetables and herbs fresh from the earth pleased her.

The scrape of gravel informed her she had a visitor and her moment of Zen tranquility vanished. Damn cat.

"Out!" she yelled, determined to get rid of that infernal mooch once and for all. She grabbed a potato from the tile counter and threw it hard, high enough that it wouldn't actually hit the cat, but simply let the animal know that her kitchen was out of bounds.

In fact, she discovered that she'd pitched the potato exactly at crotch height of a tall man when she heard a distinctly human *oomph* and spun around.

His instincts were quick, at least. He had his hands crossed over his privates as the missile hit the cupped backs of his hands and bounced to the floor with a hollow plop.

For a stunned second there was utter silence. She stood there, staring at a rangy, athletic man with close-cropped hair and a lean, intelligent face, with his hands crossed over his crotch. Slowly, he removed his hands and straightened.

"Unmanned by a spud," the man said, looking down at the potato, which had rolled, as though embarrassed by its bad temper, under the butcher's block.

"I'm sorry. I thought you were the cat," Rachel said.

"Ah, that explains it." He had a cultured voice. Crisper than George's, though. More BBC America announcer than royal family. Sharp gray eyes, she noticed, and hair that would curl if he didn't keep it so short. An athlete's build. As she replayed the protective move with his hands, she realized she'd seen that same posture during shoot-outs in soccer games.

He was looking at her as though wondering whether he dared cross the threshold. Smart guy.

"This is the private part of the house," she said, glad Max had warned her about the tourists who sometimes got lost. "The old kitchen is in the next building, around the corner. Do you want me to show you?"

"No, thank you. I came to see you."

He looked at her with those heavy-lidded gray eyes, and for the first time since Cal Moody had broken her heart, she felt the stirring of ... something. A little of that male-female thing that always led to no good in her experience.

"You came to see me?" she repeated stupidly.

"About the wedding. I understand from Maxine that you'll be doing the catering."

"Right, the wedding." She picked up a carrot and attacked it with the peeler.

Her unwanted visitor knelt to the ground and picked up the potato, then walked briskly forward and placed it beside her. "Do I detect a certain animosity toward the upcoming happy event?"

Silently, she marveled at the sheer number of words guys like George and this dude needed to say the simplest things. She also reminded herself to remain silent about her feelings referring to the upcoming "happy event." George and Max needed the money and it was up to her to make sure the catering was superb. That was all she had to do. So she forced herself to look up and try to keep her expression pleasant. She'd always stayed in the background of food preparation for good reason. She hated dealing with the customers.

"I'm sure the event will be so happy it will do cartwheels. I promise the food will be good." And she went back to her carrot.

He rolled the potato back and forth under his fingers as though it were a bumpy and rather dirty marble. She couldn't help noticing his hands. He had great hands. They looked tough and strong, like a fighter's—or a chef's. Better on a man than a woman. Hers were so scarred, burned, and generally mistreated that she never drew attention to them. On a guy, though, the roughed-up hands looked good—sexy. For a blind moment she imagined those hands on her, and then snapped herself out of her inappropriate sexual reverie.

What was wrong with her? She must be crazier than she thought.

She felt that he was watching her and wished fervently it had been the cat who'd intruded on her kitchen.

Unlike the cat, however, a well-thrown potato didn't seem to bother the man at her side. If anything, he seemed to be hanging around.

"For a guy who almost lost his privates to a potato, you're standing awfully close to a woman with a very sharp knife."

"I live for danger," he said. She glanced up, and something about the way his eyes glittered made her feel like she was the one likely to be in danger. And him a bridegroom. No wonder she'd given up on men.

"Okay, maybe we should start over." She held out her right hand after carefully putting down the knife and wiping her hands on her apron. "I'm Rachel Larraby. I'll be catering your wedding."

Chapter Three

He took her hand in his and shook it gravely. "Jack Flynt. It's a pleasure to meet you. It's not my wedding, actually. My sister is the one getting married. She's out of the country, most conveniently, so I've had to come about the arrangements."

Jack didn't know what it was about this woman that intrigued him so much. But he knew himself well enough and he'd enjoyed women long enough that he never ignored the pull of attraction when he felt it. There was something about this woman with her lethal aim, and the wild hair that she'd tried to tuck out of the way under a cap, but which still curled provocatively. He wanted to pull out every one of those hairpins and run his hands through the richness.

Her eyes were brown with flecks of green and gold, her skin pale and smooth, and her mouth full-lipped and luscious. It was a mouth designed for savoring food, or kisses.

The knife-wielding cook was voluptuous, all right, as were the scents emanating from this kitchen. He liked her efficient movements and the way she was trying so unsuccessfully to hide her irritation at his entrance into her kitchen.

Even under the apron he could see her curvy body. It

made him think of plenty. He'd known so many women on slimming diets that the words "Atkins," "South Beach," and "macrobiotic" made him want to track down the purveyors of diets and force-feed them butter, cream, and foie gras. Or better still, choke them on their brown rice cakes and meals in tins.

Rachel Larraby was obviously a woman who understood the intimate connection between food and pleasure. "Are you working on a catering job now?"

"No. The honest truth is that I am trying to get to know this kitchen. I'm starting small. Tonight I'm cooking dinner for Max and George and a couple of their friends."

"I hope you'll be joining us for dinner," he said with the smoothness of a born salesman. He enjoyed the sudden widening of her eyes and the flash of awareness that told him he wasn't the only one feeling the attraction.

"I thought it was just George, Maxine, and one other couple."

"But that would leave an uneven table," he reminded her. "It's much more interesting to have everybody paired up, don't you think?"

She was looking at him as though she wasn't entirely sure whether there was hidden meaning behind his words. Leaving her to ponder, he said a cheerful good-bye and strolled out to find his old school friend George and see about mooching an invitation to dinner.

He'd been irritated as hell with his spoiled little sister and her endless demands, but suddenly he was grateful to Chloe for introducing him to Rachel Larraby. As he emerged into sunshine, he passed an overfed, imperious-looking cat. He knelt to scratch its ears. The tabby rubbed itself against his legs and then headed for the kitchen door with its striped orange tail held high. "I wouldn't cross that threshold if I were you, old chap."

The cat didn't seem to have any better idea of self-preservation than he had himself, so he watched the open doorway in some anticipation and was rewarded by the same shouted voice. "Oh, no, you don't!" The potato that he had come to recognize came sailing out of the doorway, closely followed by the cat.

They strolled a little way together, he and the cat. Jack wasn't much for the country, but it was difficult even for a Londoner like him not to appreciate the view. Gently rolling hills, green fields dotted with contented-looking sheep, a few cottages and outbuildings. The slow amble of a river curling around a stand of fine old trees, and in the center of all, the ancestral home. Hart House.

Where his lordship might be at this time of day, Jack had no idea, but he was fairly certain that if he kept walking, somebody somewhere could direct him.

In fact, it took him almost no time at all to locate George. He and Maxine were standing on the Palladian bridge that arched gracefully over the river. They were close enough to touch, and Jack was about to think better of intruding on such an intimate scene when he noticed that Maxine was holding a clipboard and gesturing with her cell phone.

Not love, then, but business which, since he was here on business himself, he felt entitled to interrupt.

After the usual insults, without which no Englishman could greet a friend, he said, "I've just been chatting up the wedding caterer."

Maxine looked alarmed. "Oh, I wish I'd known you wanted to meet her. I'd have—"

"Warned her to be civil?"

Maxine's pretty mouth turned down. "I'm really sorry. She hates being disturbed when she's working. Was she awful?"

He thought about it. He'd been shouted at, pelted with a

root vegetable, and threatened with a chef's knife, all in under five minutes. "She was charming," he said, thinking of the gorgeous smells in that kitchen, the curvy body under that apron, and the surprising pull of lust he'd encountered in a most unexpected place.

"Oh, good," Maxine said, looking relieved. "Customer relations really aren't her strong point but she's a genius with food."

Bless Maxine. He could have kissed her for giving him the opening he'd hoped for.

"I'd absolutely love to try her cooking sometime. It smelled completely amazing in there."

Right, so he wasn't going for subtle here. George, who'd known him for as long as almost anybody, raised one eyebrow and looked at him with suspicion. But Maxine jumped in with all that enthusiasm he loved about Americans.

"Why don't you stay for dinner? Rachel's cooking a special meal for us tonight."

"Oh, well." He tried to appear surprised at the invitation. "I wouldn't want to push myself in where I wasn't wanted."

"Nothing you'd like more," George said.

Maxine chose to ignore the interruption. "Of course you should stay. You'll be able to sample Rachel's cooking and you can carry back an excellent report to the bride and groom. I wish they could have come down themselves."

"I know. Believe me, so do I. If it weren't my sister getting married, I wouldn't be poncing about acting like a wedding planner." He grimaced.

"Oh, come on. All she asked you to do was drive down here and make sure the setting is right for the tent."

"Which you could have done by e-mail."

"And we did, but she's a bride. She's entitled to be finicky on her big day."

Maxine didn't know Chloe. She had no clue that the tent placement was only the beginning. However, in the interest of a harmonious dinner he decided to spare her a better knowledge of his spoiled rotten sister. She'd find out for herself soon enough. If the wedding wasn't going to cost a bloody fortune and he didn't know that Hart House could use the money, he'd feel guilty. "Absolutely. One ought to have a final send-off before being doomed to nappies and nannies and boring your friends senseless hearing about your package holidays to Spain."

Max snorted. "Another marriage hater. You should get together with Rachel."

"I'd like that very much."

Maxine seemed rather startled by his statement and looked at him doubtfully. "I'm sure you're joking, but that's a really bad idea."

"Why? Is there something I should know about your sister?" He raised his hands in a questioning gesture. "She's got a big burly boyfriend back in America, perhaps?" Maxine shook her head, and behind her, George merely rolled his eyes. He thought harder. Recalled the violent tendencies. "She hates men?"

"Well, sort of." Max had her brow furrowed and looked both helpless and concerned in true sisterly fashion.

An awful thought occurred to him. "She's not a lesbian, is she?" Oh, please let her not be a lesbian. He thought of all that glorious hair on the sexy woman he'd glimpsed beneath the apron and the attitude. There was nothing he hated more than finding an attractive, interesting woman was out of bounds, not because she preferred another bloke, but because she preferred another gender.

"You should probably stay away from my sister."

And with that Maxine walked past him in the direction of the kitchen.

He climbed onto the ancient bridge and stood beside George, staring moodily at the slow-moving river beneath them. "Bad luck, that, her turning out to be a lesbian."

His old friend glanced sideways. "You really are a daft prick."

"What do you mean?" Renewed interest sparked. "She's available after all?"

"Maybe you should do us all a favor and forget about Rachel. Maxine's right. She's one woman you should stay away from."

George had known him too long to think he'd stay away from a woman because he was warned off without any reason. But he'd also known George long enough to realize there was no more to be got out of him on the subject.

Odd. Very odd. Oh, well, the mysterious hints only made him more curious to get to know Rachel better. "I'm looking forward to tasting Rachel's cooking. I understand from Maxine that she's a first-rate chef."

"Yes. She was head chef at a top L.A. restaurant, but it closed. Good reviews couldn't save it. Our luck, though. And your sister's, having a woman like that catering her wedding."

"I'd better run over to the pub and see about getting a bottle for tonight."

George waved him off. "We'll pull something out of the cellar." Since the Hart House cellars were legendary, Jack didn't argue. "And if we're dipping into the cellars, you'd better not drive back to London. Stay the night."

Jack glanced at the huge manor looming behind them. "If you're sure there's room."

"I'm sure we can find you a suitable garret somewhere. I'll lend you some pajamas and a toothbrush."

"Don't bother. I keep a packed overnighter in the boot of the car. Saves time if I've got to run over to the continent."

"Blimey, I wouldn't mind your life."

Jack blinked and gestured to the view. "You didn't do too badly." But he knew he wouldn't trade with George. He liked his London address, his frequent visits abroad, his uncomplicated lifestyle.

This time when Rachel heard movement in the doorway, she didn't launch a grenade. Instead she turned with a scowl, but she was also ready with a spray bottle of water in case it was the damn cat again.

"Oh, it's you," she said when her sister walked in, looking more like a model presenting Madison Avenue's idea of the country than someone who actually lived among grass and sheep and five-hundred-year-old barns.

"You weren't rude to the brother of an important customer, were you?"

For some reason she'd expected better of her recent unwanted guest, but he was a man, of course he'd disappoint. "Is that what he said?"

"No, he said you were charming, which naturally made me suspicious."

Rachel grinned in spite of herself. One point for Jack Flynt. "I wasn't exactly charming, but he certainly was."

"I know. He's famous for it." Maxine grabbed a potato and found a second peeler. Rachel moved over, so they worked side by side at the sink.

At first it was peaceful and companionable, but, like all big sisters, Maxine couldn't help dishing out a load of unwanted advice. Rachel could tell from the way Max glanced at her under her lashes that "what you should/shouldn't do" was on its way.

"Jack asked me a lot of questions about you. He seemed . . . interested."

Rachel was mildly flattered, though not surprised. There'd been that weird thing between them and she knew he'd felt it, too. "What did you tell him?"

"To stay away from you."

"Spoken like a protective big sister."

"The thing is . . . " For a few moments there was no sound but the scrape of peelers against vegetables. "His nickname is Union Jack. You know why?"

"Please tell me it's got nothing to do with flagpoles."

Max giggled. "Well, he must have something remarkable. He goes out with loads of women, gorgeous, amazing women. Most of whom go on to marry other men. He's always in wedding parties, but he never gets married himself. That's why they call him Union Jack."

Rachel went back to her potato. "So he doesn't believe in marriage?"

"George doesn't think he'll ever tie the knot. You know how men are with that *'last bachelor standing'* crap."

Rachel wasn't interested in discussing the commitment-phobic ways of all men. Only of one. "So all he wants from these women is sex?"

"I don't know that for a fact, but as you so astutely pointed out, he is a man."

Rachel had pushed her attraction to Jack aside as nothing but one more irritation in a life that seemed full of them recently. But maybe, just maybe, he wasn't one more trial sent to test her, but the answer to her dilemma. A hot English guy who wanted nothing but sex?

She was an undersexed, unemployed, depressed woman in need of a change, a spark. Some excitement. In an instant she saw that what she most craved was a crazy, self-indulgent fling. A love-'em-and-leave-'em holiday affair that would end when she boarded her plane home.

How much more perfect could Jack Flynt be?

"He's staying for dinner tonight," Maxine said.

"Yes, I know."

"So, you're okay with it?"

Rachel tried to conceal the fact that she was feeling more

excitement at this moment than she'd felt since the early days with Cal. Back when she'd still believed in happily ever after. Now she believed she was owed a little fun after all the years of Cal and the restaurant. Fun should be like back pay coming to her, with interest. She had a sneaking suspicion Jack Flynt was exactly the man for the job.

"Yes," she said, thinking about that rangy, athletic body, the come-to-bed eyes, the sizzle on her skin when he gazed at her. "I'm okay with it."

"Really?"

She sent her sister a look. "Union Jack will balance the numbers. I hate it when the boy-girl quotient is uneven."

Max gave her a one-armed hug. "I'm glad to see you. I missed you."

"Me, too. And you know what else I've missed?"

"My excellent, sisterly, levelheaded advice?"

"That, and raiding your wardrobe." Rachel glanced down at herself. "I've put on weight, but I think I can still squeeze into your clothes." She nudged up against her sister. "Or die trying."

Chapter Four

Rachel didn't normally dress for dinner. Usually she wore something lovely in white, decorated with food stains, and—adorning her hair net—a chef's hat. She'd cooked a lot of fine meals in the last few years, but it had been rare for her to dress up and join the party.

Maxine was right. She needed to get off her ass and get back to living. And having an irresistible commitment-phobe checking her out was exactly the push she needed.

Jack was staying for dinner, which she strongly suspected meant he was staying the night.

Rachel subscribed to the theory that if music was the food of love, then food was the fuel of sex. She should have realized, when she discovered she wasn't musical, that love wasn't for her. In her world, Red Hot Chili Peppers added bite to a fresh salsa and Black Eyed Peas were excellent done with tarragon and butter. Food was her gift, her talent, her favorite method of seduction.

So she wasn't in her restaurant with the professional sous chefs and servers; she'd prepared a simple but perfect meal and the ancient Homestead de George did have servants. She had everything ready, instructions for Mrs. Brimacombe, the regular cook, and a couple of hours to get herself ready.

What a blessing to sit down to her own meal and not in her chef's garb. Even better, raiding Maxine's closet was like a trip to Saks or Barneys, without any need of a credit card.

"Can I really choose anything?" This was said for form's sake, while she and her sister stood in front of a loaded wardrobe. She and Max had shared clothes forever.

"Since when did you have to ask?"

"Since you started dressing so much better than I do. The chances that you'll be borrowing anything of mine are remote."

Max's country attire today consisted of a pair of Rock & Republic jeans that hugged a body in much better shape than Rachel's, a Stella McCartney shirt in turquoise worn with chunky beads, and, adorning her feet, a pair of black Marc Jacobs flats. Her makeup hadn't smudged, her hair didn't frizz. Rachel knew she must be a very good person to be able to love her sister.

"Looks like I've gone up a size and you've gone down one." She looked at the gorgeous array of booty and pouted. "Probably nothing in here will fit anyway."

"Nonsense. Neither of us have changed that much. You haven't gained weight, you stopped working out. Besides, you've always had the curves in the family."

Rachel turned to look at herself in Maxine's full-length mirror and pulled her T-shirt tight against her belly. "I've been having a three-way affair with Ben, Jerry, and that cute European, Häagen-Dazs." She sighed and dove into the glorious bounty.

"You're already feeling better, aren't you? Admit it. Coming to England was a great idea."

She pulled out a black Dolce & Gabbana dress with tiny, expensive-looking white polka dots. "It was a great idea."

She put the dress back and withdrew a suede skirt softer than melting butter. The label was in Italian. "TV sure pays better than chefing."

Max watched her for a few minutes from the bed, then rose and gently nudged her aside. The wardrobes here hadn't been built with Max's clothing in mind and there certainly wasn't room for two to stand abreast.

Max pushed a few things aside and reached for a loose wine-colored velvet jacket with gold stitching. It had a sexy elegance to it that was still relaxed. "There's a skirt that goes with it, all loose and ethnic, and I wear it with these boots."

"It's so . . ." Rachel was almost speechless. "It's so romantic and sexy."

"I know. The color will look great with your skin tone and hair, don't you think?"

"My hair is a disaster."

"No, it's not. It's long and needs a trim and styling. But we can make you gorgeous until we get to the salon. I always liked your hair long."

"I cut it for work."

"Now you can let it grow if you want." She shoved the clothes at Rachel. "Try everything on. Oh, here's the blouse."

It was something out of *Lady Chatterley's Lover*, that blouse. All falling lace and soft linen. Victorian boho.

She yanked off her jeans and shirt and pulled on the clothes in a rush.

Max shook her head.

"What?"

"Watching you throw yourself into an outfit actually hurts me. It's how you would feel if you witnessed a diner bolt your carefully prepared food like it was a Big Mac."

Rachel grinned at her. "You were always the clothes-horse. Not me. Anyhow, I'm in a hurry to see it all on."

They looked together as she preened in front of the mirror. Maybe the button was a little snug on the skirt, but otherwise the outfit could have been made for her. The rich wine color made her eyes glow and brought out the highlights in her hair. Her skin didn't look so pasty now. It looked like old-fashioned porcelain. The style suited her, too. Loose and relaxed, but sexy. She turned in the mirror, letting the skirt sway. "I love it."

"You look fabulous. Now, I insist that you spend some quality time in your bathroom with creams, cosmetics, and bath products." Her sister's forehead creased in sudden concern. "You do have decent makeup, don't you?"

"Yes."

"Are you sure?"

She rolled her eyes. "You got some expert to do me over for that photo shoot in *Gourmet*, remember? And then you bought me all the products for my birthday."

"Right." Max's eyes twinkled. "I'm a good sister, huh?"

"When you don't make me want to kill you? You're the best."

"As soon as you're ready, come back and I'll do your hair for your big dinner date tonight."

She bent to pull off the boots. "Why are you doing this? You just warned me about Jack and now you're wrapping me up like a Christmas gift."

Max inspected her nails. Then glanced up. "Truth?"

"No. I want you to lie to me like you usually do."

Her sister took a breath. "The truth is you've seemed happier since he wandered into your kitchen than you have since you got here. I've told you what he's like. You're a big girl and can make your own decisions."

Sometimes Rachel forgot how perceptive her sister was. She walked over and perched beside her on the bed. "I won't break my heart over him."

"Of course not."

She traced a unicorn in the blue tapestry bedspread. "But I might be interested in some uncomplicated vacation sex."

Max stared at her for a moment, then nodded slowly.

"Like I said, England has a fine tradition of turning out studs."

"So you're not going to give me a hard time about this?"

"As your big sister, I reserve that right into perpetuity."

Rachel felt suddenly and unaccountably misty. "I have missed you so much," she said, throwing her arms around Maxine.

"Me, too." They hugged tightly. "Everything's going to work out. You'll see."

"I'm unemployed, broke, divorced, and wearing a borrowed dress to dinner in a castle."

"Things worked out okay for Cinderella," her upbeat sister reminded her.

A knock on the door had them pulling apart. "Come in," Maxine said, and George appeared. "Ah, sorry, didn't know you had company," he said, and prepared to depart.

"No. Don't leave," Rachel said. "I was on my way out."

"I hope you don't mind having one more guest for dinner."

"Not at all. I only hope my cooking's okay. I'm not used to the oven."

"I'm sure it will all be lovely. And if it isn't, we'll blame poor old Mrs. Brimacombe," he promised her.

"Jack seemed very eager to, um, sample Rachel's wares," Maxine said.

"Yes." George glanced at her. "He's quite taken with you."

"We know, George," Maxine said. "Did you tell him to stay tonight?"

"Yes, of course." He walked over and put a hand on Maxine's shoulder. They were always touching each other, Rachel noticed. A brush of the fingers here, a pat there. She doubted they were even aware of it. They weren't a couple she'd have imagined would work. They were so different, and yet looking at them together, she knew the mysterious couple thing she'd never been able to get right worked for them.

"Do you know," George said, "he keeps a packed case in his Jag? He often has to fly to the continent with only a couple of hours' notice."

"What does he do exactly?"

"He's a financier. Always doing complicated things with money. I think he's involved with hotels at the moment. Or is it vineyards?" George shook his head. "Both, I expect."

Jack was rather looking forward to dinner as he crunched across the gravel parking area to fetch his case. In it was a change of clothes, toothbrush, toiletries, even a modest supply of condoms. Jack didn't believe in missing opportunities, in business or in pleasure.

The housekeeper showed him to his room. It was done in greens, and the earl's coat of arms was emblazoned on the mantel of the stone fireplace which had, fortunately, been modernized so he could flick on a gas fire if he wanted heat or atmosphere.

The bed looked as ancient as the mantel, but he was pleased to find a new and firm mattress beneath the heavy, carved oak headboard.

He made a couple of calls and text-messaged Chloe to let her know that the tent was going to be brilliant, and that the chef catering her wedding had been brought over from America specially from a five-star restaurant. That ought to appeal to her. She was spoiled rotten, his little sister, and everyone knew it, including Chloe.

Duty done, he showered in the en suite bath and dressed.

They were meeting for drinks in the drawing room, and there he wandered after first checking his watch to make certain the public visiting hours were over. He'd once been trapped by a schoolteacher from East Grinstead who'd mistaken him for the earl and harangued him for twenty minutes about organic farming practices.

No lurking teachers or, in fact, anyone appeared to impede his progress and he found himself in good time for before-dinner cocktails.

George and Max were the only ones in the room.

"You're looking gorgeous, Maxine," he said, stepping forward to give her a light kiss. She did, too, in a sleek black dress and heels.

"Thank you. Rachel's checking on dinner. She doesn't trust Mrs. Brimacombe," Maxine told him and then glared at George. "Which is all your fault."

"All I did was tell her that Mrs. B.'s style of cooking is to boil everything to buggery."

"Quite right," Jack said. "The foundation of British cuisine, in fact."

"I thought that was fish and chips."

"No, darling. You're thinking of sausages and mash."

Maxine said, "I'm still waiting to try toad in the hole."

"And wait till you've tried Mrs. B.'s bubble and squeak," George said. "Which, believe me, you will. And that's not as bad as—Ah, here she is now." They all turned to the doorway.

Jack had expected that Rachel would clean up quite nicely, but he'd had no idea how well. He was fairly gobsmacked. The surly chef was stunning, with voluptuous curves in all the right places, sparkling eyes, and a mouth made for temptation. Her hair was pinned up, but a few wild curls played around her face and neck. He itched to get his hands into that thick, lustrous hair.

Whatever mysterious thing she'd done with makeup brought out her eyes and accentuated those full and extremely kissable lips.

"You look beautiful," he said.

She seemed to grow even prettier with the compliment, and glanced, half laughing, at her sister.

A tiny pause was filled by George, ever the consummate host, who said, "Dry sherry as usual, Rachel?"

"Sure, thanks."

"Everything all right with dinner?" Max enquired.

"Your helper didn't throw everything in a pot and put it on to boil?" George added.

"No. There was a little muttering, but no mutiny."

Voices could be heard in the hall, and then Arthur Denby entered, followed by an elegant, fine-boned woman. They'd never met, but Jack knew from George that she was a relatively famous American writer of terrifying thrillers. He didn't know what he'd expected—wild eyes and witchlike hair, he supposed, and that she'd be dressed all in black. But this woman, wearing a cashmere sweater and slim camel-colored trousers, could have been a solicitor or a banker. She had that calm, capable, and intelligent look about her.

He was introduced to Meg Stanton, shook hands with her and Arthur, whom he hadn't seen in months, and then chose a seat beside Rachel.

What would this odd lot find to talk about, he wondered.

It turned out that Rachel was a fan of Meg's, and Meg had twice eaten in Rachel's restaurant when she'd visited Los Angeles.

"Your cooking is amazing."

"Not as amazing as your books. I couldn't go into the meat freezer for weeks after I read *Gristle and Bone*. Honest."

Meg chuckled, obviously delighted to have scared somebody that badly who'd paid good money for her book. And people thought his business was cutthroat.

"When's your next book out?" Max wanted to know.

"A couple of weeks." Meg glanced at Arthur and a look passed between them that had Jack betting on yet another wedding before he'd had time to get his tux back from the dry cleaner's. "I'm leaving for a book tour next week. Arthur's coming with me."

Rachel sat forward in her chair, so thrilled to be talking to a favorite author that she was unaware of his scrutiny. He knew it was rude to stare, but he couldn't help himself. With the animation in her expression, the hair, the makeup, the clothes, she was gorgeous. Absolutely gorgeous, in a real way.

He needn't have worried they'd all have nothing in common. They were talking and laughing as though the six of them had known each other forever.

Wiggins, whom Jack always thought had learned his butlering from watching too many Noel Coward plays in summer rep at Brighton and Newcastle upon Tyne, stepped into the room.

"Dinner is served, your lordship."

There was a half glance, almost of apology, at Maxine. Jack wondered how soon it would be before Wiggins was announcing, "Dinner is served, your ladyship." From the way George and Maxine acted around each other, Jack—who considered himself an expert, having been involved in so very many weddings in the last few years—suspected Wiggins wouldn't have long to wait.

Another wedding.

Soon, he'd be the last of the old guard. Well, except for Haverstock, who'd last been heard of in a submarine off Antarctica. Unless he hooked up with a polar bear or a penguin, Jack felt safe. Though Haverstock was just mad enough that he might yet surprise them.

They adjourned to the small dining room, and Jack was seated beside the writer and across from Rachel. If she was nervous about her food, she didn't show it. He was curious to see if a woman who included among her talents neutering men with fresh produce from five yards could also cook.

He wasn't going to be critical. He'd eat and find something to admire even if the entree tasted like dung cakes.

It didn't.

The first course told him that Rachel could indeed cook.

Carrot soup you could get anywhere, but then he tasted it. She'd flavored it in a way that made his tongue weep with joy. She mentioned the herbs in the kitchen garden and he wondered how she'd turned those weedy-looking clumps into magic.

"Oh, mmm. This is fantastic," Meg moaned. "I remember reading that in your restaurant you only used organic ingredients and they had to be grown or produced within a certain radius."

"That's right. Fifty miles was my limit. I believe everything tastes better when it's fresh and local." Rachel gestured to the plates. "Everything on tonight's menu is made from local produce. It was fun trying different things."

Max looked at George. "This is a great marketing hook, too, you know. If we always try and serve local, it supports our farmers and growers."

"Probably more expensive, though." Jack felt somebody should mention it.

"Can you put a price on better flavor? Vitamin retention? Local goodwill?" Rachel asked.

In fact, it was his job to do just that, but when he put her food in his mouth he felt churlish arguing with her. The woman was a bloody genius.

The lamb was done with a sauce he didn't recognize, but which she informed them had quince in it. He wanted to lick the plate when he was done. Dessert was a tarte tatin made, she hastened to assure him, with apples that grew right here on the property, and even the soft cheese was local, served with pears and a Sauterne from the cellars that, like all the wine George had chosen, was not local. Some of the bottles were older than those drinking them.

Conversation and laughter flowed until the candles were low, coffee was drunk, and one of the most pleasant evenings Jack had spent in a long while wound down.

It wasn't only the food and the conversation that had made the evening exceptional. There was an energy flowing between him and the sexy chef across from him that kept things interesting. He'd catch her eye and see speculation. When he spoke, she listened intently. He found himself doing the same, though, in truth, he learned everything about her he needed to from her food.

Bold, sensuous, creative. He wanted very much to know her better.

Tonight, if her teasing and increasingly bold glances were any indication, he would.

Chapter Five

Meg and Arthur left soon after coffee, promising to stay in touch from the States. Rachel could see that George and Maxine were dying to go up to bed, too. Probably they were being polite and waiting for her and Jack to go up, but she wasn't quite ready to say good night to the man with whom she'd been secretly—or maybe not so secretly—flirting all evening.

Finally she said, "I think I'll check on the kitchen. Make sure Mrs. Brimacombe left everything in good order."

"I'm sure she will have," said George.

"I like to make a final check of my kitchen. Occupational hazard," she said. As she rose she said, as though it was an afterthought, "Jack, would you like to come with me? I can show you that local cheese you were so interested in." Okay, it wasn't the smoothest line she'd ever thought up, but it worked.

He was on his feet before she finished speaking. "I'd love to. I'll say good night, then, George, Maxine. Thanks for a great evening."

"Pleasure. See you tomorrow."

"Probably not. I'll head out early to miss the traffic."

"Right. Give us a ring, then, if there's anything more on the wedding."

"Will do."

Max said good night, but her attention was on Rachel, who sent her sister a tiny wink and hoped she'd mind her own business. Amazingly, for once she did, and suddenly Rachel found herself outside with Jack. Alone. The quickest way to the kitchen was obviously through the house, but they both knew it wasn't local cheese they were interested in.

The evening was cool, fall slowly fading.

The full moon looked like an ancient gold coin; the sky was haphazardly dotted with stars where the clouds hadn't obscured them. The air carried the scent of the river, trees, and grass. Their footsteps crunched on the pea gravel.

She tipped her head back and breathed in. "I love it here," she admitted.

"It's so quiet after London."

"And L.A.," she agreed.

"Do you miss it?"

"L.A. or the restaurant?"

"Both, I suppose." From the conversation this evening, he'd learned the sad history of her not-so-brilliant career.

She thought about his question. Tried to answer honestly. "Yes. And no. I miss the work. I loved what I was doing, but I didn't like the people running the place. So I guess my feelings were mixed. I miss some things about L.A. Being near the ocean is great. I don't know, there's an energy there that's kind of nuts but invigorating, you know?"

"Sure."

"I really needed to get away, though. I was in a bad place." She caught herself and laughed. "And if that isn't a California expression, I don't know what is."

She could see his lips curve in the moonlight. She was aware of him in every pore of her body. Felt him looking at her when her gaze slipped away, tingled when his arm brushed hers. "What does it mean exactly?"

"Me being in a bad place?" She sighed. "You really want to know?"

"Of course. I'm . . . curious about you."

The notion warmed her blood. Nobody was curious about her these days but her mother and Max. And really, the term she'd use for them would be nosy. Interfering. Bossy! Curious was a balm to a bludgeoned ego.

"My restaurant closing kind of kicked the teeth down my throat. I guess I'd forgotten it wasn't really mine. I worked so hard, it was like I was obsessed, and when things got bad I worked harder. I'm so tired."

"There was more to it than that, though, wasn't there." His words were soft, encouraging her to blurt more than she'd intended.

"Are you really this perceptive or has my beloved sister been spilling my secrets?"

"Your sister warned me away from you. It's the only clue she gave me that there's some mystery. I got my biggest clue from the way you acted with me in the kitchen. You seemed violently antimarriage, which naturally made me curious as to why."

"I'm sorry about that, by the way. If you hadn't startled me, and I hadn't thought you were the cat—"

"No, really. Perfectly understandable mistake," he said in that smooth, well-bred way that for some reason made her want to laugh.

"I got divorced," she finally admitted. "It came through a couple of months ago."

"I'm sorry."

"Don't be. He was a rat. It's only that having two such spectacular failures so close together kind of screwed me up. You know?"

"Of course. So now, due to disappointments both personal and professional, you've pledged yourself to a life of celibacy, from which all men are excluded and you will only use your considerable cooking talents as a chef for private parties."

She laughed, delighted with him.

"No," she said, turning to him. "I'm not giving up on the idea of another restaurant, and I am certainly not giving up on sex." What the hell? If there was ever a moment to take the initiative, it was this one. What did she care what he thought of her? This wasn't about courtship or love or any of those old-fashioned notions she'd once believed in. This was about admitting that the blood flowing through her veins was hot, and that she was still a young woman with needs.

The man beside her, drawing her in with the intimate message in his eyes, was reminding her urgently of how much she was a woman with needs.

"I have not taken a vow of celibacy," she promised him.

"Really?" He sounded as interested as she could have hoped. He moved closer until they were almost touching.

"Really," she said, and taking his face in her hands, she leaned up on her tiptoes to kiss him.

She brushed his lips softly with her own. She meant it to be a not-so-subtle message saying, *I'm available if you're interested.* But the second their mouths met, something happened. Shocks, sparks, shooting stars. All that stuff she no longer believed in showered around her, in her.

He made a surprised sound and pulled her forward, hard enough that she was snapped against him, body to body. He took over the kiss.

Whoo-wee, did he ever. She felt almost lifted off her feet by the impact. His mouth was warm, firm, sexy, and delicious.

Standing there in the golden glow of a harvest moon, in the shadow of a castle, wearing her borrowed finery of velvet and gold and lace, she felt as much a fairy tale princess as any woman ever had.

Why not be swept off her feet? For a few days or weeks, even a few hours? What was the harm? What could it hurt?

So she let herself go, melting against him, the way the beetroot aioli had melted over her medley of autumn vegetables. Opening her mouth to him, to taste his flavor and texture.

Her heart stuttered, her blood pounded. She'd forgotten she could feel so alive.

"I want you," he mumbled against her skin. "God, I want you."

"I know. I want you, too," she admitted, wondering if she'd ever in her life felt this urgent, this desperate. His hands ran up and down her back, over her hips. His mouth plundered and feasted.

She clutched his shoulders, then ran her hands through his short hair. His scalp was hot and she knew he was as feverish for this as she was. When his hand cupped her breast, she leaned into his warmth and touch. Wanting more.

"Where's your room?" he asked in a hoarse whisper.

"Too close to my sister's. Yours?"

"In the guest wing. We'll go there."

"Yes. Okay, yes."

"Where are you taking me?" he asked as they continued walking in the opposite direction of the massive front door. "The servants' entrance?"

"The kitchen."

"Right, of course."

She'd told Maxine and George she was checking out the kitchen, and though she suspected they knew it was a ruse, she tried to be a woman who told the truth. Besides, the kitchen drew her, she realized as she walked into the restored order of a clean kitchen between meals.

If the body had a core, as her Pilates instructor insisted, then so, she reasoned, did a house. Or even a castle. To her, that core was the kitchen. Somehow, walking into the order and efficiency of this place, where she created both art and nourishment, fed her in some indefinable emotional way.

She liked that she'd met Jack in the kitchen. She liked that he was here with her as she walked around, making sure the sink sparkled, putting the basket of eggs in the refrigerator. She and Mrs. Brimacombe were going to come to blows, she suspected, over eggs.

Jack watched her, this elegant, voluptuous woman at her homely tasks. She'd changed subtly when she entered the kitchen. She moved with a sense of purpose and control. Pride, he realized, when she ran a hand across the counter, as though patting it good night.

Arousal was a funny thing, he'd found. The older he got, the more he'd learned to appreciate the finer aspects. More than the blood-pounding urge to take and conquer, he'd discovered the slower, softer pleasures of desire. The subtle shifts in feeling, the myriad ways one woman is so wonderfully different from another. So he could watch Rachel with the fever of impatience to have her, and at the same time hang onto his ability to appreciate all the tiny things about her that added to her appeal.

She was a mystery, this woman he'd known only a few hours. Such a mystery. On the one hand he wanted to treasure the moments she remained a mystery, and yet he was as anxious to discover all her secrets as a boy on Christmas morning, holding that special package from Father Christmas.

The urge to rush forward now, quickly, pulled against the desire to go slowly, take his time, savor, so there was a fine tension inside him.

When she was done with her checking and rearranging, she flipped off the lights, plunging them into darkness.

Wordlessly, they slipped through the door that led from the kitchen into the main house.

It was quiet. The soft night lights that George had installed illuminated the way for visitors who might otherwise end up lost and wandering the old pile until daybreak.

They crept by the marble bust of a Roman emperor, watched on their way by five-hundred-year-old ancestors of George's looking down on them in various aspects from virtuous nobility to licentiousness. He imagined the naughty ninth earl giving him a nudge-nudge-wink-wink as he made his way, with Rachel's hand in his, through the long gallery to the guest wing.

Even the tireless Wiggins seemed to have taken himself off to bed, or perhaps was enough of the discreet, trusted servant to make himself scarce when a man took a lady who was not his wife to bed.

They didn't speak on the way; he felt the warmth of Rachel's hand in his, heard the slight swish of velvet as she walked.

They entered his room and he noted that the bedside lamp was on, the bed turned down. As in a good hotel, but also, he knew, the way things had been done in Hart House for generations.

Maybe they'd had to downsize the staff, but little courtesies to guests would be one of the last things to go.

Rachel let go of his hand and gazed around, as though surprised to find herself here.

He slipped off his jacket, hung it over the back of one of the wing chairs, and switched on the fire.

She'd walked to the window. Then, obviously realizing she couldn't distract herself with the view outside, turned.

"Would you like a drink?" he asked her. "No ice, I'm afraid. But there's"—he looked at the bottles arranged on a silver tray—"port, cognac, scotch."

"No. Thank you."

He walked over to her and did what he'd been dying to do all evening. He pulled the pins from her hair. She trembled when he touched her, but didn't stop him, so he took his time and watched in delighted fascination as the thick curls tumbled around her shoulders. He'd imagined the hair would go on forever, all the way down her back, but no. It brushed her shoulders, thick and wild.

Pushing his hands into it, he found it silkier than he'd imagined, but exactly as sexy.

He gazed down at her, eyeing the mouth he was about to kiss, his body so on fire he could barely think straight, when she said, "I think I would like a drink."

He noted what he should have seen before. Her eyes were wide with uncertainty, her posture tense.

"Of course," he said, releasing her. "Cognac?"

"Yes, fine."

He poured two glasses, handed her one. She didn't sip for pleasure; he rather thought she gulped for courage.

He sat in the armchair, leaning back, letting her know in as subtle a way as he could manage that a chat and a drink was fine with him. It wouldn't be his choice, but he tried to be philosophical. At least he'd seen her with her hair down. It was a start.

She didn't sit, but wandered the room, touching things. Running her fingers over the bedcover.

When she finally came back to him, she put her drink down on the table. He felt he was losing her, felt he had to make a final try to keep her with him, even for nothing more than talk.

"You have lovely hands," he said, watching them curled around her glass.

She laughed. "No, I don't." She stuffed them out of sight, at her sides.

He reached for her wrist and she let him bring it closer. "I noticed at dinner. You were the only woman not wearing nail lacquer."

"That's because I don't like to draw attention to my least attractive feature."

"But they're lovely." He smoothed the fingers onto his palm and she let him. "These are the hands of an artist."

"You're nuts. They're burned, scarred, banged up by years in kitchens."

He stroked her fingers. "A warrior's hands, then."

"More so than an artist's."

"Well, I think you are a little of both."

He brought her wrist up to his mouth and kissed it, loving the smooth, soft feel of her skin, the skip of her pulse beneath his lips.

He noticed a white scar with a line of Xs emerging from the base of her thumb. He traced it with his fingertip and felt a quiver run through her. "What happened there?"

"I was in a hurry. Tried to core an apple with a carving knife and the apple broke. I don't recommend it. I think I had seven stitches."

"So noted," he said, and kissed the line of Xs.

"Is this one a burn?" He traced the discolored, puckered shininess on the side of her hand.

"Yes," she said, her voice growing husky. "Industrial oven accident."

He touched his tongue to the mark.

Chapter Six

*H*e's *making love to my hands,* Rachel thought in amazement, *my ugly, scarred, chef's hands.*

Jack was bent over her, studying her like a very sexy palm reader. His hair was short, but thick. She glimpsed the back of his neck, the pale skin corded with muscle. She felt the warmth coming off his body, smelled the clean, somehow English scent of him.

"These are your war wounds. Honorably acquired and therefore beautiful." He kissed the misshapen nail on her left hand and she told him without being asked about the time she'd slammed it in the restaurant fridge. She watched him bending over her hands, so intent on her. So interested. Amazement washed over her along with a wash of lust that left her weak-kneed.

Sex in her marriage had been about getting to the main event as fast as possible, reaching orgasm and going to sleep. She thought she and Cal must have had the most time-efficient marriage bed in the state of California. She'd got to the point where she could slide a batch of cookies or muffins in the oven and go have sex. They'd both have their climax, Cal would be snoring, and she'd be back in the kitchen with minutes left before the oven timer chimed.

Cal hadn't been much for experimentation in bed—he'd

found what worked and stuck with it. Unfortunately, he hadn't felt the same about marriage in general.

Now, here she was, with a man who considered her scarred hands worthy of kissing. His tongue touched her fingertips and heat traveled through her body. When his lips brushed her palm, warm and slightly damp, she wanted to whimper. She started to tremble, deep inside. She'd been on the verge of leaving, thinking she was crazy to throw herself into bed with this man she'd only met a few hours ago.

But he'd seduced her by making love to that part of her that was the most accomplished and the least attractive. And somehow, she knew that a man who took this much time over a woman's palm was not going to beat a batch of cookies to the finish.

"If this was a movie," she said, "some schmaltzy music would play right now and I'd say, 'Come with me to bed.'"

"Have you been with anyone since your husband?" he asked her softly.

Her hand jerked within his grasp. "That's pretty personal."

"So is what we're about to do."

She blew out a breath. He let go of her hands but not of her, tracing the curve of her waist until his palms rested lightly on her hips. She liked the warm feeling of connection between them while he looked up with those wonderful, serious, but not-serious eyes.

And looking back at him she found she needed the truth between them. "Yes, I have. I really needed to get the taste of Cal out of my system, frankly." She shrugged, dropping her gaze to the ancient table where their barely touched drinks sat side by side. "It was quick and clinical."

"Sounds rather like mouthwash."

She thought back to the shortest affair of her life. "More like washing my own mouth out with soap."

"You don't have to do this," he said.

She looked down at him, felt the warmth of his hands against her hip, felt breathless with the anticipation that a man who could appreciate and find beauty in her hands was going to be something very special in bed.

"Yes," she said, bending over to kiss him. "I do."

His hands were back in her hair, and he kissed her with such enthusiasm that she lost her balance and tumbled onto his lap.

He tasted of cognac, complex, rich, and fiery.

His fingers played in her hair, rubbed her scalp until she wanted to purr, then he began to undress her.

Conscious that she was wearing borrowed feathers and Max might not appreciate them being tossed all over the floor, she rose and backed slowly away, slipping the velvet jacket from her shoulders. It wasn't going to be easy or natural to perform a stripper routine in this style of clothing, but she figured she'd give it her best, and if he thought it was odd that she stopped to hang each piece up neatly, she hoped he'd merely think it was part of her act, one more way of increasing his anticipation of seeing her naked.

Gack. She sucked in her stomach at the thought. If he thought her scarred, burned, and banged-up hands were a turn-on, he was going to flip at her flabby abs and I-stand-on-my-feet-all-day-in-a-kitchen sturdy legs.

She got the jacket hung up neatly, and before she could turn back to him, she felt his hands on her, tracing her ribs, stroking up to cup her breasts. The feeling was so exquisite that she forgot to worry that her boobs had gained weight along with the rest of her when her life hit the toilet.

He didn't seem to be all that put off by the expanse of flesh now cupped in his palms. In fact, judging from the contented sounds he was making and the very definite hardness pressing against her hip, he was a big boob kind of guy.

He undid her buttons and peeled the blouse off her. Then,

as she was getting ready to rescue Max's peasant blouse, he
leaned past her and hung it neatly.

Her skirt soon hung beside it.

There was something surprisingly fun about undressing
and hanging each other's clothes. "I feel like your personal
butler," she said as she hung his dress shirt.

"If I had a butler as gorgeous as you, I'd never leave my
room."

She slid his trousers off, liking the sight of muscular, furry
legs. He was such an elegant-looking man that it was a surprise to find thigh muscles thick and athletic. "You play
sports?"

"Used to. Now George and I are in a football league for
sorry old-timers who can't give up."

"It's good that you keep in shape," she said, trying not to
stare at another thick muscle that appeared in excellent
shape. He was a boxer man, which didn't surprise her, his
choice a muted navy cotton with white pinstripes. So businesslike. Pin-striped boxers.

Who would have thought, even a year ago, that she'd
find herself in an honest-to-God earl's historic mansion,
with a sexy Brit staring down at her with that particular
combination of sweetness and, oh, that so very English
word, naughtiness. Excitement skittered through her and
she thought she might be getting over her long-running
black mood.

"I am absolutely delighted that I decided to come down
today," he said.

She rose, close enough that a lot of her brushed a lot of
him as she made her way to standing. "And I am very
happy that you invaded my kitchen today," she admitted.

He kissed her. She thought she could go on kissing him
forever. He was possibly the best kiss she'd ever had. Before
she'd decided to her satisfaction that he was in fact the best

kiss she'd ever had, her breasts felt a little breezy and she realized he'd dispensed with her bra. Rather swiftly and subtly.

His hands were on her, squeezing gently, touching her nipples as though they were both fragile and precious, so the throb of desire began to build.

He lifted one, then the other, to his mouth. There was enough there that they easily reached.

"You are so beautiful," he said in a soft, reverent tone. "I don't think I've ever seen such amazing breasts."

And from feeling fat and out of shape, she suddenly felt like a voluptuous earth mother, womanly and *bring it on, baby* sexy.

She'd always loved sex, was almost embarrassingly responsive, but with him she felt it all as a gift.

She fell back on the bed, free-falling as though into a pool, letting her arms reach above her head. When she hit the mattress, she felt her breasts bounce with the impact, felt a little bit of jiggling where she'd really prefer no jiggle to be, but her soon-to-be lover seemed mesmerized with her body.

He stripped her of her panties in one smooth move and then stared down at her.

Somehow his expression told her that he liked what he saw. She started to get up so she could return the favor and remove his boxers, but he stopped her with a gesture. "No, don't move. Don't move a muscle."

How could she not feel seductive and special when he couldn't tear his eyes away? When he ripped off his boxers without looking once at what he was doing?

She looked though—*oh*—and looked some more. He was gorgeous. Fit, tough, toned, and with his body so evidently eager for her that she began to melt.

When he climbed onto the bed, she felt she would go mad if he didn't touch her, didn't kiss her, didn't take her, and now.

But he surprised her, kissing her sweetly, as though he had all the time in eternity to do nothing but kiss her.

As her passion built, she moved closer, pressing herself against him for the pleasure of feeling her skin against his. He was so warm, his skin silky smooth in places, hair-roughened in others.

She'd never in her life felt worshipped, but tonight she did. He looked at her the way he'd looked at the Rembrandt, his favorite in George's collection, he'd told her.

He tasted her the way he'd tasted her food, with eager anticipation, then slow savoring, followed by delighted satisfaction.

He played at her breasts, kissing and licking them until she felt they were swelling with the excitement that filled her. She began twisting as heat built within her. "Oh," she sighed. "Oh, yes, oh, please." She didn't even know what she was murmuring as he continued to toy at her breasts. But he didn't know her, he didn't know . . .

"Wait," she cried, but it was already too late. The wave seemed to begin at the soles of her feet and to roll upward, taking everything along for the ride.

"Am I hurting you?" He raised his head, first in concern, then with a smug grin as he saw the state she was in.

He went back to her breasts in spite of her breathless suggestion that he come inside her. He didn't seem to hear her, and then suddenly it didn't matter, it was too late, and the world began to tremble, her body began to spasm, and she cried out as an orgasm shook her.

He stayed with her through the major quake and the aftershocks, then came back up to kiss her mouth, holding her as her heart slowed.

"I've heard about women like you," he said. "Always wanted to meet one."

She groaned, torn between embarrassment and satisfaction. "It's been a while," she said. "I had a lot of pent-up horniness."

"Don't ever apologize for enjoying yourself in bed." He announced it like a lesson.

And she was feeling good enough that she opened her eyes wide. "Is that a rule?"

"Absolutely," he assured her. "Jack Flynt's rules for living. Rule number one."

She felt a little lazy, a lot turned on, and wild to see what was next on the agenda. "What's rule number two?"

"Ah," he said, kissing his way down the underside of her breasts to her belly. "Jack Flynt's rule number two is to extract the maximum pleasure from a woman." He nibbled her belly until she giggled helplessly. "To find every one of her weak spots and exploit them shamelessly."

He nudged her thighs apart and the restlessness increased again. If he was going to do what she thought he was going to do, it was her absolute favorite thing on earth. But she'd already come once, surely he'd want to . . .

"Oh," she cried as he put his mouth on her, and began to remind her why this was her absolute favorite thing in the world. He kissed her intimately, savoring her with his mouth the way he'd enjoyed her food earlier.

She wanted to hold back, to take the time to enjoy and luxuriate in the exquisite experience of his mouth on her, but he was stroking her, swirling his tongue over and around her hot button, and she knew she couldn't last. When she began to thrash, she felt the beginnings of delight take her, and suddenly, he changed his technique. Now he was light, stroking with little touches like butterfly wings that only teased, keeping her hovering over the peak but not giving her enough momentum to fly.

"Oh, oh, that's so good," she moaned, her head thrown back, feeling a drop of sweat roll between her breasts.

He spread her wide and she didn't care, she didn't care

that her thighs were built for stamina, not bathing-suit modeling, and that she had too much lust as well as too much of everything else. She let him look. Let him touch, feel, taste.

Every second he kept her on the edge was agony, and yet the most intense pleasure. She couldn't hold on, couldn't float this high without bursting into flame, and still he controlled her, holding her airborne, but not quite setting her free.

It seemed to go on forever; her heart stuttered, her breath caught, her body grew tenser, and then, when she thought she would absolutely expire from the sweet torture of those feather-light touches, he gripped her hips, holding her in place, and tongued her with deep, strong strokes. If he hadn't held her, she was certain she'd have hit the ceiling as he took her over the edge, letting her soar, staying with her until she was spent.

She waited for him to come inside her, her eyes shut and her body floating lazily in lapping waves of pleasure. She needed to open her eyes, at least one eye, and remind him about condoms, but for a second she wanted to stay here in the afterglow, enjoying the bliss.

She jerked and her eyes flew open when she felt his tongue on her again. "I can't!"

"You can." He was so sure. It was as though he'd known her body as long as she had.

And, of course, she could. Only after she'd sobbed out his name did he kiss his way up her body and reach over her for the condoms he'd placed on the bedside table.

"Rule number three," he murmured. "Always give a little extra of yourself."

"I have some rules too, you know," she said, watching, propped on her elbow as he sheathed himself.

"What are they?"

"One, never let a guy have too much control," she said. Tucking her strong, sturdy legs around him, she flipped him to his back and mounted him. When she took him into her body, she couldn't resist kissing him, feeling so intimately connected to this man on his first entering her body.

"Rule number four," he said, "never take love lying down," and he flipped her.

She laughed as they rolled back and forth, teasing each other, exciting each other, her taking him and him taking her, until they ended side by side, his hand on her hip, hers on his shoulder. He stared into her eyes and the intimacy was almost more than she could bear. She kissed him, allowing her eyes to close, and they rocked to oblivion.

She snuggled up against him. Loving the feel of his body against hers, the way his heart still pounded, which she'd caused.

Today had ended up being a surprisingly good day—the best she'd had in ages. Also exhausting, she realized, as she began to drift.

She jerked herself awake.

"I should get going," she said after a minute.

His arm tightened around her. "Don't go. Not yet."

She stared at his profile, shadowy in the dark. He had a strong, almost beaky nose and a no-nonsense jut of a chin. She wished she could read his mind. She wished she knew her own. To stay or not to stay.

So many things urged her to stay. Her body, replete and satisfied, but not so satisfied that she couldn't imagine waking in the middle of the night to another bout of amazing sex. But then, what if Maxine was up early? Or George or, God forbid, Wiggins.

"Let me think about it for a minute," she said.

"Is there anything I could do to convince you?" he said, skimming his hand down her front, bringing her tired body suddenly back to aching life.

"Yes," she said, pushing up against his hand. "You could definitely convince me."

He rolled her over, and she found she couldn't care less about what her sister or George or even Wiggins might think when she stumbled back to her room tomorrow morning.

He had her peaking before she'd even thought about it. She cried out an almost obscene number of times before they'd finally exhausted themselves and each other.

As they lay snuggled together, her head comfortably resting on his chest, his hand making idle patterns on her back, he said, "You are, without doubt, the most amazingly responsive woman I've ever had the pleasure of taking to bed."

"I got a little carried away," she admitted, turning her face into his chest.

"My dear, you have a body that was made for pleasure."

"I wish you could have seen it a year ago."

"Why?"

"A year ago I was running. I was more toned, more trim. Not so flabby."

"Flabby?" He raised his head so he could look into her face. "I've never known a woman who couldn't find something wrong with herself. You are perfect. I think you're the most truly sensuous woman I've ever known. You make art out of food, you take pleasure in eating, in touch, in your body, and in your partner's. You are a rare and special woman."

She wanted to believe him, she did, but she'd had a crappy year and her self-confidence wasn't exactly hitting an all-time high. "You don't think I'm fat?"

He shook his head. "I think you are perfect."

Well, she was far, far, far from perfect, but if he wanted to think that, hell, if he just wanted to claim he thought she was perfect while they were lying here together naked, she was not in the mood to stop him.

With a sigh, she snuggled against him and closed her eyes, her lips still curved in a smile of satisfaction.

She awoke in the cold, gray light of dawn. She wouldn't have woken at all had she not felt cold, for which, she realized, she could blame Jack, who had left the bed. So long as she'd been curled against him, warm and occasionally very, very hot, she'd been content. Now she found herself alone under crisp white sheets. She not only felt cold, but extremely naked.

The shower was running. By squinting her eyes at the clock she saw that it wasn't even six. She could roll over and go back to sleep, and chance that Jack would catch her drooling on her pillow, or that the housekeeper would find her here when she came to do the room. No. Better to haul herself out of bed now, at once.

Rachel had never been a morning person. Working in the restaurant business hadn't made her any less nocturnal, but she managed to heave herself out of bed and shove herself back into her clothes before the shower had been turned off.

Jack crept out of the bathroom a few minutes later with a furtive glance toward the bed. "You don't have to worry about not waking me," she assured him. "I'm up."

"Ah," he said, looking as good in a towel as he had in nothing at all. "Sorry to disturb."

"It's okay. I should get back to my room. Before, you know . . ."

He nodded. He glanced at the clock and shed the towel with no embarrassment, dressing with speed. He didn't even kiss her good morning. Obviously, his thoughts were already in London.

"Well," she said, "I'd better get going." She took a step toward the door. It had been fabulous, amazing. The best night of her life. She wasn't going to spoil it by wishing for more.

"Rachel, wait," he said, before she'd taken more than a step. "I want to see you again."

Her heart leapt. Oh, thank God. "I'd like that," she said.

"Why don't you come up to London?" He slipped into a clean shirt. "I'll take you to dinner and the theatre."

She sighed in pure bliss. "Sounds good."

"All right. I'll give you a ring. Have you got a mobile?"

"Yes," she said. "It's a California number." And she reeled off her cell phone number. He pulled out his and programmed her into memory. Cool.

"I could make you breakfast," she said, suddenly not wanting him to go.

He shook his head, buckling the belt on his trousers. "No time. The M5 will be murder if I don't get away soon."

She felt very unhappy with the M5. But Jack wanted to see her again. That was something.

"I never gave you a menu for your sister's wedding," she said, suddenly feeling like the worst caterer in the British Isles.

"Believe me, anything you make will be brilliant. You're a genius with food."

He came over and kissed her soundly, then grabbed his bag, which she now saw was neatly and completely packed, slipped into his shoes, and left.

It was six o'clock in the morning, and she was the only person awake in Hart House.

She didn't feel like sleeping, but she didn't feel like hanging around here, either.

She made sure any trace of her was gone, including tucking in all the blankets and remaking the bed so it looked like only one side of the bed had been used. Satisfied, she crept out of the door and stealthily made her way back to her own room, where she changed out of Maxine's clothes once more, showered, and hauled on her usual jeans and a favorite black cotton shirt.

She let her hair hang free and put on a little makeup. Nothing like a night of great sex to put a person in a good mood, she thought as she realized she was feeling better than she'd felt for months.

So the restaurant had closed, so she'd failed at marriage. Her life wasn't over. She was young, talented, attractive enough that a man like Jack Flynt could spend the night making love and paying extravagant compliments to her.

Life was good.

Feeling grateful to Maxine and George for putting up with her for the past few miserable weeks, she decided to surprise them with breakfast.

Max, annoyingly, was right. She'd needed to get back to cooking. Now she couldn't seem to stop. Something simple, she decided. An omelet with fresh herbs from the garden.

Chapter Seven

Rachel told herself repeatedly that she wouldn't expect Jack to call. Wouldn't expect anything. Just because he'd said he wanted to see her again did not mean that he was obsessively going over every detail of their night together the way she was, or even that he did in fact want to see her again.

Phrases like that should come with subtitles, as in a foreign movie. "I'd like to see you again," he'd say. Translation: *I'm really not that into you. Don't expect more.* "I'll call you," meaning *You'll never hear from me again.* "We'll have to do this again sometime." *I've already forgotten your name.*

It didn't matter. Hadn't she hooked up with him exactly with a casual affair in mind? All she wanted was some uncomplicated fun. A chance to prove to herself and her battered ego that she was still a contender.

So even as she rolled her eyes and scoffed when Max made some comment about how well she and Jack had hit it off, she felt warm all over.

And if she carried her cell phone with her everywhere, never let it out of her sight for a second, no one had to know why.

Somehow she'd fallen into the business of the estate.

Well, with Max for a sister, it was impossible not to. The woman was so full of energy and plans for raising revenue—a surprising number of which seemed to include food, and therefore Rachel's input—that she kept busy. Too busy to mope and feel sorry for herself. Even better, she was appreciated. George had appeared horrified at first to find Rachel was the chief caterer on the estate, but she hazarded a shrewd guess that Max had informed him that work would be good for her poor, depressed sister, because he never argued again. What he did was thank her, repeatedly and sincerely, for all her help.

It had been a long time since anyone had taken the time to thank her.

And he did it so charmingly. If his charm was inherited, no wonder his family had managed to thrive through centuries of turbulent history. Her sister, she had to admit, had chosen herself a great guy. How nice to know they were still out there.

Max had hinted that she and George weren't getting married until Hart House was operating in the black. How could she not want her sister to be happy? So she cooked, she catered, she sourced local suppliers, she planned.

She was in the old stables with Maxine, working out details of a corporate retreat for a big computer manufacturer who wanted to put on a medieval fair, including jousting. Her job was to create a menu of authentic medieval food, then figure out how to feed it to three hundred workers who'd no doubt be exhausted from jousting, fencing, archery, barging on the river, and learning to party like it was 1399.

"It's going to be simple fare, obviously," she said to Max. "Back then, they'd roast whatever animals they'd raised or hunted, eat local produce. No potatoes, obviously, since they hadn't discovered America yet. Honey for sweetening, I imagine. I wonder what spices were imported then? I'll check." She was scribbling notes to herself when her cell phone rang.

"Hello?"

"Jack Flynt here." He had a business voice on, she noted. "Did I ring you at a good time?"

Since he sounded so businesslike, and she was so happy to hear from him, she felt flirtatious. Turning away from Max, she took a few steps toward the open door, hoping her nosy sib would assume she was searching out better reception. "It depends what you have in mind," she said.

A short pause. "Naturally, I rang you to make lewd, filthy suggestions."

"Then you picked the perfect time," she said.

He laughed. "I may not say them"—he dropped his voice—"since I'm about to go into a meeting with the Italian trade commissioner, but I'm definitely thinking them."

"Me, too," she admitted.

"Can you come up to town on Saturday? We'll poke around and I'll take you to dinner."

He'd called. And when he'd said he wanted to see her again, he'd actually meant he wanted to see her again. She wanted to throw her phone in the air and scream with excitement. "Yes, I'd love it."

"Great. Bring your toothbrush. I'll drive you back down on Sunday."

"A whole weekend? That sounds serious."

"Once I get you naked, my sweet, I'll show you serious." He raised his voice. "Yes, I'll be right there," and then a few phrases in Italian. "Sorry, I've got to go."

"Ciao."

She turned to find Max standing much closer than was even remotely polite. "Was that Jack?"

"You have no subtlety whatsoever, do you?"

"Too many years in television. Well?"

Rachel nodded, wondering if she looked as pleased with herself as she felt. "He's invited me up to London for the weekend."

"Oh, my God. I knew it. You slept with him, didn't you?"

She nodded, unable to stop the smile that bloomed.

"And?"

"It was fantastic."

"Best ever?"

The grin widened. "No contest. I swear, one more orgasm would have killed me." She sighed, already thinking ahead. "A whole weekend."

Max's delight dimmed a notch and a worried frown creased her forehead. "You know his reputation, don't you?"

"Yes, sister dear, you warned me about him. I get it. But you know what? I don't care. He wants a casual, no-strings-attached affair and so do I." She stuck her phone back on the clip at her waist. "You were right to manipulate me into coming here."

"I didn't—"

She silenced Max with a look.

"It was for your own good," Max mumbled.

"I know. And I've finally had a chance to get over myself enough to see that I'm free. Free of a man who didn't deserve me and a restaurant that wasn't mine. So maybe I'm not such a failure after all."

"Hallelujah. She gets it," Max said, throwing up her hands.

"Maybe I can take some time for myself for a while. Time to have fun and hang out with unsuitable men who are great in bed. I can find another job. One day, I still hope to open my own restaurant. Until then, I can learn from better chefs. Maybe take some management training, so I won't make the same mistakes I've witnessed."

"Wow, three weeks in England and you're a changed woman."

"I really needed this, Max." She felt her eyes go misty as she walked up to her sister. "Thanks for looking out for me."

Maxine's eyes filled, too. "Always."

Rachel had been to London before. Once to take a course from a renowned chef and once when she'd come to visit her sister when Max was on location. But she'd never looked forward to London quite so much. She'd never had an amazing lover waiting.

Her train arrived at Victoria Station Saturday at noon. And there he was.

At a conservative estimate, there were three gazillion people in the station, rushing here and there, or loitering waiting for their trains, eating at one of the cafés, or yacking on phones in every language ever spoken.

Among all that flow of humanity, she spotted Jack almost immediately. For a moment it was as though there was a hiccup in time. There was silence, the world stilled, all those cell phone talkers were muted, all the rush of motion halted. There was only she and the man who had so easily helped her find her way back to herself.

She walked forward, so did he, and time was allowed to do the same.

Would he kiss her in front of all these people? Did she want him to?

He did. And she did. And as their lips met, she leaned into him. Oh, he was already so familiar, and her body wanted to get as close as it could to him.

"Hi," he said, taking her weekender bag in one hand and linking his fingers in hers with his other. "What do you want to do today? See the changing of the guard? Visit the Tower? Madame Tussauds?"

"We could, but I saw all that last time I was here."

"What about Notting Hill, then? Excellent shops, interesting architecture, good places to eat."

"In what part of London do you live?"

He grinned down at her. "Notting Hill."

She grinned back. "Excellent choice."

"Good. We can drop your bag off and then go out and see the sights."

She gawked like a tourist as they drove through London traffic. She loved the excitement of the city. The splendid old buildings, the surprising green spaces, the London bobbies, the Tube stations, the black cabs.

His home was a brick townhouse in a row of same, all looking Victorian and genteel. Inside, his décor tended to modern, sleek and much neater than any other man she'd ever come across. This was the kind of place where she knew she wouldn't have to shut her eyes before venturing into the bathroom, or do some Yogic, centering breathing before opening the refrigerator.

"Do you want anything before we venture out?" he asked, gesturing vaguely to the kitchen.

If a woman was launched on a short-term affair that centered around sex, then she wasn't going to waste her time on salmon sandwiches and tea. She stepped closer. Looked him in the eye. "I want you."

"Thank God," he said, and swept her into his arms. "I thought you might think I was a randy bloke who wanted nothing but a shag."

She laughed, half breathless as he pushed her coat off her shoulders and pulled her sweater over her head. "Aren't you?"

"Absolutely. But I didn't want you seeing through me quite so quickly."

There was a pool of sunlight splashed on the floor of the living area. It made the hardwood gleam and brought out the rich reds and blues in a Turkish rug. There he led her, pausing to flip a quilt she hadn't noticed from the back of a gray couch. With one flick he had it open and floating to the ground like a picnic blanket.

The thought flashed through her mind that it was a familiar move. And the quilt was washable. Very practical for a quickie in the living room. One of the intricate wooden boxes arranged on a nearby shelf no doubt contained condoms and there was a handy box of tissues tucked in behind it.

A flicker of . . . something—sadness? regret?—she banished. She'd gone into this with her eyes open. She knew what he was. He was a good-time guy, a charming rogue who'd love her and leave her unless she left him first. Which, she reminded herself, was exactly what she wanted. Some fun, some great sex, some laughs, no tears or recriminations when it was over.

And a man who had a sex station, likely in every room of his home, was a man you could trust to run an affair smoothly.

She helped herself to a cushion off the couch, in a pattern that harmonized with the rug. Stepped out of the rest of her clothes and sank cross-legged to the cushion, watching with pleasure as he stripped.

"Which little box holds the condoms?" she asked him.

If he was surprised that she'd guessed, he showed it only by the slightest flicker of an eyelid. "The middle one."

"What's in the others?"

"Why don't you have a look?"

Knowing a dare when she heard one, she rose, as gracefully as a naked, not-in-very-good-shape woman can rise from a cross-legged position, and walked to the three boxes, knowing he was watching her, feeling his eyes on her larger-than-necessary ass. She went for the middle box first, and based on their last encounter, removed two condoms. Then she opened the second box, wondering if, like Pandora, she might end up wishing she hadn't peeked.

But there was nothing more threatening than a vibrator with a variety of attachments. She glanced at him over her shoulder with her eyebrows raised.

He grinned at her. "Definitely not something you need," he said.

She lifted the lid of the third box and found a selection of flavored and scented lubricants and massage oils.

"Not bad for living room décor," she said, feeling happy that he didn't have anything that went beyond her comfort zone.

"Bring over whatever you like the look of."

"Maybe later," she said, and launched herself at him.

This sex did not need any aides.

His hands were all over her, hers all over him. He pushed her into the sunlight, so she was utterly exposed to him, and he seemed to glory in her.

Never had she felt so beautiful or delighted that her body responded so quickly. He kissed her deeply, running his hands over and over her breasts and belly. When he reached between her thighs she opened for him, sighing at his touch, blooming beneath his fingers. Her first orgasm took the edge off but also dropped her to a deeper level of sensation. Her skin was ultrasensitive, so she was aware of the subtle heat of the sun coming through the window, of the soft cotton of the quilt beneath her, aware of each quivering inch of her body as he touched her.

He didn't take the time to play as he had before; she sensed that his urgency was too keen. He took her, straight on, pushing in and up, filling her, reaching so deep inside that he began to feel like a part of her.

She watched his face change as his passion built, the way his eyes darkened and seemed to look inside her. Tiny sounds were coming from her throat, little sighs and help-less moans. She was climbing, trying to wait for him, but so excited she wasn't sure she could.

"Let go," he panted, kissing her, licking into her mouth. "Let go."

As he said it he changed the angle so he was rubbing her clit and nudging her G-spot, and it didn't take anything else to send her over the edge with a wild cry. Her body went crazy, bucking and rolling, pushing up, up, even as he thrust. She was clinging to him, feeling her body spasm around him, and then the motion grew even more frenzied as he threw back his head and groaned, spilling deep inside of her.

She wrapped her legs around him and held him tight against her. "Don't leave," she whispered, and he seemed to understand what she needed, continuing to move until she cried out once more against his shoulder.

"Any more waiting in the wings?" he whispered.

She snorted. Then started to laugh. "I can't help it."

"Darling, don't ever change."

"I was a little . . . uh, needy, I guess."

"I was fairly needy myself." He sighed. "Now I've got a few of my wits back, I can kiss you properly." And he did. So properly that it was another hour before they were ready to leave.

"Should I dress for dinner?" she called out to him from the bathroom upstairs. It was en suite to his bedroom, which was as sleek, masculine, and neat as the other rooms.

"Yes."

She had no idea how fancy dinner would be, so she'd packed a classic little black dress and borrowed a red pash-mina shawl from Maxine. Her quick shower had caused her hair to bush out, of course, but she was used to that, and pinned it back with quick efficiency.

She felt well-sexed, as attractive as it was possible for her to look, and excited about the rest of the weekend. She had no idea what the rules were for this kind of casual relationship, but a whole weekend with Jack seemed like an enormous treat and one she wasn't going to waste a moment of. By next weekend, she might well have been supplanted by an acting student from RADA or a European banking colleague.

When she emerged downstairs, he was talking on his cell phone. He waved to her and kissed his fingers to his mouth to her, Italian style.

"No, of course I understand."

She could tell it was a woman he was talking to and turned away to examine the books in his bookcase. She couldn't have said, afterward, whether he read philosophy or graphic comics—all her attention was on eavesdropping.

Instead of furtively skulking around the corner, Jack followed her into the room, phone still glued to his ear. He seemed to be doing a lot of reassuring and calming. Finally he said, "Look. Everything's going to be fine. Try not to worry so much. All right. Love you, too. Good-bye, darling."

Her spine stiffened. Every muscle in her body stiffened. Darling? Were these the rules of casual dating in Notting Hill? You banged one woman and within the hour were calling somebody else darling?

When he clicked off the phone, she smiled brightly. "I hope I'm not overdressed."

He'd opened his mouth to speak and now closed it. Blinking at her. "Don't you want to know who that was?"

She kept her face carefully neutral. "I don't think so."

He still looked at her oddly. "Well, you should. It was my sister." He grimaced. "She's having second thoughts."

"Second thoughts?" It was his sister. Yeah, sure it was. But what if it was his sister? Wouldn't she feel like a suspicious fool. "What do you mean she's having second thoughts?"

"The wedding. The one you're catering? She's having second thoughts about getting married."

"Oh. That sister." Okay, so it really was his sister, and he was right. If the wedding was off, Maxine was going to be seriously peeved. A lot of work had gone into that catering plan and the arrangements. The wedding, which would naturally be heavily featured in the society pages, was going to be a real showstopper, the kind of event that could set a trend. Maxine had hoped to see a lot of big, expensive weddings grace the grounds of Hart House. If Jack's sister cancelled . . .

"How serious do you think she is? Would she actually cancel the wedding?"

"Hard to tell with Chloe. She's chucked a wobbly in front of Mario, her fiancé. If he didn't bend to her will, she'll be in a right snit."

"Wow. I hope for George and Maxine's sake she goes ahead with her wedding." Rachel wasn't entirely sure what wobblies were, but felt confident Max wouldn't want them chucked at Hart House.

"Let's not worry about it now. She and the fiancé have had a row. Most likely they'll have forgotten all about it by tomorrow."

Rachel probably ought to have been worried for Hart House's sake, but she was too glad to find that the woman Jack had called darling was in fact his sister.

Not that she was in any doubt about his lifestyle, or under any illusions about the future, but it was nice to know he had more class than to talk to one lover in the presence of another.

"Right, we can catch a few shops, and then we'll go to dinner."

"Sounds good. I worked up quite an appetite."

"Do you fancy walking? You'll see a bit of the area that way."

"Oh, yeah. That would be great." They set out and she saw the market stalls full of everything from produce to third and fourth-hand evening bags. The street was busy with Smart Cars and Mini Coopers and cabs. They passed bakeries, independent record shops, tiny restaurants, and a sea of very trendy pedestrians.

"I thought you might be interested in that shop over there."

She followed his pointing finger. A store selling nothing but cookbooks. "Oh, how cool." She ran forward and peered into the window. "They're closed."

"Never mind. We can come back tomorrow."

She pressed her nose against the window a little longer, seeing cookbooks she'd never heard of. Mostly European and British ones. "I think I could spend days in there."

"If I hadn't ravished you all afternoon, we'd have got there before closing. Oh, well, at least we haven't missed our dinner reservation."

"Where are we going?"

"Fleur de Lys."

She stopped dead, so quickly that a man running in the opposite direction with a bouquet of flowers almost crashed into her. "Fleur de Lys? Are you kidding me?" She was so excited she was squeaking.

Jack allowed himself a tiny smirk. "I thought you'd be pleased."

"Pleased? I'm floored. Flabbergasted. You can't get a reservation there for months. I know, because I e-mailed them from the States. The chef, Jerome Smollet, is the most amazing chef in Europe." She was so excited she was talking faster and faster and her words were running together.

Finally she dragged in a quick breath. "Are we talking about the same Fleur de Lys?"

"I helped with the financing," he said. As though that answered it all. Which, she supposed, it did.

She didn't care that they were in the middle of Portobello Road and that this was a casual, short-term relationship. She threw her arms around Jack's neck and kissed him.

"This is a great surprise. It's the best surprise ever." Her heart was pounding. "This is better than meeting the queen."

He took her hand and lifted it to his mouth. "You're a lot of fun, Rachel, do you know that?"

Everything about Fleur de Lys thrilled her. She loved the blue and gold door, the black and white entrance hall, the air of laid-back, trendy elegance. The hushed atmosphere of diners who appreciate food and know they are about to have their palates pampered. The maitre d' recognized Jack and welcomed him.

This was one of the top five restaurants in the world and the maitre d' knew Jack by name. Okay, she was impressed.

They were led to a wonderful, intimate table for two in a corner that still gave her a good view of the room.

In a minute a waiter appeared with a silver tray on which sat two flutes of champagne. They hadn't even seen a menu and she hadn't heard Jack order anything, so she raised her brows.

"I told Jerome about you," said Jack.

"You did?"

"Of course. I asked him to make us a meal. He'll send out whatever he thinks we should eat along with the wines to go with each course. Are you willing?"

She leaned closer. "Other than the six orgasms you already gave me today, you could not have done anything that would thrill me more."

He reached across the table for her hand. They clicked glasses and drank. "To the most amazing woman I have ever met."

She nearly snorted French champagne through her nose. Her gaze darted to his and she was shocked at the expression she read. His eyes glowed and for a second she was shaken by the power of the connection she felt.

Tiny nibbles began to arrive. Always Jack had something different from what she did, so they shared. The sensuality of the food, of sharing with a man who got food in the way she did, was exquisite. With no menu choices to worry about, they were free to concentrate on each other and on the surprises coming out of the kitchen.

They sat long over their food and wine and coffee. It felt like she'd known him forever, and yet, because she hadn't known him more than a week, there were all her stories to tell. All his stories to hear.

When the restaurant had begun to clear, she was about to suggest they leave, when yet another tray came up with a three cognacs. Three?

And there was Jerome Smollet. Even if she hadn't read about him in *Chef* magazine and recognized him from his picture in various publications, she'd have known him from the way dining patrons oohed and aahed as he stopped to chat. He made his slow way across the room, working it like a pro, in a manner she had to admire. He didn't seem to hurry, but he didn't spend more than a minute or two at each table.

When he got to theirs, she saw that he was younger than she'd realized. Mid-thirties, she guessed. He shook hands with Jack, who'd risen at his approach.

"Jerome, I'd like you to meet Rachel Larraby."

"It is such an honor to meet you," she said, feeling quivery and girlish.

"I'm a big fan of yours, too. I ate in your restaurant in L.A. a couple of years ago."

"You did?"

"I wanted to send a message to the kitchen, but I lacked courage. You were so famous and I was virtually unknown."

"I knew who you were. I wish you'd sent a message back."

He nodded his head graciously. "Well, we meet at last."

"Okay, I have to know, was there sake in the sauce you served with the black prawns?"

And they were off. Two foodies talking about their passion.

Jack sat back, listening to the conversation but taking little part, watching her with that look. The one that warmed and chilled her at the same time.

On another man, that expression would be lovesickness. But on Union Jack? The one who was always a groomsman, never a groom?

Couldn't be.

Chapter Eight

Jack ought to have been bored rigid. He loved food. Loved good restaurants, enjoyed eating and tasting what he ate, but he wasn't passionate about how every mouthful was constructed. He didn't want the magic spoiled by seeing how the trick was done. But watching two consummate chefs sharing their art was an education in itself. And he had the opportunity to sit back and watch Rachel. Did she even realize how special she was?

She had one of Europe's star chefs at her feet.

And she completely had *him* at her feet. She'd looked startled when he'd made the toast. Was she really so unwilling to accept what had happened between them?

He'd been waiting his whole adult life for the woman who would do this to him. He hadn't remotely wanted to drive down to Hart House on wedding business for his flighty sister. And look what had happened. He'd been attacked by the temperamental chef in the kitchen and within hours, it seemed, had fallen in love with her.

Love at almost first sight was corny, mildly embarrassing, but his one consolation was that the woman he'd fallen for was someone who lived with passion. Who connected with him so immediately, so intimately, that he knew she was feeling everything he was feeling.

It was amazing to find, after all these years, that the popular songwriters had it nailed. Love really was a lightning bolt out of the blue, love was all he needed, it was every song, every poem, every greeting card message. He looked at Rachel and his whole being said, *Yes*.

Jack believed in marriage and he was ready, at thirty-four, to settle. To spend less time away and a little of his hefty savings on holidays with the woman he loved, on a larger home, perhaps, or a holiday home. Even, he thought, as he looked at Rachel with her generous spirit and loving ways, on a nursery.

He'd be terrified, but he could see Rachel with a baby in her arms. Their baby. And the notion filled him with pride.

He'd waited a long time, longer than any of the lads. But she'd been worth waiting for.

When they finally got out of the restaurant, they were the last patrons to leave and he honestly thought Jerome and Rachel would have talked right through to breakfast if he hadn't broken up the party.

He bundled Rachel into a cab for the short ride home and settled back, already trying to decide what he wanted to do first when he got her naked.

"He offered me a job." Rachel whispered the news as though if she spoke it aloud the offer might disappear.

"I know. I heard him."

"You did?" She turned to him in the cab, all eagerness and uncertainty. "You actually heard him offer me a job?"

"Yes. Jerome thinks you're brilliant. He wants you in his kitchen."

"So I didn't dream it." Suddenly she turned to him, suspicious. "You didn't put him up to this, did you?"

"Hey." He held up his hands. "I can get a dinner reservation. That's all. I had no idea he even knew who you were."

"Really?"

"Yes. Believe me. If he offered you a job, he was sincere.

Do you have any idea how many people would kill to work with him?"

"Me, for one." She settled her head on his shoulder. "Thank you," she said, "for the most amazing day and night of my life."

"You're welcome." He put an arm around her, inhaling the smell of her, enjoying the feel of her hair tickling his chin. He couldn't wait to get home and let that hair down, slip off her clothes, and get at that glorious body. Deep down, underneath the fierce desire that was pumping through his veins, was an unfamiliar feeling, but one he recognized all the same. Tenderness. He'd given her something special, and her excitement was palpable. But she'd given him something, too. He'd forgotten what it was like to have that enthusiasm for work. That passion for life.

He had a feeling that life with Rachel would be a constant banquet. A never-ending tasting menu.

"Are you tempted?"

She slipped a hand between his legs, rubbing significantly. "Yes, I'm tempted."

"The job," he said, moving his hands up her side so his fingers brushed the underside of her breast. "I'm talking about the job."

"I'd need a work permit or something before I could stay."

"Or you could always marry an Englishman," he said cheerfully.

She glanced at him sharply and removed her hand from his crotch. "Maybe."

What was that all about? He'd have liked to ask her, but his head was fuzzy from good food, good wine, and the fact that she'd caused most of the blood to drain from his head, thereby impeding his mental function.

Surely she'd felt, as he had, the clobber of destiny, the absolute knowledge that they were each other's future?

He reminded himself of two things. One, he'd known the woman one single week. Only a madman declared his love so soon. Two, the woman was skittish about men in general and love in particular.

So he'd do something that was foreign to his nature. He'd wait.

When the cab dropped them off, he looked up at his house and said, "Oh, bloody hell."

"What is it?"

"I didn't leave a light on in the lounge when we left."

She grasped his arm and whispered. "Do you think it's robbers?"

He shook his head, hearing his teeth snap together. "Worse." Of all bloody nights. He ran up the stairs and Rachel followed slowly. "Shouldn't we call the cops?"

"Not unless you want to arrest my sister for illegal entry into her brother's flat and impeding his sex life. Which, come to think of it, isn't a bad idea."

"Your sister is here?"

"The woman's got the most amazing bloody timing."

Rachel glanced back at the cab about to pull away. "Maybe I should find a hotel for the night."

He grabbed her hand. "No. I want you to meet my sister." He shrugged, trying to make the best of things. "I'd hoped you'd do it in a more civilized manner, but it can't be helped now."

He held onto her hand while unlocking the front door, then, to make absolutely sure it was Chloe and not some lout nicking things, he shouted, "Hallo?"

"Thank God you're finally home," Chloe's voice floated down to him. "I've been waiting ages!"

"My sister," he said, half sorry it wasn't thieves so he could impress Rachel with his manliness in getting rid of them, and be spared his impetuous sister's latest turn-up.

She didn't wait until they'd gotten inside properly before wailing, "I'm not marrying Mario. He's vile. I threw that utterly vulgar ring back in his face and told him this morning, I won't marry him. I should have realized when the man gave me a diamond the size of Lithuania that he simply wasn't for me. I mean, really, it was so over the top that I literally couldn't lift my arm!" As the words flowed, so did the hope he'd had that she might be here only for a bed.

"Chloe," he said, and then a little louder when the flow of words wouldn't dry up, "Chloe. Shut up."

By this time, he and Rachel had climbed the stairs and his sister's very pretty and very spoiled face was frozen in a state of surprise.

"Oh, Jack," she said, in the tone she'd have used if he'd brought her a martini made with gin instead of vodka. "Did you have to bring a woman home tonight? Of all nights?" She gazed at him with her big, violet blue eyes opened wide in an utterly helpless expression that made far too many men weak at the knees, and only warned her brother that trouble was ahead. "I need you."

"Rachel, please forgive my appallingly bad-mannered little sister. Chloe, this is Rachel. She is a top chef from America who is going to cater your wedding." He put a slight emphasis on the word *is*.

"Hello, Rachel," Chloe said from between pouting lips.

"Hi, Chloe."

Great. The first meeting of the two women he cared about most in the world wasn't a rousing success. They hadn't exactly thrown each other at their respective feminine bosoms and wept for joy.

There was a pause. "You'll have to forgive me," said Chloe. "I'm very distraught, having just broken my engagement." Her voice wobbled on the edge of tears. It was one of her more successful tricks, but he was up to them all and merely crossed his arms at his chest and gave her a *don't try it* look.

"I'm really sorry about your engagement," Rachel said, glancing at Jack. "I'm sure you want to talk to your brother privately. I'll go and stay at a hotel."

"That would probably be best," Chloe agreed, brightening immediately.

"If anyone's going to a hotel it will be you, little sister. Rachel was invited."

She was all in black, to suit the drama of the occasion, though he thought she'd gone a bit heavy on the eyeliner. "But I need you."

"What you need, my sweet, is a man who won't let you rule him, then drive you mad when he's not commanding enough."

She sniffed. "You don't understand."

"Probably not. Never mind. I am going to make you some hot milk, put you in the guest room, and take Rachel to bed. In the morning, we'll talk."

"Jack," Rachel said, turning to him with wide, shocked eyes. "How can you be so cruel? Your sister just ended her engagement. Try and be a little supportive."

Chloe blinked, and suddenly, before his bemused gaze, he saw the instant bonding he'd wanted. She sniffed. "He can be such a beast, my brother, but he's the only one I could turn to in my hour of greatest need. Don't let him throw me out."

He'd offered her hot milk and a bed, not tossed her out on the street, but it didn't seem to matter. Rachel was promising to stand by his sister and he was clearly to be cast as that horrible brother who didn't understand. Chloe patted the couch beside her, and soon she and Rachel were seated side by side and Rachel was getting the full benefit of Chloe in crisis mode.

With a shrug, he went into the kitchen and made cocoa, something he'd been doing for Chloe since she broke her first heart at thirteen.

When he returned, the two women were deep into the minute dissection of Chloe's relationship, with some very good advice from Rachel, who wasn't as blind to his sister's antics as he'd feared.

He gave them an hour, because he was a good brother and he loved his sister. But he was also a man blindly in love with a woman he'd recently met, and burning to be naked and intimate with her. Sixty long minutes passed, and the cocoa was nothing but a memory when he began yawning extravagantly and turning out lights.

When that went unnoticed, he said, "All right, Chlo. Let's get you tucked into the guest room."

"All right. I mustn't interrupt your date, must I? Thank you, Rachel. I don't know what I would have done without you."

His cleaning staff kept the guest room ready and the bed freshly made, and Chloe used his flat like a second home often enough that some of her things were permanently installed, so the only difficult part was actually getting her in the room and getting her new best friend Rachel out again.

Another quarter of an hour and he'd managed it. And finally, finally, he had his woman alone with him in his bedroom.

"Sorry about that," he said when they had the door shut. Just in case Chloe remembered something else she absolutely must tell Rachel, he surreptitiously locked it.

"It was fine. I liked her a lot."

"She's completely spoiled, but deep down she's very sweet."

He unwrapped the red shawl Rachel still had round her shoulders, folded it, and placed it on a leather ottoman in the corner.

"Will she really cancel the wedding?" she asked as she

unzipped her dress. It struck him that they were acting like a long-term couple, chatting things over while they got ready for bed. He was glad they'd got the urgent shagging out of the way earlier, so he could savor the sight of Rachel undressing before him in this matter-of-fact way that somehow struck him as dead sexy.

Odd, how love changed a man's view of things.

He'd never found himself filled with such tenderness as when he lay her back on his bed, never found his emotions tangled with his physical desires as he now did.

She lay beneath him, her hair a dark cloud on the pillow around her, her eyes large and serious. He wanted to say things he'd never said to another woman, but he wasn't sure she was ready. And yet, when he entered her, felt her so hot and wet, clinging to him as though she'd never let go, surrounding him, he felt pulled into her much more than physically.

He loved her slowly, at a less harried pace than they'd yet managed, filling himself with her sounds, her tastes, her scents. She gave herself over completely to the moment, to the sensation. She was the most utterly sensual woman he'd ever known.

He fell asleep curled around her, his hand on her breast so he could feel the heavy beat of her heart against his palm.

Chapter Nine

Rachel wasn't a morning person, but there was something about waking up to Jack kissing his way down her spine that added a definite lift to the morning doldrums.

"Morning," she said lazily, stretching as his mouth did delicious things to her.

His reply was indistinct, but she could work it out in context.

When he flipped her to her back, she was more than ready.

"Ssh," she said when he banged his elbow against the wall. "I don't want Chloe to hear."

"It's a bit like having a child in the next room. Which is truer than you might think."

"Be nice to her. She's going through a hard time."

"When you know her better, you'll understand that drama is as necessary to Chloe as Perrier Jouët."

Why did he keep saying these things to her? When you know her better? As if that was going to happen. A week or two from now, some Lufthansa flight attendant would be with Jack, writhing under the buzz of the living room vibrator, lathered up in lemon-scented massage oil. And she'd be topping her special blinis with caviar for the next scheduled function at Hart House. Did he think she was one of those women—if there were such women—who wanted to hear lies and platitudes?

She might have called him on it, but he was deep inside her body, and when he moved he nudged her G-spot, she couldn't possibly think of anything at all.

Afterward, she ran her hands idly down his back while they caught their breath, her head on his chest. "I feel so good I never want to move."

He played with her hair, and without pausing said, "Then don't."

She'd had enough of this. Now that she could think, it was time to put an end to this nonsense.

"Are you suggesting I should stay in this bed for the rest of my natural life?"

"Don't be daft." He shifted her and raised himself onto an elbow so he could look at her. "But you could stay with me forever."

Her heart stuttered, which irritated her. "Yeah," she said, rolling her eyes à la sophisticated woman of the world.

He didn't respond à la sophisticated man of the world, but stayed where he was. She felt he was struggling to say something, and finally he did.

"I love you, Rachel," he said, looking deep into her eyes, his hand touching her shoulder as though he couldn't bear not to touch her.

"Oh, give me a break," she snapped.

He blinked, and his hand fell away. "I beg your pardon?"

"I am not one of those women who needs love words. I've always known what this is and I accept it. Please don't piss me off with a load of false sentiment. It only cheapens this relationship."

He seemed genuinely puzzled. "I'm not entirely sure what you mean. You think love cheapens sex?"

"I think false declarations take away from the basic honesty of what this relationship is."

His gaze sharpened. "And what is it exactly?"

"A purely physical, mutually beneficial convenience."

Outside, she heard traffic, the low *vroom* of an airplane. Church bells from a distance.

"So, you don't love me?"

There was a pause. Her heart beat so hard it hurt. "No."

He touched her breast lightly, softly. "Your heart is completely untouched?"

Her swallow sounded loud in the sudden quiet. "Yes."

"I see."

"Oh, don't give me that brave, wounded bullshit. Every guy I've ever known wants exactly what you've got. Sex"—she gave a tiny, smug smile—"lots of sex, with no strings attached."

Instead of laughing, or stomping off, or engaging in any remotely predictable behavior, he traced her cheek with one finger. His eyes were serious and understanding. "I've never known a woman who yearns for love more than you do, and is more terrified of it."

She leapt off the bed and her laugh was harsh and sudden. "I don't have time for this. I need to—"

She found herself cut off as he flipped her to the bed so fast her back hit the mattress before she remembered moving.

He was on top of her, not pinning her exactly, but forcing her to make a big deal of it if she wanted to move. She didn't feel like making a big deal about it. She wished she were clothed, though, and that her heart wasn't beating quite so fast. It made her feel vulnerable and a little foolish.

"I don't need love," she said, staring up at him. "I don't want it."

"I've seen you around your sister and George, you know, and even around Arthur and Meg."

"And when have I ever given any indication that I want what they have? That I want to be so besotted, so blinded by emotion that I lose my common sense?"

"Oh," he said, "your words do a fine job of portraying what a cynic you are, but your eyes give you away."

She rolled those eyes now, to give him a good idea what she thought of his notion.

"I thought at first it was irritation I was witnessing, but it's not, is it?"

"You tell me. You seem to have the keys to my inner thoughts and feelings after knowing me for one week."

"It's jealousy."

Fury, hot and molten, spurted within her. She shoved at his shoulder, so he moved away, letting her up.

"I've been married. I couldn't be less jealous. It's pity you witnessed. Pity for anyone fool enough to fall in love knowing that the chances of disaster outweigh any hope of lasting happiness by about two to one."

"You had a rotten marriage, Rachel. It happens. It happens all the time to clever, successful people who you would think would choose wisely. But for every bad marriage there's a good one, one that makes you keep believing. I think Max and George have every chance of happiness. You can see that, too, that's what's making you sick with jealousy."

"That's an awful thing to say. I love my sister. I'm not jealous of her."

"She has something you want. Worse, you know it's within your reach." He reached out his arm to illustrate his point. "And that makes you crazy with fear."

She snorted. "Make up your mind. Am I jealous, afraid, or yearning? Pick one."

"You, my darling, are all three."

"I can't figure you out. Why are you doing this?" She shook her head. "Of all people, you are the last one I would have dreamed would play the love card."

"It's not a card, darling, and this isn't a game. I think I've finally found the woman I was always certain I'd meet. It was a bit of a surprise that she turned out to be you, but there it is."

She straightened, tossed back her hair. "So what are you saying? You want to marry me?"

He looked at her for a long time. "And what if I am?"

Her skin started to prickle all over, as though she were breaking out in hives.

"If you believe in love and marriage so much, then why did George and Max both warn me that you're a womanizer? Why are you always in the wedding party but never the one getting married?"

"Because I never found the right woman." He rested back on his elbows. "I wouldn't keep turning up in wedding parties if I didn't believe in and respect the institution, now would I?"

"I don't know. Wouldn't you?"

"No. Give me credit for some integrity."

"So you're saying that in all this time you've never met a woman you wanted to marry?"

"I always believed that I'd meet a girl one day, and I'd know. Pow. There'd be some cosmic bang, sparks would shower the air, and I'd know that she was the one."

"You mean you're a total romantic?" She was horrified. She felt she'd been led astray somehow, lied to in the most basic way, but of course he'd never lied. She'd merely assumed that his lengthy bachelordom meant one thing when, in fact, it meant another.

He grimaced. "It sounds a bit soft when you put it that way, but yes, I suppose I am. In the last couple of years, I admit, I began to feel that it wouldn't happen after all."

She almost dreaded what would come next, but still had to ask. "And?"

His smile was tender, and uncomfortably intimate. "And then I met you."

"I don't recall seeing sparks flying, or a cosmic shake-up when we met."

"If you'd had a potato hit you in the balls, believe me you'd have felt a cosmic shake-up, and seen stars."

She grinned, as he'd meant her to, and the atmosphere lightened a little. But she also felt utterly confused and vaguely wronged. "I don't know what to say."

He turned his head, regarding her. "At the risk of sounding ridiculous, can I ask if you felt anything at all?"

"When we first met?"

"Mmm."

She thought back to the first moments when he'd come across her, irritable and twitchy in the kitchen. The sense she'd had of instant attraction. Not more. Surely not more. "I felt attracted to you," she admitted.

He flopped back onto the bed so he was staring up at the ceiling. "You never think, when you read about meeting the one person who was meant for you, that it might be a one-sided affair. Nobody ever warns you that you might feel love at first sight while the other person thinks, 'What a wally.' "

"Since I don't know what a wally is, I certainly never thought of you that way. Like I said, I was . . . attracted."

"You don't sound very happy about it."

"I wasn't. At the time. Very inconvenient. I felt like I'd been kicked around by life, and then Maxine had manipulated me into coming to England to work on, of all things, a wedding. I admit I was pretty down, and Max is a relentless do-gooder when she thinks she knows best for a person. Which is far too often."

"So your sister encouraged you to have it off with me?"

"No. She hated the idea. She thought I'd be too vulnerable, that I might end up hurt again."

"And you knew different?"

Did she? Had she? It was so difficult now to look back to a week ago and recognize anything she'd felt. "I don't know. I don't even know what I thought or felt except that you made me feel excited about something and a holiday affair seemed uncomplicated. Easy."

"Easy because you could walk away at the end of it with a few good memories?"

"Don't make it sound so . . . I don't know, so . . ."

"Cynical?"

"But I'm not cynical. I'm practical."

"You, my dear, are terrified of love."

"Oh, just get over it."

"I hope I don't have to. I believe that you and I may have found that rare and amazing thing. True love, the kind that lasts."

She scratched her leg. Maybe the hives weren't visible, but she could feel them, beneath the skin. Emotional hives. Great. She'd invented a new mental illness.

Chapter Ten

"Can we please talk about something else?"

He should have kept his mouth shut. He'd known she wasn't ready. Now all he could think about was that he loved her and she either didn't love him back or couldn't admit to loving him.

For a number of reasons, he hoped the latter was true.

He could conquer her fear, he was certain. Indifference was impossible to contemplate. Surely, after all this time, he ought to be able to tell when a woman really cared?

Or was he projecting his own feelings onto her?

He had so little personal experience of being in love that he was out of his depth. All he knew was that instead of having Rachel throw herself onto his chest and whisper those magic words of love back to him, as he'd more than half hoped she would, she was lying beside him, stiff as a board, staring up at the ceiling, in the same posture he was in.

"I met you a week ago," she said, sounding aggrieved.

"Look, I don't say it makes sense. Only that it is."

"I thought this would be easy, uncomplicated."

"Do you want easy and uncomplicated?"

"Yes!"

"I'm sorry I offended you. I didn't mean to. But I think

you're going to have to begin thinking of this in a new light."

"They warned me that you were the love 'em and leave 'em type. Which happens to be exactly what I'm looking for right now."

"If you pass up what we have, you're more of a coward than I believed."

"Okay, I can't do this right now. I simply cannot do this." She rolled out of bed and unzipped her overnight case, dragging out the jeans and sweater she'd brought.

He leapt off the bed and followed her. "Look, forget I said that. You're not a coward. I'm a complete and total git. Where are you going?"

"Home." Irritation sluiced through her system. "No. Not home. Back to the castle where I will stay in my kitchen hiding behind the ashes whenever any Prince Charming comes near."

"But you've barely seen Notting Hill. And I want to take you for afternoon tea at the Ritz. You'll love it."

He was stalking up to her, naked, when she reminded him, "Chloe is here. She needs you."

"Rachel."

"Let me go now. I'll call you."

For a long time he stared at her, his eyes full of concern. "All right. I'll get dressed and drive you back to Hart House."

"No. I'll take a cab to the station and get a train."

She was so panicked she barely knew herself. She knew she wasn't being rational, or fair, or remotely mature, but the urge to flee was so strong she couldn't resist it.

She was dressed in seconds and within five minutes had brushed her teeth, dragged a brush through her hair and stuffed the tangle of curls into a clip, swiped lip gloss over her passion-swollen mouth, and flicked the mascara brush over her lashes.

When she returned to the bedroom, he wasn't there.

She packed her dress and Maxine's pashmina into her case and left the room.

She found Jack in the kitchen with his sister. Chloe wore the most gorgeous silk robe and looked like a movie star from the twenties. Rachel almost expected her to light up a cigarette on a long holder.

Jack wore a look on his face that tore at her heart. And that made her furious. They'd only known each other a week. This was ridiculous, unfair, manipulative. She was a recently divorced, unemployed mess. She didn't have the mental or physical energy for a complicated love life.

"Have some coffee," Chloe said. She was messing around with a French press and it was obvious that somebody else usually made her coffee.

"No. Thank you." She looked at Jack. "If you could just call me a cab?"

"I'll drive you to the station."

"You should spend some time with your sister." She paused, feeling like a total, miserable bitch. "All right. Maybe you could drive me to the station."

They were no sooner pulling out of his parking garage than he said, "Rachel, I'm sorry. I didn't mean to put you off."

"No. It's me who is sorry. I didn't expect, I didn't know . . ." She heaved a sigh and tried again. "I would really like for you not to think I am a total loser."

He sent her a wry grin. "I'd like you not to think the same about me."

She laughed. "Agreed."

"How long do I have?"

"I beg your pardon?"

"When's your return ticket home?"

"Oh. It's open. I can stay up to twelve weeks, I think."

"Well, that's not so bad. I've got some time to convince you to stay."

She looked at him, truly curious. "So if I said right now, yes, let's get married . . ."

"I'd be driving straight back so I could cancel all my appointments tomorrow and we'd get married."

"How can you be so sure? No one's ever wanted me like this."

He sent her a look that melted her heart. "Maybe no one's ever loved you enough."

Wow. There was a zinger. As much as it hurt to admit it, she thought he was right. "I've failed so much in the last year. I don't have much faith in my own judgment."

"Never mind. I'm not going anywhere. We'll take it as slowly as you like." He turned to her in alarm. "You won't stop shagging me, will you?"

She glanced at him, all crisp and clean and gorgeous, not a big overblown mess like she was. "I may be stupid, but I'm not crazy."

He pulled into the station. "You know, if I didn't have Chloe waiting at home, I'd drive you down in spite of your protests."

"I know you would. But the train's fun for me. And—"

"Yes, all right. You need some time."

He'd stopped the car at a drop-off point by the taxi rank. Now he got out and retrieved her bag. He stood before her and she saw this tall, gorgeous, successful Londoner who loved her. Or at least who believed he did enough to say so.

Suddenly, she threw her arms around him and kissed him like there was no tomorrow. "I had a really wonderful time. Thank you for last night. Thank you for everything."

"I'll ring you."

"And be nice to Chloe."

"I'm always much nicer to Chloe than she deserves."

Rachel chuckled. "She's lucky to have you."

He gave her a quizzical glance.

"No, really. She is. And"—she took a deep breath— "thank you. For loving me."

"My pleasure."

Chapter Eleven

"You're back early," said Max when Rachel finally tracked her sister down in the long gallery.

"Jack's sister Chloe showed up."

"Ah, yes, the bride. Definitely puts a cramp in the affair to have little sis hanging around."

"Yeah, I need to talk to you about that."

"You don't have to," Max said. "Chloe rang. God, listen to me. She rang. I'm turning into a Brit. Anyway, she's canceling the wedding. Can you believe it? Our big society wedding, the one that was going to put us on the map. Gone. Poof. And I already put a deposit on the tent."

She'd done a lot more than put a few pounds down on a tent, but she was obviously trying to stay cheerful, even though, the way things were going, she and George were going to be too old to get married before they ever dragged Hart House into profitability.

"We'll figure something out." Jack's words echoed unpleasantly in Rachel's mind. Was it possible that she was jealous of Maxine? She hadn't exactly been super-supportive of her sister, and yet, look at her. She was glowing. "You're really happy here, aren't you?"

Max laughed. "Amazing, isn't it? I keep waiting for the other shoe to drop, but things keep getting better."

She knew Max had made up her mind not to marry George until they were in the black, and maybe it was stupid, but Maxine was not one to budge after she'd made up her mind. So it was up to Rachel to help bring in the bucks. Already, she knew they'd made a sizable dent in the bank loan. What they needed was a big, splashy success.

"Don't cancel that tent. There must be a replacement couple who want a splashy wedding. Let's brainstorm later. I'm going to shower."

"It's not your problem, Rach."

She took a deep breath. "Okay, maybe I'm not being clear. In my subtle way I'm giving you my blessing. George is a wonderful man and you two belong together. I've been pretty whiny and self-involved recently so maybe I wasn't as enthusiastic as I could have been, but I'm telling you right now that I'm going to do everything I can to help raise revenue. With the two of us on full throttle?" She grinned. "England doesn't have a chance."

She patted her sister's shoulder as she walked by. "Now close your mouth and start thinking."

Rachel had contemplated Jack's words all the way down on the train. First, she had to take in the astonishing fact that he'd said her loved her, and even more astonishing, that she believed him. Then she replayed the accusations he'd lobbed her way. She was scared, jealous, yearning for love. When she got past the sting, she thought maybe he wasn't completely wrong.

Even if he was right and she was too terrified to accept love for herself, she could at least be big enough to help her sister reach her happy ending.

A little scary warmth stole through her every time she replayed the moment when he'd looked at her with his sexy eyes all serious and said he loved her. And what about her? Was he right? Was she so terrified of love that she'd turn it away?

A person didn't fall in love in a week, she told herself furiously. One didn't!

She showered, and then went into the kitchen and baked shortbread cookies with chunks of candied ginger, a lemon pound cake, and thick, gooey espresso brownies. The baking soothed her and the scents coming from the oven lifted her mood. The kitchen was her place, where she felt in control, and while she worked her mind was free to brainstorm money-making ideas for Hart House.

"Rachel?" She heard George calling her and turned to find him striding into the kitchen. He was so impossibly cute. "I thought I'd find you here." He stopped to breathe. "God, it smells fantastic in here." He scoffed a shortbread cookie in a practiced fashion. "Can you come into the drawing room?"

"I've still got one batch of cookies to bake."

"Oh, do come. I'm opening a rather nice bottle of bubbly."

"All right." She felt more like being alone—a recluse, in fact. Having her meals sent to her on trays and writing in her journal. She'd have to buy a journal somewhere. What she needed was an elegant journal bound in leather where she could write her thoughts and feelings with a fountain pen. She smiled to herself. She'd just bet that Chloe was at this very moment writing in her journal.

Instead, she was going to have to play nice with two people she adored, but who were going to have her believing in love again if she wasn't careful. Champagne was for celebrating. George couldn't have picked a worse time to pop a cork.

George seemed chattier than usual as they walked back to the great house. Given that Chloe had cancelled her extremely expensive and already planned wedding, she was surprised at how buoyant he seemed.

When Rachel walked into the parlor, Maxine was closing her cell phone. "Mum and Greg say hi," she said.

"You talked to them on Friday. Why are you—"

Then Maxine looked up at her and she noticed the glow. She'd never seen Max look so beautiful, or so happy.

She glanced at George, who'd broken into the widest, most heartfelt grin she'd ever seen.

"Oh, my God," she squealed. "You're not?"

"I am. We are. We're getting married."

The two of them screamed like five-year-olds who'd drunk too much pop, and were suddenly hugging, laughing, and crying, and hugging some more.

When Rachel pulled away, she glanced at George, who was looking a little shy but pleased. "I'm so happy for you both," she said, and threw her arms around George, too. "I think you'll be an excellent big brother. I always wanted one."

"I'll do my best," he said simply, and she believed him with all her heart.

"But how did you get Maxine to agree? She's got this thing about paying off the debt first."

"I managed to convince her that she was wrong. No one should postpone happiness for silly reasons."

The words sent an odd pang through her. Was she doing that? Pushing away happiness for stupid reasons? Like she'd decided never to love again because it had gone wrong once?

George hugged her back and then extricated himself to open the champagne. The business of opening and pouring gave them all enough time to pull themselves together.

He handed them each a flute of golden, bubbling wine. He'd obviously raided the family cellars for something fabulous.

"I'd like to toast my future wife. The woman I'd almost ceased to believe existed. My countess. My love."

Rachel watched him, heard the sincerity of his words, but what struck her was the way he was looking at Maxine. It was so familiar, that look, and she realized it was the way Jack had looked at her this morning when he'd told her he loved her.

Love. How could you avoid it when it hit you any more than you could hold onto it when it was gone?

"I wish you every happiness," she said, feeling emotion choke her. She turned to her sister, feeling that it was all becoming too much. "And I don't care if you do become a countess. I'm not curtsying to you."

"Throw her in the dungeon, Earl!"

And by dint of being very silly they managed to bring the atmosphere down from its almost painful high to a more rollicking foolishness.

"So when did you decide to get married?"

"We started talking about all the work we've already done for Chloe's wedding. It wasn't any old wedding, but a pretty big society deal. I told George what you'd said. That we should start working the phones for another society wedding to slot in its place."

Max reached for his hand. "And he said that perhaps our wedding would do. He said he's not as rich as the guy Chloe's going to marry, but his family is much older."

"You're such a snob, George," Rachel said.

Maxine grinned at her. "And there's bad news for you, I'm afraid."

"Oh, I know. Even though I am fundamentally opposed to the entire patriarchal institution, you're going to make me cater your wedding."

"Worse. You're a bridesmaid."

Chapter Twelve

Jack didn't ring Rachel for a week. He cursed himself up and down for being such a stupid prat as to blurt out the fateful words that had made Rachel run from him. He decided a woman that petrified of love needed space and time to come to terms with the possibility that she was in it.

Of course, she loved him. He was almost positive that she must. He'd rushed things, that's all. He, who'd somehow managed never to fall very hard in thirty-four years, had gone arse over teakettle for a rather bad-tempered chef with violent tendencies almost the moment he met her.

When he could stand it no longer, he rang and she sounded pleased to hear from him. Phew, he thought. First hurdle passed. She hadn't hung up and told him she never wanted to see him again. And she hadn't gone back to America. He suggested a date for next Friday and she accepted.

He took her into Salisbury, to an ancient pub he thought she'd like. The food was good, and he didn't think Los Angeles could boast many places as old. The spires of the cathedral rose in gray majesty and the day was perfect.

With George and Max's wedding as well as Chloe's rather surprising decision to study painting in the south of France, there was plenty to talk about. None of it personal.

He'd brought her a cookbook from the shop round the corner from him, the way he'd have brought another woman flowers. She was so pleased with her present that she kept opening it and reading bits of recipes to him.

After the pub lunch, they strolled the narrow streets of the medieval village and toured the cathedral. He wondered if it was a mistake to visit a cathedral, such a grand, solemn place that rather reminded one of the serious ceremonies of life. Birth, death . . . marriage. But she seemed entranced by the cathedral and when the choir began to practice, she held his hand and stood, rapt.

When he took her home, he was prepared to make do with a quick snog and drive back to London. She gave him her mischievous smile. "Why don't I practice on you? I'll cook something from my new book. For dinner tonight." He helped her in the kitchen, finding pleasure and companionship in being her sous chef. They ate dinner with Max and George, and then she took him to her room, where they made love with quiet sweetness. Her mind might not have been ready to face up to her love, but her body told him everything he'd hoped to hear. They ate breakfast on their own, rising much later than anyone else.

After that it became a regular thing for them to spend Friday evenings, which turned into Saturdays, together. Sometimes they had the entire weekend, but she often did the catering for a small wedding, or an afternoon tea for the ladies of the straw hat society or some such thing. He regretted the hours they could have spent together, but not the way he could see her becoming more and more a part of the estate.

He thought it was a very good thing for her to be exposed to so much successful love as she was surrounded by, not only at the great house, but also in the pub where Arthur and Meg's affair progressed most satisfactorily. They were back from America and the novelist was hard at work on the next bit of terror she planned to unleash on unsuspecting readers.

Where they'd settle permanently was anyone's guess. He thought Arthur would follow Meg anywhere.

Would he? he wondered. If Rachel wanted to go back to California, would he be willing to go with her?

He wasn't sure if being willing to relocate was a true test of love, but he rather thought he would. If his choice was London without her or L.A. with her, he thought he'd be wearing Oakleys, striping his nose with zinc, and ordering half-caps with wings quite happily on Sunset Strip.

One Friday, as he arrived at the estate after a hellish slog down the M5, George said, "Can I have a word?"

The earl had obviously been on the lookout for him, for he'd even beaten Wiggins to the door.

"Yeah, sure," Jack said, loosening his tie.

George took him into a book-lined library that his father had used as a study. George kept an office on a different floor, out of the way of the tourists, so the library still had the formal atmosphere of the old earl.

George chatted idly about football, but Jack could see there was something on his mind, and after two and a half hours of driving that had consisted of jerking forward a few feet then idling for several minutes, he was more than ordinarily anxious to see Rachel.

Finally he interrupted a pointless treatise on Manchester United's last match. "What is it you want, George?"

"Well, the thing is, I'd like it very much if you'd be one of my groomsmen. For the wedding."

The irritation that had begun to build dissipated immediately. He felt the grin spread on his face and shook George's hand heartily. "I'd be delighted. Thank you for asking me."

"I hesitated, because I know you've been in about a hundred wedding parties."

"Not so many. Not quite fifty, I should think. But I'd be truly happy to stand up for you."

"Thanks." George blew out a breath. "There's such an awful lot to think about with a wedding. You were starting to look so cross I thought you'd refuse."

"Actually, I thought you were about to ask me what my intentions were with regard to your future sister."

"God, no. None of my business, really," George said, walking behind his father's desk and pouring out two stiff whiskeys. He handed one to Jack and sipped his own. Then he said, "At least, well, I suppose it is my business in a way. Not that the lady would thank me for interfering."

He glanced at Jack, obviously enjoying his position of power, however bogus. "Just out of interest, what are your intentions?"

"Oh, I'm going to marry her."

Jack had the satisfaction of seeing his old friend snort thirty-year-old single malt up his nose and cough until his eyes watered.

"Really? But you never marry them. They always marry someone else."

Jack settled into one of the leather wing chairs and regarded George. "You know the way you feel about Maxine?"

"Yes, of course." He nodded, as it all came clear. "You, too?"

"I thought it would never happen."

"Stunning when it does."

They sipped for a quiet moment. "And what do you reckon for Manchester's chances in this week's match against Cheltenham?"

And so the two were comfortable again, having done as much emotional sharing as they were ever likely to.

The year had ticked over and spring was unfurling all

over the estate. Rachel hadn't gone home. He never asked how she managed to stay in the country, or for how long. He'd rushed his fences once; he wouldn't do it again. Instead, he tried to show her how their life could be. He introduced her to his friends, he flew her to Paris for a very decadent weekend, and they'd all spent Christmas at Hart House, including various brothers and sisters and George's odd relatives.

He was waiting, he knew. And wooing the hell out of the woman he loved.

Maxine and George's wedding day dawned as blue and glorious as the wedding of a titled gentleman marrying his true love on an ancient English estate ought to dawn.

Rachel was probably as happy about the fact as the bride was. They'd worked out contingency plans in case of rain, there was a big tent on the grounds, and loads of room in the house, but it wouldn't have been the same. Max wanted to get married in the village church and celebrate the event on the grounds of Hart House. The society photographers would be there, and blooming roses and sparkling water photographed so much better than sodden branches and dripping umbrellas.

And, of course, Rachel's food would present so much better without a drenching.

Her dress—thank God for Maxine's excellent taste—was a soft, sage green. Designer simple, it fit her perfectly and brought out the green in her eyes.

The bride wore antique satin and carried the softest pink roses.

The ancient church was hushed as they walked in. Rachel followed two flower girls, and while George looked down the aisle behind her to where Max would appear, Jack looked at her, so she felt as every step brought her closer that she was making a tiny vow. Their gazes held and she saw his lips curve, ever so slightly.

It was a strange moment to have an epiphany about her own heart while celebrating her sister's union, but perhaps it was appropriate. For she saw Jack standing there at the front of a church, ready to celebrate a marriage, and she knew without a doubt that he was waiting for her. As she'd been waiting for him.

The next wedding Union Jack took part in was going to be his own. It might not happen for a while, but she knew in her heart it was right.

I love you, she told him with her eyes.

I know, his said back.

They stood together while Maxine took George to be her lawfully wedded earl and George took Max to be his lawfully wedded countess.

The tiny village church contained royalty, TV people from L.A., Meg and Arthur, who'd flown home for the event, and family and friends. Rachel's eyes widened slightly as she recognized Chloe, who'd flown back for the wedding. Like the latest Prada bag, she sported the latest darkly handsome boyfriend.

There'd been enough media to guarantee a lot of publicity on both sides of the Atlantic. Rachel strongly suspected that Maxine, ever the overachiever, had accomplished her goal. The Hart House Wedding Package was booked through the summer at rates that had made George's eyes bug out when he'd first heard them.

Of course, Rachel didn't believe in a perfect love, but she had to admit while watching her sister and her brand-new brother-in-law walk down the aisle, with quiet joy pretty much radiating off them, that they had found something very special.

Then she felt Jack take her arm and walk her down the

aisle behind them, and she knew she'd found something special, too.

Will you take this man? The words of the wedding service echoed in her head as they emerged into sunshine and a shower of rose petals.

Did she have the courage to risk her heart again? To let go of a painful past and take a chance on an unpredictable future?

Will you take this man?

"Yes," she said aloud.

"What's that, darling?" Jack asked, turning to look at her with that special look he kept just for her.

"Yes," she repeated, while bells rang and rose petals floated and laughter danced on the air. "Yes, I believe I will."

And, now a look at Jamie Denton's
romantic suspense novel,
THE MATCHMAKER.
Available now from Brava . . .

Travis winked at her and she tossed him a narrow-eyed hiss before walking back to the open grave and Manny. "Get rid of that reporter," she said irritably to Travis. "Make sure he knows he's not to print a word until he hears from me."

Travis's smug expression faded into one of confusion. "What reporter?"

She pointed to where she'd last seen the *NYT* wannabe. "That . . ."

"Hello, Greer."

The husky undertone of *that* voice slammed into her with all the subtlety of a runaway freight train. ". . . reporter," she finished weakly as she turned around and faced her past.

The air between them sizzled. She looked into the breathtakingly handsome face of the one man from whom she kept no secrets.

The high-pitched ringing in her ears deafened her. The ground beneath her feet shifted. This simply could not be happening. Why did that damned loose end she'd left dangling for so long have to become a noose tied around her neck today? Why now?

Ash.

Her every dream, her every regret rolled into one painful reality staring her in the face. Those delicious dark brown eyes once filled with affection were now colder than the granite headstone behind him. She expected or deserved, nothing more.

"What the hell are *you* doing here?" she blurted rudely. The suit. She should've known. Standard FBI blue, she thought, remembering her own closet once filled with the same dull rainbow of subdued hues.

"The report you filed with VICAP. It was brought to my attention."

"Faith." Who else? Faith worked closely with Ash, and had been the only person she'd kept in contact with at the Bureau for a short time after she'd left. Of course Faith would've passed the report on to him. She was Ash's eyes, ears, nose and throat for crying out loud.

Ash nodded. There was an underlying arrogance to the slight curve of his mouth that set her teeth on edge one second, then made her as nervous as a whore trapped in a confessional with a judgmental priest the next.

"And you thought you'd just come on down and take over my investigation, is that it?"

Travis cleared his throat. "I thought you—"

She glared at her boss, warning him to shut up. True, she wanted no part of the investigation, but having Ash breathing down her neck wasn't something she was anywhere close to being able to handle.

Thankfully, Travis wasn't a stupid man. "Never mind," he said, then clamped his teeth around a half smoked, unlit cigar.

A glinting flash of light caught her eye when Ash moved his hands to tuck them into the front pockets of his trousers. Probably just the sun reflecting off his watch, she thought. Anything else was unthinkable.

"You know how the system works, Greer," he said with a slight shrug of his shoulders.

"You're right. I do. And this case doesn't come close to meeting the criteria for ISU's involvement. I don't recall a section in the manual about steamrolling an investigation, either. You're not wanted here, Ash." She didn't want him anywhere near her. "Go home."

He leaned toward her and she breathed in his scent. Flashbacks of a different kind peppered her conscience. A private celebration. Candlelight. Champagne. Making love until dawn. His hands, his mouth. Never getting enough of each other.

"You develop a sudden understanding of the word?" he said in a low voice with enough of a hint of controlled anger to push her past the edge of reason.

Have a peek at Dianne Castell's
I'LL BE SEEING U
Available now from Brava!

Quaid answered the door, surprise slipping across his rugged, incredibly handsome face. "Hi," he said with a smile. "I'm glad you're here."

"Well, you won't be." Cynthia folded her arms, trying to add some menace to her words that she didn't feel at all. Hard to be stern with Quaid right in front of her. This was much easier when she practiced in the hall mirror. "I'm here on business, personal business, between-us business."

"Sounds serious." He came outside, closing the screen door quietly behind him, another member of the napping baby club. His familiar unique scent of hot sexy guy filled her head, making her a bit dreamy, until she caught the aroma of . . . "Oh my God." She walked past Quaid and pressed her face to the screen door, not caring that it left little tic-tac-toe marks on her nose. She inhaled deeply. "Fried chicken. Real, honest-to-goodness fried chicken."

"Well, it isn't rubber."

"I know, I had that one over at my house last night." She sniffed in another lungful. "Any leftovers?"

"You came here for Dad's chicken?"

"Not exactly." Maybe a little.

"Kitchen's down the hall to the right. Chicken's in the fridge."

She glanced back at Quaid but the lure of fried chicken dragged her onward and she followed the scent to the fridge in the neat yellow and blue kitchen. She pulled a drumstick from the platter covered with plastic wrap and eyed a thigh that somehow found its way into her other hand. She took a bite, euphoria washing over her and she nearly succumbed to one of Ida's swoons.

"Good?" came Quaid's voice from behind her.

"Terrific," she managed around a mouthful while nudging the fridge door shut with her hip. She took another bite. "I'm starved."

"You're not eating over at your place?"

"Ida and I can't cook. Totally suck at it. Pea soup for dinner, tasted like BBs. Rocks for rolls. Very sad." She licked her thumb.

"Lawrence told you about Dad's chicken, didn't he?"

"He might have mentioned it in passing, right after telling me about steak on the grill, but that's not why I'm here."

With his index finger he swiped a smudge of gravy from her cheek. "Could have fooled me."

He licked the gravy from his finger and for a moment all she could imagine was doing the same thing, then maybe tasting him all over. He had a great all over, she was sure, and she didn't get a chance to lick one single part on the dock, but she'd like to do it now. Except she was preoccupied with the chicken and this was business. *Business, business, business.* She wagged the half-eaten drumstick at him. "You sent Preston to Ivy Acres. And you bribed him to stay by offering him free dinners at Slim's. What in the world were you thinking?"

Quaid propped his hip against the counter. "That you run a bed-and-breakfast and he needed a place to stay and you could do with a little extra cash? And the dinner wasn't a bribe so much as an incentive. Dad hired Preston, and springing for some food seemed like the right thing to do."

"Well, last night Mr. Wright sprang into the shower with Ida, doing the full monty, and his head ruined a perfectly fine antique vase that was my great-grandmother's."

"Preston did all that?" Quaid stood straight. "Damn. He doesn't seem like that kind of guy. Rory checked him out. He's a retired teacher, impeccable reputation. Oh, he's got this Magnum thing going on but he's harmless. Is Ida okay?"

"She's fine, but I want you to butt out of our lives. The Landons are not a charity case. We just can't cook." She stiffened her spine, suddenly aware that she probably looked beyond charity and more like something the cat dragged in that happened to be hungry. Landons were proud, they were better than this . . . until lately. She hated lately, but she really loved the chicken. "We may not be the high and mighty O'Fallons, but we can still manage on our own. Lawrence does not need your money and neither do Mother and I and—"

"Hey, hold on. I apologize if Preston didn't work out but leave my family and Lawrence out of this. It seemed to me you've been going through a rough patch and I wanted to help you out, that's all there is to it."

"We are not going through any patches." *Oh, no,* she thought. *What if he . . .* She jabbed the drumstick in the direction of the docks and lowered her voice. "You didn't . . . I mean *we* didn't . . . because you felt *sorry* for me?"

"Holy hell, Cynthia." He raked his too-long black hair. "Did I act like I was feeling sorry for anyone?"

Well, thank heavens for that.

And now here is Kathy Love's
I ONLY HAVE FANGS FOR YOU.
Coming next month from Brava!

"Why are you so scared of me?" Sebastian asked softly.

She shifted away as if she planned to move down a step and then bolt. He couldn't let that happen, not before he understood what had brought on this outburst.

"Wilhelmina, talk to me." He placed a hand on the wall, blocking her escape down the stairs.

She glared at him with more anger and more of that uncomfortable fear.

"You can bully your mortal conquests," she said, her voice low. "But you can't bully me."

Sebastian sighed. "My earlier behavior to the contrary, I don't want to bully you. Or anyone."

'You can't seduce me, either," she informed him.

"I don't . . ." Seduce her? Was that what all this was about?

"Do you want me to seduce you?" he asked with a curious smile. Maybe that was the cause for her crazy outburst. She *was* jealous.

She laughed, the sound abrupt and harsh. "Hardly. I just told you that you *didn't* want to seduce me."

"No," he said slowly. "You told me *I can't*. That sounds like a challenge."

Irritation flared from her, blotting out some of the fear. "Believe me, I'm *so* not interested."

He raised an eyebrow at her disdain. "Then why do you care about me being with that blonde?"

"That blonde?" she said. "Is hair color the way you identify all your women? It's got to be a confusing system, as so many of them have the same names."

He studied her for a minute, noting that just a faint flush colored her very pale cheeks.

"Are you sure you don't want me to seduce you?" he asked again, because as far as he could tell, there was no other reason for her to care about the identification system for his women.

She growled in irritation, the sound raspy and appealing in a way it shouldn't have been.

Sebastian blinked. He needed to stay focused. This woman thought he was a jerk—that shouldn't be a draw for him.

"Why did you say those things?" he asked. "What have I done to make you think I'm so terrible?"

Her jaw set again, and her midnight eyes locked with his. "Are you going to deny that you're narcissistic?"

He frowned. "Yes. I'm confident, maybe, but no, I'm not a narcissist."

She lifted a disbelieving eyebrow at that. "And you are going to deny egocentric, too?"

"Well, since egocentric is pretty much the same as narcissistic, then yes, I'm going to deny it."

Her jaw set even more, and he suspected she was gritting her teeth, which for some reason made him want to smile. He really was driving her nuts. He liked that.

He was hurt that she had such a low opinion of him, but he did like the fact that he seemed to have gotten under her skin.

"I think we can also rule out vain, too," he said, "because again that's pretty darn similar to narcissistic and egocentric." He smiled slightly.

Her eyes narrowed, and she still kept her lips pressed firmly together—their pretty bow shape compressed into a nearly straight line.

"So you see," he continued, "I think this whole awful opinion that you have formulated about me might just be a mix-up. What you thought was conceit, which is also another word for narcissism," he couldn't help adding, "was just self-confidence."

His smile broadened, and Wilhelmina fought the urge to scream. He was mocking her. Still the egotistical scoundrel. Even now, after she'd told him exactly what she thought of him. He was worse than what she'd called him. He was . . . unbelievable.

"What about depraved?" she asked. Surely that insult had made him realize what she thought.

"What about it?" he asked, raising an eyebrow, looking every inch the haughty, depraved vampire she'd labeled him.

"Are you going to deny that one, too?" she demanded.

He pretended to consider, then shook his head. "No, I won't deny that one. Although I'd consider myself more debauched than depraved. In a very nice way, however."

He grinned again, that sinfully sexy twist of his lips, and her gaze dropped to his lips. Full, pouting lips that most women would kill for. But on him, they didn't look the slightest bit feminine.

What was she thinking? Her eyes snapped back to his, but the smug light in his golden eyes stated that he'd already noticed where she'd been staring.

She gritted her teeth and focused on a point over his shoulder, trying not to notice how broad those shoulders were. Or how his closeness made her skin warm.

He shifted so he was even closer, his chest nearly brushing hers. His large body nearly surrounding her in the small stairwell. His closeness, the confines of his large body around hers, should have scared her, but she only felt . . . tingly.

"So, now that we've sorted that out," he said softly, "why don't we go back to my other question?"

She swallowed, trying to ignore the way his voice felt like a velvety caress on her skin. She didn't allow herself to look at him, scared to see those eyes like perfect topazes.

"Why are you frightened of me, Mina?"

Because she was too weak, she realized. Because, despite what she knew about him, despite the fact that she knew he was dangerous, she liked his smile, his lips, those golden eyes. Because she liked when he called her Mina.

Because she couldn't forget the feeling of his fingers on her skin.

She started as his fingers brushed against her jaw, nudging her chin toward him, so her eyes met his. Golden topazes that glittered as if there were fire locked in their depths.

Once again she was reminded of the ill-fated moth drawn to an enticing flame. She swallowed, but she couldn't break their gaze.

"You don't have to be afraid of me," he assured her quietly.

Yes, she did. God, she did.